W9-BEK-996

"I don't usually like brown eyes. Yours are exceptional."

The man was not without charm. "You have a lot of prejudices. Doctors, social workers, brown eyes."

"Let's focus on the things I do like, such as the way your mouth trembles a little when you're annoyed."

He wasn't the simple, attractive flirt she'd thought him to be. But he was still bad news, and Dionne wasn't having any. "I came here to work, Colby. It's not a good idea to mix business with pleasure."

"This is after hours, Doctor. Don't you ever turn off that analytical brain of yours?"

"Dinner's ready," said a grumbling voice from the doorway. When neither moved, Colby's housekeeper spoke again. "Better come now, before things cool down."

She needed to cool down, Dionne thought as she broke eye contact with Colby and got to her feet, feeling somewhat shaky. She was oddly pleased to see he was none too steady, either. She hoped she didn't look as flushed as she felt.

Perhaps she had overestimated her ability to handle Colby Winters.

Dear Reader,

Welcome to Silhouette **Special Edition** . . . welcome to romance. Each month, Silhouette **Special Edition** publishes six novels with you in mind—stories of love and life, tales that you can identify with— romance with that little ''something special'' added in.

And this month is no exception to the rule—June 1991 brings *The Gauntlet* by Lindsay McKenna—the next thrilling WOMEN OF GLORY tale. Don't miss this story, or *Under Fire,* coming in July.

And to round out June, stories by Marie Ferrarella, Elizabeth Bevarly, Gina Ferris, Pat Warren and Sarah Temple are coming your way.

In each Silhouette **Special Edition,** we're dedicated to bringing you the romances that you dream about— the type of stories that delight as well as bring a tear to the eye. And that's what Silhouette **Special Edition** is all about—special books by special authors for special readers!

I hope that you enjoy this book and all the stories to come.

Sincerely,

Tara Gavin
Senior Editor

PAT WARREN
An Uncommon Love

Silhouette Special Edition

Published by Silhouette Books New York

America's Publisher of Contemporary Romance

To Vicki Lewis Thompson,
a class act and a super roommate,
"for the good times"

SILHOUETTE BOOKS
300 East 42nd St., New York, N.Y. 10017

AN UNCOMMON LOVE

ISBN: 0-373-09678-X

First Silhouette Books printing June 1991

Printed in the U.S.A.

Books by Pat Warren

Silhouette Special Edition

With This Ring #375
Final Verdict #410
Look Homeward, Love #442
Summer Shadows #458
The Evolution of Adam #480
Build Me a Dream #514
The Long Road Home #548
The Lyon and the Lamb #582
My First Love, My Last #610
Winter Wishes #632
Till I Loved You #659
An Uncommon Love #678

Silhouette Romance

Season of the Heart #553

Silhouette Intimate Moments

Perfect Strangers #288

PAT WARREN,

the mother of four, lives in Arizona with her travel-agent husband and a lazy white cat. She's a former newspaper columnist whose lifetime dream was to become a novelist. A strong romantic streak, a sense of humor and a keen interest in developing relationships led her to try romance novels, with which she feels very much at home.

Prologue

The office was dark as she entered. Shoulders slumped, she walked to her desk, sat down and turned on the antique lamp with the Tiffany shade. A golden glow fell onto the papers she'd left scattered on the desk when the call had come and she'd hurried out three hours ago. She lit a cigarette with trembling hands and inhaled deeply.

The line of work she'd chosen was never easy, but days like this one were the worst. From the depths of her cluttered purse, she withdrew a snapshot and propped it against the tinted base of the lamp. Drawing again on the cigarette, she leaned forward and studied the photo through the spiraling smoke.

Such a beautiful boy. Curly brown hair framed a face that had only recently lost its pubescent look, the brown eyes always too serious, the full mouth still vulnerable. Denny had set up his camera—the one she'd given him for his fifteenth birthday—to snap their picture, then he'd dashed over and self-consciously put his arm around her shoulders. She was looking at him and smiling and, for an instant, he looked happy, innocent—carefree, even. Six months later, he had died.

She held the smoke in her lungs a long, shaky moment, fighting for control. *Oh, Denny, why did you stop coming to me when things got worse? Why did you give up instead of continuing to fight, to hope? Didn't you think I could see past the brave smile, the nonchalant shrug? When I asked how you were getting along, your cavalier answers were always followed by a quick change of subject. Why didn't you trust me enough to let me help you?*

Viciously, she ground the cigarette out in the big, glass ashtray. "We failed you, Denny, all of us," she said aloud, her voice ending on a choking sob. "Oh, God, I'm so sorry."

Eyes on the picture, she decided she would keep it always, to remind her of the fragility of life.

Lowering her head onto her crossed arms, Dionne Keller wept.

Chapter One

"We want *you,* Dionne. Only you. Because you're the best."

The voice on the other end of the phone was gently persuasive yet maddeningly insistent, as was the man who owned it. Dionne leaned back in her desk chair thoughtfully. "You wouldn't resort to flattery, now would you, Zac?"

She heard the soft chuckle and pictured her best friend's husband of six months with his warm smile and his shrewd gray eyes. She'd liked Zachary Sinclair from the day she'd met him, mostly because he was straightforward and honest, traits she valued above many others.

"I don't have to flatter you, Dionne," Zac answered. "You *are* the best. I'll never forget what you did for my wife."

Dionne searched about for a cigarette. "I believe you played a large role in Lainey's recovery, my friend." She closed a drawer and opened another, fingers exploring.

"I'll be around to play a role in this project, too, though you'd be working mostly with Colby."

Therein lay the problem, she thought. "Colby and I didn't exactly hit it off, if you'll remember."

Dionne abandoned her search of the desk and unzipped her large handbag, thinking her comment a masterpiece of understatement. She and Colby Winters, Zac's business partner and closest friend, had stood up at their friends' wedding and had clashed from the start. She saw Colby as cocky, arrogant and a man who thought himself irresistible to women. All women. Not *this* woman, she thought as she tossed her bag aside with a frustrated frown. "Oil and water rarely mix well, Zac."

"I promise you that Colby will stay out of your way. Will you at least consider my offer, Dionne? I know you could do one hell of a job, and we really need your help."

Caught between a rock and a hard place, she thought. The word *need* never failed to get to her. "Let me sleep on it, all right?" She could picture him smiling at that.

"Sure. And Dionne, thanks."

She hung up the phone with a disgusted shake of her head. She was an easy touch to but a well-chosen few, but those few did know the right buttons to push. And she was out of cigarettes besides. How had she let that happen? Grabbing her bag, she rose as the door to her office swung open.

"Hilary, hello. I don't suppose you have any cigarettes?"

"Out again?" Hilary's long brown hair fell forward and framed her small face as she bent to the credenza drawer and withdrew a pack. "I hid one in here last week."

Smiling, Dionne reached for the pack and ripped it open as she sat back down. "You're a wonder."

Hilary dropped her slender frame into the chair facing Dionne's desk. "Mmm. It's easier than watching you go through withdrawal. When are you going to give up those things? Haven't you heard, nonsmokers are in?"

Blowing smoke into the air contentedly, Dionne leaned back. "Everyone's entitled to one or two vices. Haven't you any?" she asked, though she doubted that her new partner did.

"I wish I had time to develop a few," Hilary confessed, and Dionne laughed.

Dr. Hilary Drake had joined Dionne's practice just three months ago, and Dionne had felt fortunate in getting her. Hilary had needed to move from Detroit to the small resort town of St. Clair on Michigan's eastern shoreline to be near her fiancé who was a resident at a nearby hospital. As the only clinical psychologist for miles around, Dionne's patient list had grown to an almost unmanageable size over the past four years. Specializing in trauma victims, particularly children, had made her even more sought after. The results of her caring technique had brought in referrals that had finally necessitated the dividing of her workload. Hilary was an experienced psychologist, who shared Dionne's philosophy and her concern, and they'd quickly discovered they worked well together. An added bonus was that they'd become friends.

Thoughtfully studying Hilary, Dionne wondered if her partner could manage the practice alone if she took off for a few days. Uncertain of her decision, she nonetheless told Hilary about Zac's request. "The problems have escalated over the past few months," she went on to explain. "Midwest Construction employs over two hundred people and, although less than a dozen are involved in repeated absenteeism, Zac now tells me they've traced several on-the-job accidents to substance abuse."

Hilary crossed her legs and nodded. "Drugs *and* alcohol, I imagine. Yes, I've heard that even the smaller companies are being affected. So what exactly is it that Zac asked you to do?"

Dionne took a pull on her cigarette, then answered. "Before I went into practice here, I spent a year in Chicago, and one of the things I got involved in was training key management personnel at various companies on how to treat their employees who suffered from alcoholism. I worked with this large airline on intervention, codependency, family counseling, and even put in some time at a detoxification center. Zac knows this and wants me to set up something like that at his company, on a smaller scale, of course."

"I sense a bit of hesitancy on your part. If you're worried about the practice here..."

"That's not it," Dionne said, dismissing the thought with a wave of her hand. "If Zac were running the Detroit operation, I'd go in a minute. I like him, and the challenge interests me. And I believe you can handle things here for the short time I'd be gone. But, as you know, since his marriage, Zac's busily building a branch office in St. Clair and rarely goes to Detroit. That end of it is being handled by—"

"Ah, yes," Hilary interrupted, a gleam in her blue eyes. "Zac's partner, Colby Winters. I remember him from the wedding pictures. You have something against tall, blond men with football shoulders and a smile that would melt an iceberg?"

Snubbing out her cigarette, Dionne shook her head. "No, but I'm not crazy about self-assured men who think they're God's gift to women." She'd fallen for that confident magnetism once before and could recognize it at fifty paces. She'd also sworn never again to let herself become vulnerable to that kind of deliberate charm. "Let me tell you, they're bad news, personally and professionally."

"So you've turned down Zac's request?"

Dionne ran a hand through her short, red hair. "I just hate to. Zac's so nice, a really sincere guy."

"Oh. So you've accepted?"

"I don't want to. And yet..."

Hilary smiled. "I like a woman who knows her own mind."

Dionne gazed out the window pensively. "Maybe it's the dimples. A man over thirty shouldn't have dimples. He flashes them at a woman and expects her to believe every word he utters." Nathan had had dimples and had used them like lethal weapons. Unfortunately, she'd been one of his casualties.

Swinging back, she saw Hilary watching her with amusement. Clearing her throat, Dionne sat up straight. "I'm sorry. I got off track there. I'll decide this later."

"It's all right. I know I'd have difficulty working closely with someone I was attracted to."

Dionne's eyes widened. "Attracted? To Colby Winters? Good Lord, no. He looks at every woman as if she were dessert on his plate."

Hilary shrugged. "He finds you attractive and lets you know it. What's wrong with that?"

"Everything's wrong with that, especially if he acts that way while we're working together on a serious project."

"Do you honestly think he'd behave the same way as the head of his company as he did at a wedding? What are you afraid of, Dionne?"

In the short months of their friendship, Hilary had become a confidant, one who read Dionne quite accurately, which was why her question wasn't offensive. It did, however, give Dionne pause.

She remembered how Colby had swirled her into his arms for a dance at the reception. He hadn't asked; he'd just taken over, assuming she'd want to go with him. He'd held her close, unabashedly flirting with her and, despite her best resolve, her blood had heated. For a long moment, she'd lingered, basking in that addictive warmth, then she'd pulled back and left him alone on the dance floor.

She didn't want an involvement, not with Colby Winters, not with any man. Her life was complete the way it was, as complete as it was likely to get. If she had a few regrets, if occasionally she shed a few hot tears for things that might have been, she had learned to live with them. And she would allow no man to hurt her again. Perhaps the way to reemphasize that to her own satisfaction was to go to Detroit, to work alongside Colby and prove to herself and to him that she was in control of her life.

Dionne turned back to Hilary. "I'm not afraid. I think I will go. It might prove interesting, matching wits with Colby Winters."

Hilary nodded, pleased. "Good for you. And may the best man—or woman—win. Now, do you want to go over these files before we call it a day?"

Yes, that's what she'd do, rearrange next week's schedule, update Hilary on pending cases and call Zac tonight. She'd leave Monday morning, spend the week with Midwest Construction's management team and be back by Friday. Decision made, Dionne felt better as she leaned forward to review the files.

Colby Winters stood gazing out the second-story window at the maple trees bordering the perimeter of the paved parking lot. His eyes moved beyond the newly constructed ten-thousand-square-foot building that housed Midwest Construction to the neatly fenced lumber yard and the brick works alongside that. He never tired of looking at his domain, the one he shared with Zac. Not bad for two men who'd both come from the wrong side of the tracks, growing up in the inner city.

He took a sip of coffee from the mug he held and watched the late-afternoon sun dapple the trees as the breeze shifted the leaves. It was unseasonably warm for mid-September in Michigan, with barely a hint of autumn in the air. Colby slid the window open wider, knowing his secretary would probably close it when he left the office. Most everyone preferred air-conditioning, but he loved the freshness of the outdoors and found a climate-controlled office difficult to put up with for long periods of time. Which was why he spent as much time visiting the sites of their many projects as he did behind his desk. But today was an exception. Dionne Keller was arriving today.

Frowning, Colby walked over to where the coffeepot sat warming on a corner table and refilled his cup. Zac had sounded so enthusiastic on the phone explaining that he'd finally persuaded Dionne to agree to work with them. Colby hadn't had the heart to mention that he felt that having her here was a rotten idea. Taking a careful sip, he sat down in his swivel chair and stretched out his long legs.

First of all, Dionne Keller didn't *look* like a doctor of anything, much less a clinical psychologist of some reputation, as Zac was always reminding him. She was short, five foot three tops, with a terrific body, creamy skin, curly hair such a perfect red that he knew it hadn't come out of a bottle, and a smile that made a man keep on looking, except she seldom flashed it. Then there were her eyes, huge and brown and usually frosty. Colby wished he knew what the hell it was about him that had Dionne turning cool and distant the minute he so much as looked at her.

But it wasn't because of her looks or her indifference to him or the fact that they hadn't particularly hit it off the few times they'd been thrust together that he didn't want her here. It was because he didn't think she was the one to help their men. Hell, these men were rugged construction workers—carpenters, electricians, roofers, plumbers, bricklayers. What made Zac think men like that would listen to this little slip of a woman, that they'd pour out their problems to her, problems that might cost them their jobs? Draining his cup, he shook his head. It would never work.

Of course, he knew where Zac was coming from. Dionne was not only Zac's wife's best friend, but she'd helped Lainey to face her fears and learn to trust again after she'd been traumatized by a stranger who'd raped her. And Dionne had worked some minor miracles with a couple of kids up in St. Clair. But these men were different. Colby knew his men, knew which ones drank or took drugs. Knew because he'd lived among them, and because his own father was an alcoholic.

Colby felt he owed Zac, so he had to let Dionne take a shot at helping. But when she failed or gave up, whichever came first, then he'd get his own man in here to counsel the men. A male doctor, tough and unbending, preferably one from the inner city who understood gut-level problems. He wasn't convinced even someone like that could make some guys turn around. But certainly a pampered woman who looked as though she ought to be listening to the complaints of the country-club set didn't stand a chance of getting through to them.

Restlessly, Colby strolled back to the window. Where the hell was she anyway? Zac had said she'd be arriving before noon, and it was nearly three. Real dedicated, he could see. Probably stopped to have her hair done, maybe a manicure. He'd have to keep an eye on her while she was here and—

He heard the roar of the engine through the open window before he saw the red car zoom into sight, brake through a turn into the parking lot and then whip into an empty space. A Corvette convertible, top down and a redhead behind the wheel. It would seem the good doctor had arrived. He remembered seeing her in that car on one of his visits to St. Clair. So she loved speed and flashy cars. It didn't fit the cool, controlled image.

Leaning closer, he saw her remove her sunglasses and glance up at the building, her gaze finding his and holding. Bracing himself, Colby tried to remember that he'd promised Zac he would not only behave, but that he'd impress her with his professionalism and be the perfect host.

He was waiting for her. She should have known he would be. Dionne tossed her sunglasses into her bag and glanced down at her reflection in the rearview mirror. Her hair was windblown and hopeless, she thought as she ran her fingers through it. Too bad, because she wasn't about to sit here and comb it as long as his eyes were still on her.

Quickly, she got out and put on her beige suitcoat over the brown silk blouse she wore with the matching skirt. She'd learned long ago that her diminutive size and her wholesome Irish face gave people the impression of youth and inexperience, though she was twenty-nine and had been out on her own since college. So she always dressed as professionally as possible and wore high heels nearly everywhere. There were still times when she had to prove her credentials. Dionne guessed that this was probably one of those times.

Colby hadn't moved from the window, she noticed as she walked toward the door. Though she couldn't see their color, she knew his dark blue eyes were trained on her every step of the way. Unbidden, the memory of the dance they'd shared six months ago, the sweet hot pleasure of being in his strong arms, washed over her. Shaking her head free of such disturbing thoughts, she pushed through the swinging door.

He was in the hallway as she stepped off the elevator, his eyes coolly assessing. Mr. All-American with his blond hair, his perfect teeth and his tanned skin. Dionne put on her best professional smile—just a tad warm, not quite friendly. "I apologize for being late," she began.

"No problem," Colby said, guiding her toward his office. "Run into a lot of traffic on the drive down?"

She owed him no explanation, but she'd give him the reason anyhow. There was no point starting off on the wrong foot. "No. I had to stop at the courthouse and give a deposition on one of my young patients who's involved in a nasty custody suit."

"And whose side are you on, the mother's or the father's?"

"The child's. Always." She saw him nod approvingly, as if she'd given the right answer to a test question, and felt her spine stiffen.

"Did you have time to stop for lunch? We have a cafeteria on the ground level. Or I've got coffee in my office."

"Coffee would be fine, thank you."

Colby led the way, stopping to introduce her to his secretary and right hand, Marianne, and then seated her on a leather couch in his office before handing her a cup of steaming coffee. "I like your car," he said, seating himself at the far end of the couch.

"Thanks. So do I." She swallowed the coffee gratefully. She had skipped lunch, but she wasn't particularly hungry. Nerves, she supposed.

"I wouldn't have guessed you'd choose a sports car."

He was trying to slot her. She knew he had an engineering degree and guessed that he was probably a logical thinker, very methodical. She wasn't going to make it easy for him. "Did you picture me in a sedate little sedan, gray perhaps, with seat covers and a small plastic waste container hanging from the dash?"

Colby shook his head. "That's what I'd expect from a little old country doctor. That's not how I see you at all." He stretched his arm along the back of the couch. "You're more the country-club doctor, aren't you? Swimming, tennis, golf and consultations in the locker room. 'Doctor, my husband doesn't understand me. What shall I do?'"

Carefully, she set down her cup and turned toward him, more annoyed by the amusement in his eyes than at his slight. "You don't have a very high opinion of my work, do you?" Before he could answer, she went on. "For your information, I've never been inside a country club, not that there aren't some people there who are legitimately troubled and might need help. Problems have no gender, Colby. No age limits, no financial criteria. All of us, any one of us, have had, do have or might have a problem of a serious nature. Psychologists are not the only answer, but we are *one* answer, and I like to think we make a difference in some lives.'' She paused a moment, letting that sink in. ''If you don't want me here, why don't you say so now and save us both a lot of time and trouble?''

He appeared neatly put in his place, and swallowed tightly. ''Zac wants you here. He's a good judge of people.''

So that's how it was. She'd suspected as much. ''Then is it psychologists, psychiatrists or doctors in general that you don't trust?''

He shrugged and drank some coffee. ''Shrinks tend to probe around in someone's mind, find a textbook description and toss on a label. For instance, they discover the man's a drunk. They poke around in his past and come to predictable conclusions such as his father beat him, so he drank. His mother made rotten chocolate chip cookies, so he drank. His dog ran away, so he drank. Did anyone ever stop to think he may drink because he likes to drink?''

There was something personal here, Dionne thought, watching him over the rim of her cup as she took a sip. ''I agree. Labeling is wrong. But I disagree that a man drinks to excess regularly simply because he likes to drink. Alcoholism is an illness, not a conscious choice.''

He doubted that they'd ever see eye-to-eye on this. ''So you came here with your mind already made up on that. I wouldn't have thought a doctor would have preconceived notions.''

"My opinion on alcoholism being an illness is not a notion but a learned fact. And I dislike preconceived notions, too. For instance, that everyone who works with his hands is a dumb, uneducated clod."

If he'd been wearing a hat, he'd have tipped it to her. A reluctant smile touched his mouth. "Good point. So are you ready to meet my staff and start working your miracles?"

Dionne almost sighed aloud. This was going to be uphill all the way. "Colby, I don't want to mislead you. I can't work miracles. But it would be nice if you'd reserve judgment until I've at least met your people and heard their concerns."

"That sounds fair." He held out his hand. "Truce?" Did he really want a truce, or did he just want to touch her?

She ignored his hand. "I wasn't aware a war had been declared." She stood. "Are you ready to show me around?"

Colby rose. "Let me have Marianne check to make sure the people I want you to meet are available."

For the next hour, he escorted Dionne into every nook and cranny of Midwest Construction. While Marianne gathered the management staff together, Colby walked Dionne about the brickyard and lumber lot, explaining that they'd recently expanded their operation into providing some of the basic building materials, not only to cut costs on their bids, but to be assured of getting quality goods. Dionne could sense Colby's pride in their new facilities as he showed her the billing department, the sales showroom, dispatching, purchasing and finally, the conference room.

It was there he introduced her to his department heads, Dave Peters, Ron Henry and Dottie Philips. They were the three key employees she'd be training to assist in counselling the men. Leaning against the conference table, Colby listened while his people asked Dionne a few tentative questions. She briefly outlined the methods they'd be using, much of it based on the Twelve-Step Program begun by Alcoholics Anonymous. They listened with growing interest.

"But will a program designed for alcoholics also work on, say, drug users, for instance," Dottie asked. As office manager, she saw fewer troubled victims than the other two, yet even those few worried her.

Dionne nodded. "Alcohol, drugs, prescription-medication abuse or a combination of several, all can benefit from the same concept. Overeating is another. Many companies are now realizing that obese employees cost them a great deal in excess insurance costs for high medical risks, so they're instituting physical-fitness procedures and weight-loss programs for their employees. Intervention methods for all these disorders are similar. In teenage delinquency, it's sometimes called 'tough love,' a caring approach that has had good success in causing an offender to rise to the level of parental expectation."

"And you've started these programs at other companies and succeeded with them?" Dave Peters asked. The skepticism in his voice was all too clear. As one of the construction crew bosses, he'd seen a lot of men try to kick habits and fail.

"This isn't a miracle cure. The progress is slow, the outcome usually uncertain. The person with the problem has to *want* to get well. To remain sober, to be drug free, to bring his weight to a normal level—whatever the addiction. And of course, the addiction is often a symptom of a more deeply rooted problem. We'll need to tackle all these issues."

"Sounds like a tall order," Ron Henry added. As the other crew boss, he had the look of a man who thought this whole idea a waste of time.

Colby straightened. "We agreed, before Dr. Keller arrived, that something had to be done about our absenteeism problem and done soon. Let's keep an open mind and let's meet here again tomorrow morning at nine. Is that agreeable with everyone's schedule?"

There were murmurs of assent, and the three department heads left. Colby turned to Dionne as Dave closed the door. "A tough sell, wouldn't you say?"

Dionne shrugged. "Pretty much as I'd expected. The initial reaction at most firms is skepticism as to the success ratio and/or an expectation of instant results. The staff that counsels needs to learn that these people didn't develop their problems overnight, nor will they be free of them quickly. It simply doesn't work that way."

"I guess you have to be patient in your line of work."

"Patience is handy to have in most any line of work."

"It's never been my strong suit," Colby admitted ruefully. He watched her as she stepped back and tilted her head to study him.

There was a restlessness about him, Dionne decided, even in his deceptively casual stance. As if he were ready and eager to spring into action. "No, I don't suppose it is." She glanced at her watch. "Well, I think that's about it for today. Zac told me you'd make reservations for me at a nearby motel. If you'll tell me how to get there, I think I'll go check in."

"He asked me to, but I didn't call the motel." Colby coughed into his fist, wondering if she was going to balk at the change in plans he'd impulsively decided on.

She paused in midmotion, about to arrange the strap of her bag onto her shoulder. "Really. Why?"

"My house isn't far from here, and I've got a very private, very comfortable guest wing. I've even got a live-in housekeeper, who's probably making dinner for us as we speak. In case you're afraid to stay alone with me."

Dionne narrowed her eyes as he flashed those devastating dimples. There was that word again—*afraid*. He seemed to be challenging her, yet underneath all his snappy remarks, she sensed he'd had a bad experience somewhere in his past that had colored his opinions. Perhaps the real challenge was in earning his respect as a doctor while at the same time unraveling the puzzle that was Colby Winters. Even as a child, she'd always loved puzzles.

She could still find a place nearby and check in. But maybe she needed to prove to Colby—and perhaps herself—that not only could she handle the job she'd come to do, but handle being around such an attractive man and not crumble as so many others before her, she was certain, had. She sent him an equally challenging smile. "Okay."

His expression told her she'd caught him off guard. "You're full of surprises," Colby said, opening the door. "You'd better follow me. I like to keep within the speed limits."

"I'll bet," Dionne muttered as she walked out after him.

The housekeeper's name was Aggie, and she seemed to hover over Colby and distrust Dionne on sight. Hanging her clothes in the closet of the spacious guest room, Dionne frowned as she thought of the short, gray-haired woman's quick perusal and grumpy greeting. Dionne wondered if Aggie disliked all women under fifty, or her in particular? Ah well, she wouldn't be in Colby's house long enough to let it upset the housekeeper.

He'd built his house himself, he'd told her with almost boyish pride, and what she'd seen was lovely. A large ranch on a secluded acre in North Bloomfield Hills, it rambled and twisted into an uneven U shape, with an enormous pool and hot tub nestled within the curve. Generous windows brought the outdoors inside, bleached wooden beams accented high ceilings, and the warmth of a builder's loving touch was evident from pillar to post.

Somehow, she'd pictured him in the careless disarray of a bachelor apartment, a place to merely hang his hat. As she changed into brown linen slacks and a yellow cotton shirt, she decided he was more complex than she'd originally thought. Colby Winters, homebody. A new thought. She put out her cigarette and left the room.

She found him in the kitchen, arguing good-naturedly with Aggie.

"Needs more pepper, Aggie," Colby said, lowering the wooden spoon after a generous taste.

Aggie swatted at him with her dish towel. "You get away from my pot roast. There's plenty of pepper in there."

Colby turned and spotted Dionne, waving her over to join them. "You like hot food, as in spicy?"

"Mmm, yes, I do," she answered, breathing in the delicious aroma.

Aggie scowled at her. "All them spices eat your stomach lining away. Not good for you."

"Ah, but what a way to go, Aggie!" Noticing his housekeeper's distraction, Colby shook a generous sprinkle of pepper into the pot before replacing the cover and turning an innocent face back to her. "Are you making cheese biscuits?"

"Don't I always with pot roast?" Aggie turned her frown toward the oven. "Go on out of here so I can see to dinner."

"Yes, ma'am." He held a glass toward Dionne. "I took a guess. White wine?"

"That's fine, thanks." She let him lead her from the kitchen. When they were out of Aggie's hearing range, she stopped. "Is she always this sweet natured?"

Colby laughed. "Don't mind Aggie. She was born complaining, but she's got a heart of gold. Unfortunately, she has a tendency to be overprotective." He liked Dionne Keller in casual clothes. Her business look put him off. He hadn't realized she was so small without those heels she always wore. Small, delicate, almost fragile.

Sipping her wine, Dionne strolled to the patio doors. A lush green lawn, well-trimmed shrubs and lots of tall trees lay beyond the pool area. And every few feet, there were flower beds, each displaying a riot of fall colors. "What a beautiful yard."

"I think so." Colby pushed open the sliding door and stepped out with her. The sun was just setting. "I try to get home in time to watch Mother Nature's evening performance as often as possible. You should see the sunrise from my bedroom window. You can see the whole show from my bed." Suddenly, he seemed to realize what he'd just suggested and grinned.

Keeping her expression bland, Dionne walked over to an old-fashioned glider and sat down under the shade of a young birch tree. A homebody and a nature lover. Interesting. She watched him walk closer and stand looking at the view. He was so very tall, his shoulders broad under a navy shirt, his arms muscular from years of physical labor. The jeans he'd changed into were comfortably worn and hugged his solid frame appealingly. Dionne took another swallow of wine, very aware that she hadn't eaten since early morning. And very aware of the man who came to sit alongside her.

"The pool's heated if you want to try it later, and the hot tub's ready at the press of a button."

"Thanks." He angled toward her, and she caught the clean, fresh-showered scent of him.

"Do you own a house up in St. Clair?"

"No, I live in an apartment. I'm not there much with my long hours." She let her gaze travel around the yard and for a moment, felt a pang of envy. "This is nice, very nice. I've never found the time to plan a house. It's a big commitment."

"I suppose. Some people need a solid place of their own. I grew up in a third-floor walk-up apartment, one bedroom, one bath, tiny kitchen. I slept on a lumpy couch in the living room and my sister on a cot. I always wanted a place of my own."

A familiar story, one she'd heard many times, but no less poignant. "Looks like you've got it. Are your folks still around?"

Colby took a swallow of iced tea, set the glass down, then leaned back and crossed his hands behind his head. "My mother died when I was ten. My father walked out on my sister, Kathy, and me four years later."

"Walked out? You mean left the two of you alone?"

"Yeah. He probably did us a favor. He drank like a fish and liked to hit things when he was feeling good. And sometimes he hit us."

Now she understood his earlier comments about drunks and drinking. She felt her sympathies rising and her resolves weakening. Again, it was a story she'd heard various versions of before, and she struggled to keep her distance. She didn't want to warm toward this man. It was not only unprofessional, but it could be dangerous. "That must have been rough."

The calm comment of a dispassionate doctor. What had he expected? Colby wondered. Had he brought all this up as a test to see how she'd react? If so, she'd reacted exactly as he'd guessed. Detached. He wondered if after years of hearing sad stories, perhaps ice ran in her veins. "Yeah, rough. Really hard on my sister. She was only twelve. But I didn't care."

No, of course he didn't. "What did the two of you do?"

Gently, he swayed the swing back and forth. "I took Kathy to Zac's house, and his folks took us in." He reached for his glass and finished his tea. "People like my father should raise puppies, not kids. Only they'd probably hurt them, too."

"Does Kathy live near you?"

"No. She married young. Tom's a big man, but gentle as a kitten. Kathy lives in Iowa, raises corn and kids. They have three."

"Do you know where your father is?"

"He surfaced about ten years ago. He lives downtown in some crummy apartment. Every once in a while, I have to bail him out of jail after some brawl. So you see, I have more than just a passing acquaintance with drunks."

Unable to stop herself, she touched his arm. "I know you don't think so, but your father is a sick, tormented man."

He turned to her then, his eyes dark with bitterness. "He didn't have to hit my mother though, did he? And Kathy?" He didn't mention the many times Harold Winters's open-handed slaps had caught him off guard.

Dionne heard the pain and wished she could erase his bad memories. She kept her voice level. "No, he didn't have to do that."

Slightly appalled that he'd revealed so much, Colby cleared his throat and turned to her, his smile a little off center. "So, Dr. Freud, what do you make of my inauspicious beginnings? Think I can rise above all that?"

She would play it light, since that's what he seemed to want. "I think you already have. Your story sounds a lot like Lainey's. Thank goodness she found Zac, too. You know her background, I imagine." She saw him nod. "Only her parents specialized in verbal abuse and emotional blackmail—not physical neglect. The results are just as devastating."

More labels, pat answers, a classic textbook analysis, he thought. "Yeah, there are a million stories in the big city." His tone was a shade more caustic than he'd intended.

She caught the bitterness and searched for something to say. "In the long run, it's not what happens to us that matters as much as how we handle it. I'd say, for a boy of fourteen, you handled a potentially destructive situation very well."

A woman who always said the right thing. He wondered if it was her training or her personality. His sense of fair play warred with his long-held prejudices as he nodded. "So the social worker who used to come around told me. She was a real do-gooder.'' *Like you,* he'd almost added. Fran Ellis had been her name, and she'd been cool and impersonal, too.

"The school used to call her before we moved in with Zac. She'd make out her reports and shake her head at the way we lived. She told Kathy and me that we were socially, morally and economically deprived. She tried to reform my father, get him jobs, keep him sober. After her visits, he'd go on another binge worse than the last one. Finally, I told her to butt out."

"Maybe she was honestly trying to help. People don't go into social work for the money."

"What drew you to psychology?"

She studied his relaxed pose, his hooded gaze, yet she could sense the tension in him. She didn't know him well enough to go into the real reasons. Not nearly well enough. "Sometimes, in helping others, you help yourself."

"That's too simplistic."

"Sorry, it's the best I can do. What drew you to construction work?"

He gave her the cocky answer, the one that won over the ladies, accompanied by a charming smile. "I'm good at it."

She didn't buy it. "Try again."

He raised an eyebrow. "Predinner analysis, Doctor?"

"It's all right if you don't want to tell me."

For the first time, he thought she could be a dangerous woman to know. She saw more than most, heard things he hadn't even said. "I'd rather talk about you. I don't usually like brown eyes. Yours are exceptional."

The man was not without charm. "You have a lot of prejudices. Doctors, social workers, brown eyes."

His eyes were drawn to her mouth, soft and tempting in the shadowy twilight. "Let's focus on the things I do like, such as the scent you're wearing and the way your mouth trembles a little when you're annoyed."

He was defensive, stubborn and arrogant. He wasn't the simple, attractive flirt she'd thought him to be. But he was still bad news, and Dionne wasn't having any. "I came here to work, Colby. It's not a good idea to mix business with pleasure."

"This is after hours, Doctor." Colby gave in to the need to touch her and raised his hand to trail a finger along her full lower lip. He saw her eyes darken, heard her breath catch. "Or don't you ever turn off that analytical brain of yours?"

"Dinner's ready," said a grumbling voice from the doorway. When neither moved, Aggie grew annoyed. "Better come now, before things cool down."

She needed to cool down, Dionne thought as she broke eye contact with Colby and got to her feet, feeling somewhat shaky. She was oddly pleased to see he was none too steady, either. She walked inside, hoping she didn't look as flushed as she felt.

Perhaps she had overestimated her ability to handle Colby Winters.

Chapter Two

Someone had put flowers in her room, a small bouquet fresh from the garden out back. Dionne stepped closer to the nightstand and touched the delicate petal of a pale rose, the velvet sponginess of a deep red snapdragon.

They surely hadn't been placed there by the sullen-faced Aggie, whose only comment to Dionne during dinner was that smoking could kill her. But Colby? She'd been out of his sight only briefly since leaving her room earlier. Yet it had to have been him. She leaned closer and inhaled deeply.

What a paradox he was, she thought as she undressed for bed. He was home loving, fiercely protective, a nature lover, an independent thinker, a survivor and a closet romantic. He was also judgmental of his father's weakness, but she understood. He was coming from a position of pain and abandonment. He'd asked his personnel to keep an open mind about her program, yet she wondered if his mind-set left room for change.

The breeze ruffling the curtain at the window over her bed was warm as she slid between cool, crisp sheets of pale blue. The house was far enough out in the country that no city noises intruded to drown out the call of night birds skittering in the trees. A peaceful place, yet Dionne felt restless.

She'd left Colby after their delicious dinner, explaining that she was tired, and she was. Just not sleepy. Ordinarily, in her own apartment, she'd arrive home around seven, change clothes and fix a light dinner, then work on files or do required reading until her eyes would no longer stay open. Yet tonight, she felt keyed up, and she didn't need her psychology degree to explain why. Colby Winters.

Dionne couldn't remember the last time she'd lain awake at night, thinking of a man. Years, she was certain. It wasn't that she wasn't interested in men, but rather that through the years, she'd grown fussier. Mature, available men in her corner of the world seemed few and far between. Dating took time and energy, and she had precious little of either left over at the end of a work day. It was easier to choose that good book or dinner with Lainey and Zac or a movie with Hilary on one of the many nights her fiancé was stuck at the hospital. Sometimes, Dionne worried that she was not yet thirty and turning reclusive.

Tossing off the top sheet, she rolled over. The house was silent. Aggie had evidently finished in the kitchen and turned in. Colby's bedroom was way on the other side. When he'd shown her around, she'd glanced in from the hallway and glimpsed a wall of books—some standing, some leaning, several open, suggesting frequent use. There'd been blueprints spread on a large oak table, soft lighting and an old Beatles album playing on the stereo. An inviting room.

She shifted, trying to picture him there, then sat up, disgusted with herself. Maybe she'd try the hot tub. Anything to relax her racing mind and restive body.

Minutes later, wearing her black one-piece suit, she slid the door open and stepped onto the back patio. Colored Malibu lights illuminated the walks and flowerbeds, and the pool was a shimmering aqua invitation. She eased into the adjacent hot tub and pressed the button once. A quiet gurgle, and the water began to churn. Leaning back on the seat, Dionne spread her arms on either side, laid her head back on the ledge and gazed up at the heavens.

A few clouds moved lazily across a midnight sky while scores of stars winked a welcome. A perfect night. The scent of flowers drifted on the light breeze. From a distance, an owl hooted, and she remembered passing a wooded area. Yes, she could see why Colby loved it here.

She smiled, thinking of how Aggie had fussed over him at dinner, all but buttering his rolls. Protective wasn't the word. Possessive was more like it. Perhaps Colby made it a point to bring women home and the little housekeeper felt that none of them were good enough for him.

Well, Aggie could relax if she was worried that Dionne was trying to snare her employer. She would like to have assured the little mother substitute that she had no interest in serious entanglements with any man. Long ago, she'd come to the conclusion that marriage was not for her, and she'd never wavered in that decision.

Three of her four brothers, all married and reproducing regularly, and her parents still prodded, still reminded, still nagged. Dionne needed someone special in her life, they'd told her countless times. No, she did not. Not ever again.

Dionne closed her eyes. Once, she'd had someone she'd thought very special. Nathan Eagleton—bright, funny and handsome to a fault. They'd met in their junior year, she hesitant and nervous, Nathan aggressive and confident. She'd fallen hard, and when he'd mentioned love and marriage, she knew she'd have to tell him her dreadful secret.

She'd been seventeen when she'd developed endometriosis and nearly died. She'd come through, but afterward, when the doctor had told her that they'd had to do a hysterectomy in order to save her life, she almost wished she hadn't. No children, not ever.

The news had all but shattered her.

Trailing her fingers gently through the water, she remembered her family's devotion in helping her get over her pain. Somehow, she'd adjusted and even managed to convince herself that there were other ways to be happy—and a husband, strong and loving, could fill the empty places. And Nathan had been her choice.

She'd dreaded telling him, but she knew she had to. He'd taken the news better than she'd dared hope. Their love for each other would be enough, he'd told her, and she'd loved him all the more for his generous understanding. They'd started sleeping together then, and through the next two years, right up until graduation. Right up until the night he'd broken her heart.

Looking back, she wondered why she hadn't noticed the signs of restlessness in him. Perhaps she'd been too caught up in finals and the rush of graduation, and too much in love. His ardor for her in bed had never cooled, so she'd assumed his feelings hadn't, either. When he told her—rather breezily, she thought—that he was moving East, going on to law school and breaking it off, she'd felt as shocked as she undoubtedly had looked. The quarrel that had followed had stunned her.

Even now, Dionne shivered despite the hot tub's warmth. It's been fun, Nathan had said, especially not having to worry about an unwanted pregnancy. But for marriage, he'd need a *real* woman, one who could enhance his career and give him children. Devastated a second time, she'd gone home, feeling broken, feeling used.

Dionne stretched her legs in the steaming water, welcoming its soothing heat. Thinking back, she recalled that whenever she'd mentioned wedding plans or a home together, Nathan had been vague, disinterested. She'd chalked it up to distraction over his studies. Men, she'd surmised, weren't that interested in discussing orange blossoms and vine-covered cottages. What a fool she'd been to disregard such obvious signs.

Broken hearts do mend, she'd realized during that hideous summer she'd spent recuperating. But scar tissue remains forever. She'd had to face some terrible truths, that it would take a rare man to offer the type of uncommon love she would require, and that she wasn't about to go searching for needles in haystacks.

She would go it alone, with the help of her family and friends, and become a doctor, one who could help others. Eventually, her love and need for the company of children had led her to specialize in treating traumatized kids who needed her more than most. From them she received more than she gave. It wasn't the life she'd have chosen originally, but it was the life she now loved. Life, after all, was filled with compromises, and she was luckier than many.

But she had her pride. So she'd convinced nearly everyone that the family life wasn't for her, that her career meant so much more. Everyone except her mother. The lie came more easily to her tongue these days, and only she and her pillow knew the price she paid to utter it.

But she would not be pitied, not ask a man to share her life again, nor would she open herself up for a repeat of that kind of pain. Her problem would remain *her* problem. Too bad she couldn't tell Aggie to relax, that her precious Colby was perfectly safe around Dionne. There was no need to—

Suddenly she felt the water sway and shift. Her eyes popped open and she sat upright. Across the narrow space, she saw Colby seated on the opposite side of the hot tub, his face shadowed in the dim lighting.

"I couldn't sleep, either," he said. "I hope you don't mind if I join you."

She ran a wet hand over her steamy face. "No, of course not. It's your hot tub." He sat high out of the water, on the top ledge, wearing an ordinary bathing suit. Yet she was acutely aware of his physique, the curly hair on his chest. Averting her gaze, she slid lower into the tub.

"Lovely night, isn't it?"

"Yes." Small talk. Lord! Dionne struggled to get a grip on herself. "I want to thank you for the flowers."

He eased into the water and smiled. "You're welcome. Zac's mother loved flowers. She taught me about the many varieties, how to raise them, their names."

"She must have been quite a lady." Dionne had met Zac's father at the wedding—a big, husky man, yet gentle like Zac—but she knew Zac's mother had died several years ago.

"She was the best." The one who'd taught him about the gentle ways of woman. Colby found himself wondering if the woman across from him had a gentle side under that cool exterior. "It occurs to me that you know a great deal about me and I know very little about you."

Dionne trickled water through her fingers. "Do you think it's necessary for us to know about each other in order to work together?"

He thought she had a maddening habit of answering a question with a question. "Perhaps not necessary, but kind of nice. Tell me about your family." He wanted to know her. He stopped asking himself why.

It seemed a safe enough topic. Dionne smiled, thinking of her folks. "My parents were born in Germany, immigrated to Canada when they were young, met there and married. But there was more work available in Detroit, so they came there. In my late teens, we all moved to Frankenmuth, Michigan, where they still live in a big old house on a lake. My father was a plumber. He's retired now. And my mother's an anachronism, a housewife and mother who's never worked outside the house."

"By choice?"

"Absolutely. Bertha Keller believes that the trouble with the world in general and America in particular is that women don't stay home and raise their own children."

He caught the affection, the warmth. "And though you don't agree, you love her very much."

She sat up straighter, surprised at his perception. "Yes, I do."

"Are you an only child?"

She laughed. "Oh, my, no. I have four brothers, Karl and John, who are older than I, and Konrad and Werner who are younger. I'm the middle child."

"You don't look like you'd come from a German background."

"I know. I'm the black sheep, or I should say, the redheaded sheep, a throwback to my Irish grandmother on my mother's side. Everyone else is tall and blond, and here I am, the runt of the litter." She smiled at her father's favorite description of her.

"Is it true that redheads have bad tempers?"

She considered that a moment. "Mmm, I suppose, if riled. But so do blondes or brunettes."

He let his legs drift toward the center, his toes touching hers briefly, and felt her quickly pull back. "Do you ever answer a question spontaneously, without giving it thoughtful consideration?"

"It depends on the question and who's asking."

A cloud shifted and suddenly the moon shone down on her. Her face was flushed from the heat of the water, her skin flawless, framed by wisps of damp hair, her brown eyes wary as she watched him. Colby slid closer, almost but not quite touching her. Maybe if he talked about the job she'd come to do, she'd stop looking as if he were about to attack. "Do you really think you can help our men?"

Dionne felt on safer ground with this subject, though Colby's nearness was not helping her nerves. "In Chicago, I helped set up a program that's still working today. When management discovers that an employee is chronically late or absent or suddenly not performing well, they arrange meetings with him or her. They determine the problem and, if it's a type of addiction, they refer the employee to specific programs designed to treat that problem."

"You mean like the Alcoholics Anonymous methods you mentioned earlier?"

"Yes. Many hospitals now have drug rehabilitation programs, some on the premises and some on an outpatient basis. But the other beneficial part is intervention, getting the families of the addict involved. A wife who doesn't admit her husband has a drinking problem, a parent who feels experimenting with drugs is just a phase her teenager is going through—these people are codependents who enable the sick person to continue his unacceptable behavior. Until that person faces the problem, admits he's hooked on something he can't lick alone, he or she can't even start on the road to recovery."

Colby rubbed his left arm absently. Broken twice when he'd been young, it often ached. "You really think these people are ill?"

She angled toward him, wanting him to understand. How could she make the program work at Midwest Construction if the boss was unconvinced? "Yes, absolutely. I've worked with too many addicts not to believe exactly that."

"Maybe you should meet my father. You might change your mind."

"Maybe if you sit in on some of our sessions, you'll change yours." She propped her elbow on the tiled rim. "But maybe you don't want to see things differently."

Frowning, he looked at her. "Why wouldn't I?"

"Because if you admit to yourself that your father is ill, not just a drunk, then you have to forgive him for what he did to your mother and your sister. And to you."

His eyes flashed with anger, making him look suddenly dangerous. Then he got himself under control. "You play hardball, don't you?"

"I've always thought beating around the bush was a waste of time."

"So have I." Facing her, he reached to touch the ends of her hair and found the damp strands silky soft, then dropped his hand to rest on her shoulder. "I'm attracted to you and I don't especially want to be."

She felt the unfamiliar tug of desire even from his light touch, and fought her reaction. "I don't want that, either."

"But you feel something, too." It wasn't a question.

It would be foolish and stupid to lie when he was looking into her eyes. "Yes, but that doesn't mean I'm going to do anything about it. We have separate lives, different beliefs, nothing in common."

"Oh, I don't know. We're both workaholics who put in more than the usual eight hours. We both like pot roast, sunsets and hot tubs."

"Not much to base a relationship on."

"I'll bet there have been marriages based on less, if they also had that strong attraction."

"I'll bet the marriages didn't last."

He gazed up at the stars thoughtfully while his fingers skimmed her arm lazily. "Well then, let's see. Do you like the opera? Or reading those thick Russian novels? How about sushi?"

She made a face. "No, none of those."

He gave her a triumphant smile. "Neither do I. How about bird-watching, stamp collecting or eating chocolate-covered ants?" He saw her smile as she shook her head. "See how much we have in common?"

"Not enough, I'm afraid." She'd tried to scoot away from his touch, but he'd only drifted closer. It was time to end this cozy chat, Dionne thought as she feigned a

yawn. "I think I've about had it in here. My skin's going
to shrivel like a raisin."

Colby ran his hand along the length of her arm, then
laced his fingers with hers. "Your skin's beautiful." He
rose, taking her up with him. He was easily a foot taller
as he stood looking down into her dark eyes. "Do your
patients ever forget you're a doctor when they get this
close to you?"

The water had sapped her strength, or was it his nearness? "They don't get this close to me, except the children." Quickly she pulled free of his hand and gingerly
stepped out of the tub. "And I like it that way. Good
night, Colby." She hurried to the sliding doors of her
room and slipped through.

Colby switched off the motor, climbed out and
grabbed his towel. Settling it on his shoulders, he
watched as the drapes were pulled closed across her
window. He'd caught a glimpse of vulnerability there,
but then she'd slid the guard back up.

He saw the light go on behind the drapes. Was she
lying there thinking of him? Most likely not, but instead, dwelling on one of her cases. She was dedicated,
all right, but could she get through to anyone to really
help them? Or was she like Fran Ellis, the social worker
who'd tried to reason with his father?

The night air had turned cool with a hint of fall in it.
Colby stood a moment longer staring at the door of
Dionne's room. He badly wanted to believe she could do
it, make a difference in the lives of his men, perform a
few minor miracles. But he'd stopped believing in Santa
Claus before he'd entered kindergarten.

Turning, he strode to his own room.

She wore glasses, large oversize ones, with wire rims.
They made her brown eyes look softer, Colby thought as

he sat at the far end of his conference table while Dionne talked to his staff. He'd driven her to the office early, and she'd made several calls, then rounded up Dave, Dottie and Ron and left with them. He'd learned she'd taken them to two AA meetings, one for victims and one for family members, called Al-Anon. Then they'd gone to Charter Hospital and been familiarized with the methods used in rehab procedures. Colby had met them upon their return in midafternoon, surprised at how impressed his people had been at the thoroughness of the programs.

It was nearing the end of the day, and yet Dionne was as fresh as when he'd seen her walk into his kitchen that morning. You had to love your work to have such untiring enthusiasm for it. He sat back and tuned in.

"You've all got a copy of the Twelve-Step Program, and we've gone over each step. By far the hardest one is the first, that the troubled individual has to admit to himself and then to one of you, that he's powerless over his particular addiction and that his life has become unmanageable. This is one step you can't hurry. Until they see this in themselves, they won't believe and they won't begin to recover."

Dottie crossed her legs, looking puzzled. "But I don't see why the director at Charter Hospital said that most people have to hit rock bottom before they seek help. Why can't we get a hold of them *before* that, lead them into the proper program and get them help earlier? I mean, rock bottom! In some cases, that means loss of family, job, home—everything!"

Dionne nodded. "Yes, I'm afraid it does. But the reason you're setting up this employee-assistance program is to move that bottom up, to force that individual to face his situation sooner. Intervention is not confrontational but rather a loving approach. It's saying to him, 'Look we know you have a problem. We can no longer sweep it under the rug because we now have a liability in you. Your work performance is affected and in many cases endangers the lives of others as well as your own.' Of course, you can't get someone to hear you until they're ready to listen. Anyone here have a teenager?"

Both Dottie and Ron nodded.

"Did you ever try to talk them out of dating someone you didn't approve of? They appear to listen, even nod and say the right things, then see that person on the sly anyway—at least that's the case with most teenagers I've run across. So you sit back, helpless to keep them from getting hurt. When they're hurting real bad, then they realize you were right. But not until *they* see it for themselves. It's the same with drinking, with drugs. The addict may *want* to stop, but when he's low, he remembers only that he felt good when using the dangerous substance. He doesn't remember the morning after or the pain or that his life is getting out of control. When he finally does see it, then he's ready. That's when he'll listen."

Ron shook his head. "It seems almost cruel."

"Perhaps it does," Dionne continued, "but you sometimes have to be cruel in order to be kind."

Dave glanced at his watch. "So when do we start the actual hands-on stuff? I've got to get back to my men."

Dionne checked her notepad. "I realize this was a long session, but necessary. Tomorrow morning, I'd like to take you to the detoxification center, just so you know what it's like. And to visit an after-care clinic in a local hospital. Without structured follow-up, the employee may quickly resume his former activities, even after completing the program. And in the afternoon, if possible, I'd like to set up a group or individual counseling sessions with a couple of people you feel are recognized problems." She glanced toward Colby, her first acknowledgement of his presence since he'd quietly entered, though she'd been keenly aware of his intent gaze and undivided attention. "Is that all right?"

Colby rose. "Sure. Why don't you each submit a name and we can go over the files in the morning before you leave. Then, while you're away, I'll make sure the men are available for the afternoon session."

"Or women," Dionne interjected. "The number of addicted women in the last decade has almost doubled."

Dottie gathered her papers. "Why do you think that is?"

"More women in the work force, pressure to succeed, the high divorce rate, single parenting. Women need escape, diversion. Just as much as men."

The three agreed with her assessment as they left, saying good-night as they closed the door.

Colby strolled over to where Dionne was sliding her papers into her leather briefcase. "I'm impressed. You seem to know what you're doing."

Dionne struggled with a smile as she shot him a quick look. He would surely turn her head with such lavish praise, but then, she was well aware of his doubts. "Did you think I'd come this far on a bluff?"

"It's not you I have trouble believing. I know you're very qualified. It's your whole line of work I have little faith in."

She snapped her case closed and turned to face him. "I thought you were going to reserve judgment for a while?"

She wore blue today, a pale blue wool jacket over a navy skirt. Redheads had trouble with certain colors, yet she looked good in all of them, Colby decided. And she was busily putting him in his place again. "You're right, I did say that. Our methods may differ, but I believe we have the same goal. You may not think so, but I want to help these people, too."

She believed him. He was a man as hard as the steel and lumber he worked with, yet she'd spotted a core of sensitivity in him. He would fight her methods until she convinced him that they worked. "I have no doubt of that," she told him.

"Good." It was time for a change of subject. "So what would you like to do tonight? Have pizza and beer and go bowling, or go to a schmaltzy restaurant and dance a little?"

Amused, she raised a questioning eyebrow.

"You said women need escape and diversion as much as men. What's your preference?"

"It's been a long day, Colby."

He took a step closer. "After a hard day's work, what do you usually do for relaxation?"

She picked up her purse, angling back from him. "I go for a long drive or I sleep. I never seem to get enough sleep."

"But it's still light outside, a little early to sleep. How about if I pick up a Chinese assortment and we catch a movie. I've got a large library of oldies and a new VCR."

Why did that sound so inviting? Dionne sighed. "What about Aggie? Won't she pout if she can't feed you?"

"I already called her. Told her to go visit her sister tonight."

"Pretty sure of yourself, aren't you?" Alone in the house with Colby. It sounded like a mistake. "I don't know..."

"I've got every picture Bogie ever made," he teased, sensing her weakening.

She cocked her head. "Including *Casablanca* and *To Have and Have Not,* in which Bacall teaches him how to whistle?" She saw his confident nod. "You've discovered my two weaknesses, Bogie and Chinese. All right, you're on."

"Do you do this often?" Dionne asked as she stared down at the scene. After she'd changed into shorts and a cotton shirt, she'd come into the living room to find Colby had spread a plaid blanket in front of the hearth and lined up the cardboard cartons of Chinese food in the center. Picnic plates and cutlery were waiting, as were frosty glasses of iced tea.

He grinned up at her. "You don't like picnics?"

She hunkered down opposite him. "Actually, I do. My brother Karl especially loves picnics. He'd talk the rest of us into going on them regularly. He and my mother would fix all the food and we'd all pile into Karl's Jeep and drive up into this wooded section near the house. And we'd swim and play baseball and climb trees, then eat ourselves silly."

Colby busily opened cartons and stuck spoons in each. "Sounds like you were a tomboy."

"Was I ever. I tried to get a girls' football team organized in grade school. I was so insistent, they threatened to put me on probation if I didn't stop riling the other girls every chance I could." She shook her head.

"My poor mother. I must have given her a few gray hairs."

He found he liked her like this, relaxed and chatty. "Weren't you a little small for football?"

Dionne nodded, chewing on a fried wonton. "And I was too short for basketball. But my height didn't matter in racing."

Colby spooned himself healthy helpings as he balanced his plate on his lap. "You mean track?"

"No, race cars. Karl got me interested. I had this old souped-up Corvette and I loved speed. So he thought I'd be better off on a track."

"This was in high school?"

"No, later. There are sanctioned races in lots of states, many classed out for women. I only entered about half a dozen and never came very close to winning." She took a tangy bite of pepper steak and closed her eyes in appreciation.

They ate in companionable silence for a few minutes before Colby went on. "Racing's fairly dangerous. Weren't you afraid?"

"Sure, some. But it's also exciting. After college, I went through a reckless stage. I wouldn't do it now, but at the time, I seemed to need to prove something." Or maybe take her mind off Nathan. She looked up. "Didn't you ever do anything daring and stupid when you were young?"

Colby nodded as he reached for his tea. "More than once. Zac and I both were wild there for a while."

"What made you change?"

"I had to work two jobs in order to go to college, so I didn't have the time or the money. And Zac had Nancy, his first wife, who tamed him in a hurry." He paused a moment, considering his next question. "You ever been in love?"

Dionne pushed a mound of sweet-and-sour pork around her plate. "I was involved in what I thought was love at the time."

"Kind of like a bad case of chicken pox, isn't it? Not terminal, but damned uncomfortable and sometimes leaves you scarred."

She smiled at his apt description. "Yes, kind of. You, too?"

"Yes. She was very beautiful, and I was too young and stupid to look for more. Raging hormones account for a lot of early mistakes." Finishing, he set both their plates aside.

Dionne lit a cigarette. "Aren't you glad you've outgrown that silly phase?" She watched the sheepish smile appear.

"Does any man ever outgrow that phase?" Shifting, he moved to sit close alongside her. "Does any woman?"

"Speaking clinically? Probably not."

He slid his arm along her shoulders. "And speaking personally?"

"Doctors never speak personally, didn't you know?" Rising, she strolled to the television across the room, wondering if he was going to be a problem or let her watch the movie. "Where're these Bogie movies you promised me?"

Sighing, Colby joined her and pulled out a couple of storage drawers. "Your choice, madam." While she read through the titles, he stashed the remnants of their picnic in the kitchen.

"How about *The Big Sleep?*" Dionne asked as he came back in. "I've almost memorized the dialogue from most of the others."

"One of my favorites." He turned on the set and shoved the cassette into the VCR. Turning, he saw that she'd settled herself on the floor, her back against the couch, and he walked over to sit alongside.

The credits came on as Dionne put out her cigarette and leaned back. In moments, Bogie was on the scene, his ever-present cigarette dangling from the side of his mouth.

"It's odd the way this man's movies are still so popular years after his death," Colby commented as Bogie stepped into the foyer of a large home. "I mean, he's not very tall, not exactly handsome and has a lisp. How do you explain it?"

"It's hard to explain appeal. Some ordinary men have it while some extraordinary men don't."

Colby stretched out his long legs comfortably. "Would a man like him appeal to you?" He wasn't sure why he was asking, but there was so much about Dionne Keller that had him wondering.

"Possibly. Not all of us are drawn to the conventionally attractive."

"This man you thought you loved, what did he look like?"

Colby would have made a good detective, Dionne thought. "He was tall and blond with blue eyes."

"Uh-huh." He got the picture. "So now you're looking for a short, dark man with brown eyes?"

"Throw in a cute lisp and you've got a sale."

Colby shook his head and turned his attention back to the movie, wondering how Bogie would have handled Dionne Keller.

She lost herself in the movie, letting her mind relax with the familiar dialogue, the complicated plot and Bogie's understated acting. She was watching two thugs work Bogie over in an alley when she noticed that Colby had moved closer and had stretched one arm along the couch back. Tensing, she waited until his hand settled on her shoulder before she turned to face him.

"Look at that old Packard they're pulling out of the water," Colby said, his eyes on the screen. "Now there was a car. Built like a tank." He could feel her eyes on his profile, so he turned toward her.

"What are we doing here?" she asked.

"Watching a movie."

"That doesn't require body contact."

He smiled. "I've always loved contact sports." Slowly, he lowered his head toward hers.

The thing to do was to be an adult, get this over with, because until she let him kiss her, he was going to keep on trying. Once he sampled for himself and learned that she was cool and unresponsive, he'd back away and stop this silly game. Leaning her head back, Dionne waited, her eyes half closed.

"Looks like you got a little sun today. Your face is kind of pink."

Her eyes fluttered open. "What?"

"With your skin, you have to be careful, even in the fall." He ran the back of his hand along one cheek and down the line of her throat, trying not to smile at the confusion in her eyes.

Embarrassed she flushed deeper as she sat upright. The laugh was on her, Dionne thought as she stood. "It's getting late. I think I'll turn in."

More quickly than she'd have thought possible, he was on his feet and close beside her. "That's too bad, because we haven't come to the good part yet."

She knew he wasn't referring to the movie. "There is no *good part* between us, Colby." She pushed against his chest and freed herself, then took a step backward, half expecting him to grab her. "We're doing business together, and that's *all* we're doing."

He widened his stance challengingly. "I could have kissed you just now and you know it. You wanted me to. I would have thought a shrink would know better than to deny her feelings."

Any moment she'd betray her feelings if she didn't get away from him. It wasn't anger at him that had her nearly trembling, but anger at herself. He was right. She'd wanted to discover what his hard mouth would feel like on hers. Quickly, she turned away.

"I don't have time for games. Go find yourself another playmate." Bending, she snatched up the blanket and began folding it.

Colby grabbed the loose end and moved close, settling his hands over hers. He saw her eyes grow stormy.

"I didn't think you were the type of man who would push."

"You're right. I'm the type of man who'll walk away from the obvious. But only once." Turning, he left her standing there, holding the blanket.

Chapter Three

It was raining, and she was fuming. But her anger had little to do with the weather, Dionne thought as she glanced at the directions she'd scribbled down hurriedly. The site wasn't much farther, she decided as she aimed the Corvette up the winding hillside street.

After her narrow escape last night, she'd left the house early, needing to avoid Colby. She'd spent the morning with his three supervisors, snagging them before Colby arrived. They'd toured the detox center, talked with the staff and, through a special window, had even been able to observe a patient going through the hell of drug withdrawal. Dottie had been shaking when they'd left.

The after-care clinic at a nearby hospital had been easier to handle, learning about the follow-up counseling sessions, the job-placement center and the twenty-four-hour care line manned by former patients. The doctor in charge had introduced them to members of the

Aim Group, recovered users who spotted troubled people and tried to convince them to seek treatment.

At lunch, they'd discussed their impressions, and Dionne had been elated that all three seemed to find merit in the programs they'd seen, even the skeptical Ron Henry. It was all she could hope for at this point.

Things had gone well until she'd returned to Colby's office and found his terse message. Marianne had handed her his note saying he'd set up two individual counseling sessions for her at his trailer parked on the building site in a neighboring suburb. She was to change clothes before meeting him there or to be prepared to get wet and muddy. It had sounded too close to a command as opposed to a request to suit Dionne.

Gritting her teeth, she'd gone to the house and changed into jeans and shirt, grabbed her jacket and headed for the site. She must have looked more than a little annoyed, for even Aggie had given her a wide berth as she'd rushed out the door. Of course, she could have called and cancelled, or just not shown up. But she never took her commitments lightly. Turning left into the fenced construction area, Dionne decided she still felt as stormy as the rain that pounded on the roof of her Corvette.

She spotted only one trailer and saw Colby's pickup parked near the door. Pulling alongside, she groaned at the mud splashing her low-slung car. Why had this wild man demanded she work out here when he had a perfectly dry office available? She hoped he had a plausible explanation as she zipped up her jacket and ducked outside.

Scooting up the stairs, she shoved at the door and didn't lift her head until she was inside. The air was warm, humid and smoke filled. Rolled up blueprints mingled with those spread out on a table with scarred red booth seats. A narrow convertible couch ran toward the back, where a closed door indicated the bathroom. A two-burner stove and small refrigerator were also in the rear. A short, dark-haired man stood wrestling with a tray of reluctant ice cubes, swearing ripely. Looking up and noticing her, his face reddened and he quickly apologized.

"It's all right, Frenchy," Colby said, sliding out of the booth. "The doctor here has heard worse, I'm sure."

Shaking the moisture from her hair, Dionne unzipped her jacket and looked up at him with an icy glare. "Yes, and I'm about to use all the four-letter words I know so you'll understand I'm not thrilled at being ordered around."

Colby accepted the glass of iced tea from Frenchy and sent Dionne a lazy grin. So she did have a redhead's temper. "Couldn't be helped. Foreman didn't make it in today, so I had to cover for him. I thought an experienced professional like you could counsel anywhere, Doc."

He had a rough-and-ready look about him that contrasted with his more polished office demeanor, she noticed, and she wished she didn't find it suited him. He wore leather boots, jeans and a denim shirt rolled up high on powerful arms. His hard hat rested on a filing cabinet, and she wanted to pop him with it.

Frustrated, she balled her fists at the amusement on his tan face. "Let me remind you, Mr. Winters," she said, low and frosty, "that I don't work *for* you, but that I'm here at your partner's request, granted during a weak moment that I'm beginning to regret. House calls went out with the horse and buggy, haven't you heard?"

Despite her soft delivery, Colby heard Frenchy give a short laugh that the man tried to cover with a cough. He turned to stare at him. "You want to make yourself useful, go to Unit Twelve and send over first Dan, then Terry."

Nodding, Frenchy grabbed a slicker and left.

Colby took a long sip of tea before answering, hoping the icy drink would cool him down. Why was it that this woman could set his teeth on edge with only a sentence or two? Remembering his promise to Zac, he frowned.

"I didn't think it was such a big deal. Besides, I thought you might enjoy seeing one of our work sites."

Dionne glanced pointedly out the window where a leaden sky and gray sheets of rain kept visibility to a mere dozen feet. "You thought I might want to tour the area in a downpour?"

He shrugged. "A little summer shower." He reached to touch the ends of her damp hair. "Most women don't look good when they're wet. You do."

She closed her eyes a long moment, praying for patience. "Lord, you're exasperating." Moving to the side, she grabbed a towel and took a stab at drying her hair. Her own fault, Dionne decided. She should have laid down more explicit ground rules from the onset. No matter. She'd get through this and be gone by the weekend.

"Would you like something cold to drink?" he asked, watching her get her temper under control. He wondered idly what it would be like to let her lose it, *really* lose it. To have her fight with him, then make up with him on the narrow couch while the rain sounded against the roof.

"Yes, I would, thank you."

She had the towel up around her head as he tried to pass. A slow, sliding step and he was close up against her in the narrow aisle of the trailer. "Lemon or sugar?"

Dionne felt a shiver race up her spine and wondered if he could feel it, too. No matter how much her mind wanted her to ignore this man, her traitorous body was keenly aware of the press of his hard thighs against hers, of his warm breath on her cool face. Damn him for making her forget her intentions so readily and so often. "Neither." Shifting, she eased away and past him, seating herself at the table. Where the hell were those men? "I thought you were setting up appointments with three of your people this afternoon."

"Dottie's working on the third one. Our head bookkeeper. There aren't any obvious signs, but her friends think she's a secret drinker. Hopefully, you can talk with her tomorrow."

"Closet drinkers usually take a long time coming around."

Colby placed her tea in front of her, then leaned against the file cabinet, crossing his feet at the ankles. "How'd it go this morning?"

"Very well. Are you going to remain while I talk with your men?"

"I checked it out with both Terry and Dan, and they prefer I do. They know me and trust me. I've also assured them both that we're not looking for excuses to fire someone. We're trying to help anyone with a problem." He flashed a quick smile. "Besides, they're probably afraid to be left alone with the big, bad doctor."

She chose to ignore that. "Tell me about their backgrounds before they get here."

Brisk and businesslike, he noticed. That was fine with him. He'd take care of business first. But then... "Terry

Hanson's twenty-four, a bricklayer, very good at what
he does, as long as he stays dry. He comes from a family of drinkers, father and two brothers. He tries, but he
falls off the wagon frequently. Do you believe in the
heredity factor?''

She sipped her tea, feeling her control return. "The
tendency toward inherited weaknesses and behavior
disorders has been documented. Genetics play a part, as
does environment. If everyone around you drinks as
you're growing up, chances are you'll do the same.''

"Or you'll be disgusted by it and never drink.''

It occurred to her that she'd never seen him touch alcohol. Because of his father? "In some cases, yes.''

"But more often than not, they drink.''

"Children are apt to follow a monkey-see, monkey-do
behavior pattern. Has Terry had any serious problems?''

"Sporadic absenteeism mostly. He binges with his
buddies, then is regretful and leaves the stuff alone for
a while. Recently, he got engaged, and I've been hoping
Jean would help straighten him out. So far, no luck.''

"She can't do it if he fights her. What about Dan?''

Colby shook his head. "Dan's about thirty, a big guy,
six-three, weighs about two thirty-five. He's a master
electrician, and that's a tricky job if you come in hung
over. He claims he doesn't have a drinking problem, that
he works hard and deserves his play time, including
wine, women and song. What's surprising is he comes
from a very solid background of clean living. His father's a minister.''

"He could be rebelling against a repressed childhood. Have there been any incidents?''

"Yeah, the last one about two weeks ago. He and an
apprentice were working on this condo and somehow, a

hot wire was left uncapped before lunch break. The apprentice found it later and told Dan, but he got real defensive. Nothing happened—*this time*. But somebody could have wandered in, picked up the wire, fallen, any number of things. There's no proof, but several of the men feel that Dan's gotten careless, especially on the mornings after."

"Sounds like Dan's still in the denial stage."

"You bet. He's going to give you a rough time."

Colby called that one right, Dionne thought later as she sat across the table from the heavyset electrician. His small eyes were more than a little wary, his body tense and his feet were pointed toward the door, the only avenue of escape. Restlessly, he fiddled with a book of matches as she started out with preliminary questions, then zeroed in.

"Would you be opposed to a blood-testing program as a work requirement?"

"You mean for drugs?" Dan asked. "I don't do drugs. Man, that stuff'll kill you."

"And you don't think alcohol will?"

"Listen, lady, I'm a big guy with a big tolerance. I can drink more than a little guy and it don't bother me."

"I see. No health problems?" She watched him shake his head emphatically. "Then you wouldn't be opposed to having a general physical?"

His large fist wrapped around the matchbook. "I'll bet I'm healthier than you are," he challenged.

"It's possible. I suffer from migraine headaches occasionally."

"Me, too. Terrible headaches some mornings. I—" He stopped, looking as if he suddenly realized he'd walked into a trap. "I guess everyone has headaches."

Dionne glanced down at his file. "I understand you're divorced, Dan. Do you have any children?"

His smile broke through. "Yeah, I got a boy. He's seven. Going to be an electrician like his old man. Great kid."

"Have you got a picture of him?"

Smiling now, Dan got out his wallet and handed her a snapshot of a young boy with sandy hair and a mischievous grin. "His name's Kevin."

She studied it carefully, then crossed her arms and leaned forward. "Tell me, Dan, when your son's an apprentice, would you want him working under a master electrician who might be hung over, whose reflexes might be just a little slow that morning, who might be tired and get a little careless?"

His face reddened as he sat up straighter. "That's not fair. I do my job."

"Answer my question, Dan."

He clasped his big hands together and slammed them down on the table. "I'm not an alcoholic, dammit!"

Dionne forced herself not to react, to keep her eyes steady on his. She heard Colby stand up behind her and hoped he'd stay put. "Think about this, then. Have you ever taken a drink in the morning, just to steady your nerves? Have you ever not remembered what you did the night before? Have you ever—I mean *ever*—had the fear deep inside that you might be becoming an alcoholic, that you're losing control, and it scares the hell out of you? Don't answer aloud, but be honest with yourself."

For a long minute, Dan just stared, conflicting emotions evident on his florid face. Then slowly, he bent his head and averted his gaze.

"It's hard, I know." She pointed toward her cigarette pack lying on the table. "See those? I've tried for years to kick the habit, and I haven't yet. But I'm only endangering myself, bad as that is. You could be hurting others, including not being there for your son as long as he needs you." When Dan raised his head, she saw a haunted look in his eyes that made her want to reach out and reassure him. But she kept her face free of emotion. "Would you agree to go to a meeting or two? Most of us can't lick these things alone. Would you accept help from people who've been there themselves, who won't judge you?"

Dan ran a hand across his face, obviously torn. "I don't know. I'm not like those guys downtown, bums who steal or beg for a bottle. I pay taxes, I hold down a responsible job."

"How long will that continue if you keep drinking and possibly make mistakes that could get you fired or begin not to show up because you feel too lousy the next day?"

Again, Dan shot Colby a quick glance, but he was silent.

"Will you go to a meeting I arrange?" Dionne persisted.

After a moment, Dan let out a deep breath. "I'm not promising anything once I get there, you understand?"

"I understand. I only ask that you show up and listen with an open mind." She handed his picture back. "Kevin's a beautiful boy."

Dan returned the snapshot to his wallet. Rising, he glanced toward Colby, then back at Dionne. "When do I have to go to this meeting?"

"Tomorrow night, seven o'clock. I'll call to remind you, all right?"

"Yeah, all right." He moved toward the door, then turned back to her. "You're not what I expected."

"What had you expected?"

"I don't know, but you're not it. No, sir." Shaking his head, Dan opened the door and left.

As Colby came up beside her, Dionne looked up at him. "What do you suppose he meant by that?"

"I'm not sure, but I agree with him."

She didn't know what to say, so she shifted her thoughts back to Dan. His capitulation had come about too quickly. It was a victory too easily won, and she never trusted those. Dan, like many alcoholics, could be very good at mouthing the right responses with little intention of doing as asked. Time would tell.

"I can't believe you got him to agree to go to a meeting. I've talked with him three times and he flat out refused."

"Don't let's celebrate just yet." She badly needed a cigarette and quickly lit one, inhaling deeply.

Colby thought that she didn't look elated or particularly troubled. She looked cool and detached, like the social worker who'd visited his father. At least Fran Ellis had pretended to care. He struggled with a surge of unreasonable anger. "You enjoy this, don't you?"

Dionne looked up in surprise. But before she could answer, Terry bounced up the stairs, dripping wet and smiling.

"Hi, Colby," he greeted breezily, then turned to Dionne. "I'm Terry Hanson." He wiped his hand on his jeans, then thrust it toward her. "You wanted to see me, Doc?"

He was short with sandy hair, a freckled face and a cocky grin. Dionne approved of his timing. Colby's presence was unnerving, and she wished she could tell him to take a hike. However, he was in charge here, so she swallowed her displeasure. She put on a smile for

Terry and shook his work-roughened hand. "Yes, please sit down, Terry."

She heard Colby walk back to his seat as she reached for Terry's file. He was affable and charming. Yet, as they chatted, Dionne asking questions and Terry giving flip answers, she found herself growing concerned. He was treating his addiction as if he'd had a minor head cold and it was over now.

"I told Colby only last week," Terry said, "I'm all through with the heavy stuff. Can't afford booze, for one thing. I'm getting married soon, saving my money. I have an occasional beer, that's all." He leaned forward, flashing his boyish grin. "So you can cross me off your list, Doc."

"How often do you have an occasional beer, Terry?"

He shrugged. "Weekends. Friday night, maybe Saturday."

"And you stop with one, two at the most?"

"You bet. Jean's on my case and she can be mean. She even said she wouldn't marry me if I didn't quit. That did it."

"I see. So you're clean now?" She watched him nod emphatically. "Then you wouldn't mind if Midwest Construction set up a blood-testing program, especially for their employees who have potentially dangerous jobs?"

His steady gaze wavered slightly as he glanced back at Colby seated at the far end of the trailer. "If everyone else has to take a test, I will, too." Reaching into his shirt pocket, he took out a roll of mints and popped one in his mouth.

"Do your friends drink?"

"A few. Not falling down drunk, you know. They just like to have a good time."

"What do you do for a good time when you're all together?"

"We go boating on the river, sometimes fish. We bowl, play cards, that sort of thing."

"Do you take a cooler on the river, buy drinks at the bowling alley, play cards at someone's home where they provide sandwiches and beer?"

Terry shifted uneasily, his smile slipping. "Yeah, there's beer around. But I don't drink much of it. Not anymore."

"Are you then the designated driver for your friends when you all get together, since you're the sober one?"

He gave a short laugh. "Not in the past, but since Jean's been with me—"

"Does Jean drink?"

"No, makes her sick."

"Do you ever get sick from drinking too much? Do you ever come to work feeling ill, hung over? Do you miss many days?"

Again, Terry sent Colby a quick glance. "I've got a nervous stomach, so once in a while, I miss a day or two. Occasionally I'm late 'cause my car won't start. But I do my job. Ask anyone around here."

Dionne flipped open his file. "I have. Last month, you missed six days and were late four more." She looked up into his suddenly defensive gaze. "Would you be willing to attend a couple of meetings where people who have similar problems talk and help one another?"

"You mean AA? No way! I'm no alcoholic, Doc." He ran a shaky hand through his damp hair. "Maybe I used to drink a little too much now and then. No more. I'm through with that. I'm not like my old man. He used to drink damn near a fifth a night, but he still made it on his own to bed every night."

Dear God! She took a gamble. "Where is your father now?"

Terry shifted in his seat. "He died two years ago. But not from cirrhosis or any of those drinking diseases."

"What did he die of?"

"Heart attack."

"How old was he? Fifty? Fifty-five?"

Terry glanced back to where Colby was shuffling through some papers, seemingly not listening. "Fifty-three, but lots of nondrinkers die of heart attacks."

"Yes, they do. But excessive drinking can harm the heart, especially over a long period of time."

"I know. That's one reason I quit."

Slowly, she closed his file. "All right, Terry. That's all, then."

He cleared his throat, looking confused. "You believe me?"

"I believe it wouldn't hurt you to attend the meetings. But I can't force you to go."

Terry shoved out of the booth. "If I needed to go, I would. Nice meeting you, Doc." He waved to Colby. "See you." Hurriedly, he left the trailer, closing the door with a resounding thud as a rainy mist blew in after him.

Sighing deeply, Dionne lit a cigarette and gazed up at the drifting smoke as Colby came alongside and took the seat Terry had vacated.

"You don't believe him," he said.

"Do you?"

He shook his head. "I've heard a lot of drunks swear they had drinking under control. Too many."

Dionne frowned in annoyance. "Not drunks. Men who have a sickness."

"Call it whatever you like, it's the same thing."

Dionne pulled on her cigarette, feeling her frustration building along with a healthy dose of anger. What could she say to convince this pigheaded man? "Dan's drinking is getting out of control and he's beginning to worry about it. But will he attend the meetings and is he frightened enough to quit? Anyone's guess. Terry's convinced himself he's licked the problem, but his absentee records indicate otherwise. He's lying to himself, to Jean and to us because he can't face his weakness and refuses to accept help. They're both sick, not drunks. I wish you'd understand the difference."

"*I* don't understand? Listen, lady, I understand more than you think. I'm the son of an alcoholic, remember? My father could have hit me just a little harder in one of his drunken rages and maybe I wouldn't be here today. I sat back there and listened to Dan talk about his son, Kevin, with love and pride. But what's he like when his brain is foggy with booze? And what's going to happen to Jean if she gambles and marries a drunk like Terry? Will she wind up broken and beaten like my mother did while he struts around saying he's not an alcoholic because all he drinks is beer? These guys ought to be... to be..."

Angrily, she ground out her cigarette. "Ought to be what? Locked up? Beaten until they agree to stay sober? What punishment would you give them?"

Her calm voice made him even more furious. He narrowed his eyes and leaned closer. "How do you do it? How do you remain so clinical, so unaffected, so damn detached when a guy's spilling his guts out to you, when he's close to tears?"

"My sympathy wouldn't help him. What good am I to a patient if I crumble and cry with him? Both of those men need firm guidance and direction, not a shoulder to cry on. And not punishment.''

She could tell she wasn't reaching him. So few understood how difficult it was for a doctor to remain uninvolved and professional for the good of the patient. Especially with children. She'd broken her own rule a few times and paid a high price. He couldn't begin to imagine the private grief that tormented her, nor would he believe her.

Her silence was irritating him further. Colby rose, too agitated to remain sitting. ''Clichés. Textbook answers. Where are your *feelings* in all this? Are these men just a case to you, a problem to solve, then you move on to another? How do you keep from letting it get to you? Or does ice really flow in those professional veins of yours?''

Dionne knew that part of his anger was directed at himself because of his own past situation, and part was misdirected. But she didn't have to take this from him or from anyone. Quickly she slid out of the booth, grabbed her jacket and hurried down the steps.

''Where are you going? We're not through here.''

A gust of cold, wet air met her as she pushed open the door. ''Oh, yes, we are.'' Ducking her head, Dionne stepped onto the muddy ground and headed for her car.

''Wait a minute, dammit.'' He ran after her, unable to remember when he'd last been so angry. Who did she think she was, walking away from him in the middle of a discussion? He didn't care if she was a doctor with ten degrees. He caught her at the Corvette, jerked her around by the arm and trapped her against the door. ''I want to talk to you.''

The rain had drenched her in moments, plastered her hair to her head, soaked her shoes. Dionne scarcely noticed as she glared up at him, her dark eyes blazing. "But *I* don't want to talk to *you.*" She struggled but his strong hands gripped her arms like twin steel vises.

Never had a woman infuriated him so regularly, ignored him so maddeningly and aroused him so swiftly. He didn't give a damn if he pushed her over the edge or if half his men were near enough to stop and watch them.

"Let me go, you—"

His mouth covered hers and he swallowed the rest of her words. At the first taste of her, Colby's anger drained. He felt her stiffen in shock, then fury had her fists striking his back once, twice. He needed to know if he could chip away the ice and discover a smoldering heat he suspected was inside her. Winding his arms around her, he dragged her closer, twisting his body until it was in intimate contact with hers. She tried to yank free, but he held her fast. His lips moved over hers until finally he felt her fingers unclench, then tangle in the material of his shirt.

He remembered how she'd looked the night he'd touched her lips with his finger in the hot tub, the way her eyes had turned smoky and aware. And he remembered how her breasts had felt against his chest when he'd pulled her up close last night, desire flushing her face at the contact. He remembered and grew hard as he swayed with her now. He wanted to release that avalanche of emotion that she thought she'd buried so thoroughly. He wanted her to feel the aching need that had him throbbing.

What had happened to the cool almost disdainful response she'd given most men over the years? Dionne asked herself through a haze of desire. Where was the woman who'd always been able to control, to subdue, to turn off a man who persisted? It was shattering to have her choices narrowed, her free will neatly squashed.

Her head was swimming. With no small effort, she pulled her mouth from his. "Stop this!" she said in a voice surprisingly thick. But he paid little heed, trailing his lips down her throat, then back up to take her mouth again. When his tongue mated with hers, she heard herself moan. Suddenly, she was clinging to him, unable to fight the rush of heat, the awakened need that had her trembling.

She was far from inexperienced and cautious by nature and design, yet she gave herself up to the moment and the madness even as she questioned her own sanity. This was crazy, this had nowhere to go and could lead to nothing but disaster. Yet her arms held him tightly, her mouth responded avidly, her body strained to his shamelessly.

Colby felt desire slam into him like a powerful fist. He'd suspected a fire within her, but he'd been unprepared for a roaring blaze. He'd thought her cool, controlled, detached. But that had been before she'd taken his breath away. It was only natural to want a woman who responded so unexpectedly. But this was the wrong woman to want. He pulled back, breathing hard.

Dionne drew air into starving lungs, her chest heaving as she stared up at him. He took a step backward, and she all but sagged against the car door as she dropped her gaze. "All right," she said, her voice almost normal. "You proved your point. I'm human."

Colby swiped at the water dripping off his chin. "I wasn't trying to prove anything."

Slowly, she raised her head. "Weren't you?"

He looked off toward the units being built and noticed several men huddled outside and turned their way.

Let them look. He turned back. "Maybe. Maybe I got more than I bargained for."

His unexpected admission threw her off balance. "Perhaps I should leave town. This...alliance isn't working out." She needed a cigarette and she needed to move away from him.

Colby thought of Zac and frowned. "Professionally it is. Personally is another matter."

"Actually, we think alike on very little." She squared her shoulders, remembering her commitment to Zac. "I'll finish out the week. I'm sure you can take it from there."

He knew her suggestion made sense. A smart man shouldn't want to stick his hand into the flame twice. Yet, now that he'd tasted her, felt her response, did he want her to leave? "Let's wait and see. No rash decisions at emotional moments. Okay?"

His eyes were no longer angry, but what she saw there frightened her more. Determination. She'd been wrong. They weren't oil and water. They were kindling and a ready match. She shook the water from her hair, then shook her head. "Look, Colby, this is hardly the time or place for true confessions, but as I mentioned, I was involved once and it ended badly. I won't go through that again. I think we should do each other a favor and go our separate ways."

The rain was letting up, but his emotions weren't. Colby braced himself against the car and looked down at her. "I've been that route, too. I even married her. When we broke up, I went on a six-month binge that nearly killed me. I don't want this either, but here it is. Only a fool would deny what's between us."

He wasn't the only one with determination. "I've walked away from attraction before. I can again."

He couldn't resist the challenge. Before Dionne realized his intention, he touched his lips to hers again, his hands gentle on her back. Where before he'd aroused, now he captivated. Where before he plundered, now he seduced—slowly, softly, tenderly.

She should push him away, she knew she should. But his mouth on hers felt suddenly right, suddenly irresistible. Far more potent than his devouring kiss was this sweet seduction. Her lips invited, her body demanded as she took from him.

At last, Colby released her, his eyes smoldering. "*Can* you walk away?"

"Maybe not," she answered honestly. "But I can try." She opened the car door as she groped in the pocket of her sodden jeans for her keys. Inside, it took her two tries to get the key into the ignition. When she finally managed, she wiped the moisture from her face and turned on the windshield wipers. Chilled, shaken and suddenly exhausted, she backed up, shifted into first, then paused.

He was in front of the trailer, his stance arrogant, his clothes soaked, his boots muddy. And his eyes on hers were defiant and challenging. With a small shudder, Dionne stepped on the gas and headed for the gate.

The phone started ringing as Colby dashed inside the trailer. Grabbing a towel, he slung it on his head as he picked up the receiver. "Hello."

"Hello, Colby. How goes the battle?" Zac's voice was as clear as if he were in the city instead of fifty miles north in St. Clair.

What a day for him to ask that, Colby thought as he sat down somewhat heavily. "Been pouring since dawn.

Otherwise not so bad. How are things with you and Lainey?''

"Good. It's raining here, too. The outer shell of our new building's up, but they're not getting much done today.''

Rubbing the towel through his hair vigorously, Colby asked a few questions about their expansion project, trying to appear interested, though his mind kept wandering. Dionne had zoomed out of the parking area like a bat out of hell. She ought to know better than to drive that powerful car so fast in a downpour. He'd have to talk to her and . . . He became aware of a silence on the other end. "What'd you say, good buddy?''

There was a pause before Zac answered, a note of concern in his voice. "I said you appear distracted. Is anything the matter?''

Yeah, something was the matter, all right. There was this redheaded bundle of energy who weighed about a hundred pounds and had somehow managed to crawl under his skin. She was intuitive and intelligent, and she had a way of kissing that knocked his socks off. She'd messed up his plans and his concentration, and he was damned if he knew what he was going to do about her.

"Hey, are you there, Colby?''

"Yeah, yeah. Nothing's wrong. I'm just wet and tired." He pictured his partner in the kitchen of the house he was remodeling, his gray eyes thoughtful, his quick mind trying to assess the situation. "Not to worry, pal.''

"Uh-huh. How are the supervisors taking to Dionne's employee-assistance ideas?''

Standing, Colby tugged off his wet shirt. "Surprisingly, they like her. They're impressed with the facilities she's shown them and the programs she's introduced.

Today, she started her counseling sessions, talked with two men over here."

"Did you listen in?"

"She's got a lot on the ball."

"I think so. I've watched her with these kids up here. She never gets ruffled, never loses her cool, professional approach."

Well, almost never, Colby thought with a slow smile.

"I was hoping you two would get along. You are, aren't you?"

Colby shifted the phone to his other ear. "She's not what I expected, but I have to admit she knows her stuff. I'm still not convinced all this will work, but she is trying."

"Don't expect miracles in a few days. Just give it time. Dionne's been known to change lives, if the person meets her halfway."

But what if he didn't want his life changed? Colby pulled a fresh shirt out of a cabinet. "Well, listen, I've got to get out of these wet things and call Marianne before she leaves."

"Why are you so wet, Colby?" Zac's voice was suddenly curious. "Did you run into a problem outside?"

"Yeah, you could say that. But I've taken care of it." Sure he had, in so much as he'd stuck a finger in the dike wall. "I'll get back to you later in the week, all right?"

"Sure. Give Dionne our best."

"Right, you hug Lainey for me." Colby hung up with a relieved sigh, hoping his astute partner hadn't read between the lines. Punching out his office number, he waited for his secretary to answer.

A shower and shampoo and some dry clothes had her feeling much better. Dionne made her way to the laundry room to throw in a load of wet things and found Aggie there. Dionne's spirits sank again. "I hope you don't mind if I use the machine. I got caught in the rain."

"I'll do it," Aggie said, reaching for the bundle.

"No, really, I can—"

"Don't like people messing around my washer." Aggie tugged the pile from Dionne and began sorting it. "You sure run out of here in an all-fired hurry this afternoon. By the looks of these, you must have been hiking in the mud."

Dionne almost groaned aloud, but she tried for a smile. "I was out at a building site with Colby, interviewing some of his men. It's pretty messy out there." Suddenly, a sneeze shook her. Pulling a tissue from her pocket, she blew her nose.

"How'd you get so soaked?" Aggie shook her head, turned on the washer and marched back into the kitchen. "You likely caught a cold. I'll fix you some hot tea."

Dionne's eyes were watery, perhaps from an oncoming cold, or maybe from the first kind word Aggie had sent her way. She leaned against the counter. "Have you been with Colby long?"

"Seven years come October. I moved in same as him, the day they finished the house."

"How'd you come to work for him?"

"It's a long story." Aggie poured hot water into a cup and carried it to where Dionne stood. "Let this steep, then drink it down."

"Thank you." Maybe Aggie was human after all.

The older woman wiped her hands on a spotless dishtowel. "My Albert worked for Colby, and Zac before him. Fell off a scaffolding and died that summer. We didn't have no children and very little insurance. Colby come to me, said he really needed me to cook and clean for him, asked if I'd move in." She sent Dionne a quick glance, her eyes shiny. "We both know it was me who was doing the needing. I packed that same day and been here ever since. Colby's cantankerous, but he's the best there is."

Dionne was beginning to see the basis of Aggie's devotion. Setting the bag aside, she sipped. "Did you know Colby's wife?"

Aggie turned to face her, her frown deep. "I knew her, all right. That woman wasn't fit to shine Colby's shoes. I used to clean the old office building way back before Colby bought in. He worked long hours, and she'd come sashaying in, wearing two-hundred-dollar dresses and smelling of expensive perfume. She never looked right or left. None of us was good enough for her to talk to. She had mean eyes, you know. Except when she flashed them at some man. Deciding to leave her was the hardest thing Colby ever done, but he's better off without a woman like that."

"Perhaps you're right."

"I'm right as rain." Aggie tossed the towel and came closer. "A career woman, you know. Always traveling, never having no time for her husband, didn't want kids. My Albert and me couldn't have kids, though we wanted them real bad. And this high-and-mighty lady gets rid of hers."

"You mean she miscarried?"

Aggie gave a short laugh. "That's what she said, but I don't believe it."

"You think she had an abortion?"

"Yes, ma'am. Damn near killed Colby. He left his job, Zac, everybody, and just wandered around. It took him nearly a year to get his life back together. Man's better off alone than to be with a woman like that."

Dionne finished her tea. "You're right." Her heart went out to Colby for what he'd been through, if Aggie was right.

"I told him over and over, look out for them career women. They got no business marrying, I say." She cocked her head at Dionne. "You got someone special back in St. Clair?"

Not too obvious, was she? Dionne shook her head. "No, but then, I'm not interested in marrying. I don't believe careers and marriages mix well." How easily the lie slipped from her these days, Dionne thought disgustedly.

For the first time, Aggie gave her a genuine smile. "Good for you. I knew you were smart the first day I saw you."

Dionne rubbed the back of her neck where a tension headache was beginning. The hum of an approaching engine had her glancing out the kitchen window. Colby's pickup pulled into the garage as she turned back to Aggie. "I believe I *am* catching a cold. I think I'll skip dinner and go straight to bed. Thanks for the tea. Please tell Colby I'll see him in the morning."

"All right. You sure you don't want a little soup?"

"Nothing, thanks." She'd had more today than she could comfortably swallow as it was. "Good night, Aggie."

Hurrying to her room, she hastily closed the door and leaned against it, her thoughts on Colby.

She didn't want to think about him, to feel pain or sorrow for him. Yet she pressed her knuckles to her mouth as she felt both.

Chapter Four

"Would you like a piece of candy, Doctor?" Theresa Abbott asked. "They're Sanders Chocolates, hand-dipped and simply wonderful."

"No, thanks," Dionne said as she took a seat across the desk from the slender head bookkeeper and studied her. In her early fifties, she guessed, quite thin, with high cheekbones, pale skin carefully made up and silver-blond hair wound into an intricate French twist. The woman was dignified, well-educated and a bit of a snob.

Theresa finished her candy and wiped her slim fingers. "I'm really not sure why Dottie wanted me to speak with you," she commented. "I've heard about the employee-assistance program you're implementing and I heartily approve. Is that what you wanted to hear?" Carefully she emptied the contents of a Coke can into a glass with ice.

"That's part of it, yes." Buying a little time, Dionne opened the file she held and pretended to peruse it, though she'd read it thoroughly yesterday. Miss Abbott hadn't been in, so she'd had to wait to interview her today. Dottie felt strongly, as did several other office personnel, that the lady was a secret drinker, but their suspicions were more conjecture than fact. Getting this somewhat haughty woman to admit she had *any* problem, much less a major one, wouldn't be easy.

Dionne smiled and started with a bit of honest flattery. "First, I'd like to commend you. I understand the accounting department—headed by you—is the most efficient in the company."

Theresa brightened, though her eyes flitted about the room as she talked. "Yes, it is, with no small effort, I might add." She lowered her voice conspiratorially. "It's hard to get good help these days. Young people don't seem to have the work ethic that was almost commonplace years ago."

"Do you have many problems with absenteeism in your department?"

"No more than the other departments, I imagine."

Dionne glanced down at the manila folder, then back up. "We need you to check your personnel files to see if anyone misses more than one or two days a month. Especially Mondays. As you know, we're trying to spot substance abusers. People who drink to excess often have trouble getting going in the morning, so I'd also like to know if anyone is chronically late."

"Certainly, I'll be happy to cooperate." She took a long swallow of her drink, then set down the glass and clasped her hands together on the desktop.

"I understand you often aren't in until ten many mornings, although the workday begins at eight. Is that a special arrangement you have?"

Color moved into Theresa's pale face. "Does that file also mention how many evenings I work late, that I've been known to take work home, that I've even come in on Saturdays to clean up a mess created by one of our sweet young accountants out there—" she waved her hand indicating the work area outside her private office "—most of whom are more interested in flirting than doing their work correctly?"

Obviously Theresa didn't think too highly of her staff. Or was it jealousy? "Your devotion to your job is in no way being questioned. However, everyone here is being asked certain questions, for the record, at the request of Colby and Zac. So, do you have a special arrangement with the office manager that you be allowed to arrive later because you also stay later?"

Theresa leaned back in her swivel chair as if searching for patience. "Dr. Keller, perhaps you don't know that my mother, who lived with me, died last year and it's taking me some time to adjust. However, I believe in honoring my commitments. I've worked for Midwest Construction for thirty years, since before Zachary Sinclair purchased it. I don't *need* to make special arrangements. My integrity is not under question here, is it?" Taking another candy, Theresa popped it into her mouth and chewed almost viciously.

Dionne had expected the defensiveness. "Not your integrity, no." Again she glanced at the file. "However, there was a problem in your department several months ago, forms that were incorrectly filed with the IRS, causing a rather costly audit. Is that correct?"

With a shaky hand, Theresa picked up her glass and drank. "I've explained that, more than once. I don't pretend to be a tax expert or a CPA."

"There's also something in here about a second-quarter report that was filed late, thereby incurring a fine? The company CPA had approved it, sent it to you, and I believe you told Dottie that you'd misplaced it. That was in June and—"

"I was ill a good deal of June." She coughed delicately. "I'm plagued with allergies."

"I see." It was time to win her confidence again. "I do understand. You've also had quite a turnover in staff, which is always a problem."

Theresa nodded. "Yes. Silly young girls not checking their work, giggling on the phone during business hours. It's up to me to keep a firm hand on them."

"And I'm sure you do. Tell me, what do you think of a blood-testing program?"

"For drugs, you mean? I truly don't believe we have anyone addicted to drugs here, not in my department."

"Not just for drugs. Random testing would also bring to light anyone who comes in hung over, for instance. Alcohol remains in the bloodstream quite a while. Are you aware of any problem drinkers on your staff?"

"Not that I know of personally."

"Do you drink, Miss Abbott?"

"Me?" Her eyes finally met Dionne's, shiny with surprise at the question. "The occasional social glass of wine. Doesn't everyone do that sort of thing?"

"No, not everyone drinks, not even wine. I suppose a problem drinker wouldn't be able to hide it long in bookkeeping. An accountant who's impaired could make some serious errors in the books, which would be noticed sooner or later. Our testing program would reveal a person with a problem and perhaps avoid that. What do you think?''

Theresa drained her glass before answering. ''I suppose the girls would go along with that.''

''Of course, management would have to be tested, also. We wouldn't want your staff to think they were being singled out.'' As Theresa grew even paler, Dionne stood. ''I really appreciate your cooperation in this. It's Friday afternoon so it's too late this week. But I'll arrange the tests to begin next Monday. I'll see that you get permission slips that will have to be signed.''

Theresa's hands were twined in a white-knuckled grip. ''So soon?''

Dionne sent her a smile. ''The sooner, the better. If we find someone with a drinking or drug problem, we can then recommend proper treatment. It's for their good as well as for the good of the company.''

''Yes, of course.''

''Thank you for your time.'' Dionne walked out of the bookkeeper's office and made her way to the room adjacent to Colby's that she'd been using. Sitting down at the desk, she picked up her pen to make her notations while her impressions were fresh in her mind.

She couldn't help feeling sorry for Theresa Abbott. A woman who'd never married, instead devoting her life to caring for her invalid mother. She must have some dreams unrealized, some regrets to live with and a somewhat lonely life. Theresa thought herself above the women who worked for her and didn't even realize she envied their youth, their busy social lives, perhaps their men friends. Maybe alcohol had become her only friend.

What a shame, Dionne thought, staring at the thick file that represented thirty years of Theresa Abbott's life. Not much to show for all that time. Dionne suddenly wondered if maybe she herself would be like that one day, bitter, envious, unhappy—searching for escape in a bottle.

Leaning back, she lit a cigarette thoughtfully. Addictions were insidious. They snuck up on you and had you hooked before you realized it. Her own included, she thought as she stared at the cigarette she held. Maybe she should try to cut down. Regretfully, she drew on it once more, then put it out in the ashtray.

No, she would not become like poor, sad Theresa. She had interesting work that challenged her, lots of family and friends who cared, a diversified life. She was a little low right now; the five days she'd spent away from St. Clair had been filled with emotional upheaval. Trying to prove to the people in charge the worth of the program, trying to break down the barriers addicts erected so she could help them, and trying to keep her distance from Colby Winters.

Yesterday he'd spent the whole day at one of his building sites and she hadn't seen him. He'd returned home late, and again she'd closeted herself in her room early, eating a light dinner and spending some time reading. She'd used a cold as her excuse to Aggie when in fact she felt fine. A little white lie had warded off a great deal of temptation. For she hadn't forgotten the kiss she and Colby had shared in the rain, not for a moment.

Dionne stared off into space, letting her mind drift. It had been a long time since a man had made her heart pound with that edgy excitement, that sensual pull that was as impossible to ignore as it was to fake. She'd never taken lovers lightly, but she'd had a few strong relationships after college. She didn't want permanence and had made that perfectly clear up front. When things had ended, neither had had regrets.

Now there was Colby, and from the start, things had been different. He pursued her despite his own reluctance, he challenged because it was his nature, he attracted when she wanted no part of attraction. She didn't want to start things with him, yet she didn't want things to end between them, either. Ambivalence was something she rarely suffered with, yet she was truly torn. She had no right to lean on him, for she couldn't afford to get involved. Forcing herself to remember Nathan's cruel words, *"I want a real woman for a wife,"* she shivered.

Still, she couldn't avoid Colby forever, for there were files to go over before she left and a couple more people to talk with next week. She'd thought she'd be finished by now, but there were too many loose ends that needed tying. She missed her familiar apartment, her own office, her patients. Especially Shelly Morgan.

Dionne smiled as she thought of the sweet blond, blue-eyed seven-year-old who'd been her patient for months. Shelly had gotten to her more deeply than Dionne had planned. The child was finally overcoming the trauma of being in an automobile accident with her parents. She'd watched her mother die and had to live with fear for her father, still hospitalized, in a coma. After the accident, Shelly hadn't spoken a word.

But slowly, with counseling sessions, with learning to ride horses at Lainey's ranch and with time and attention from her relatives and from Dionne, Shelly was finally talking again. Still, she was far from over the shock, and Dionne's heart, the one she tried to harden, had a special chamber reserved for Shelly.

She'd been so pleased to learn that Shelly was visiting her grandparents in Detroit for several days while school was closed for a teachers' meeting. She'd called Mrs. Morgan to ask if she could take Shelly on an outing tomorrow. Sounding tired, her grandmother had readily agreed. Having their son in a coma all these months had taken a toll on the elder Morgans, both of whom were in their late sixties.

It would be good to spend a day with the child, Dionne thought, to relax and have fun and to be away from the devastating effect Colby Winters had on her nervous system. Looking forward to her Saturday plans, Dionne closed the Abbott file.

"So how about it, find another?" Colby leaned against the doorway of her office, aware he'd startled her. He'd been watching her for some minutes as she'd sat lost in thought. She'd been avoiding him since that stunning kiss they'd shared in the rain, retiring early, rising at dawn and dashing into the office. He knew why; he'd had no small amount of trouble wrestling with thoughts about her, too. And he was still undecided as to what to do about her unsettling presence in his life.

She glanced up at him, then down at the file. "You mean Theresa Abbott? Yes, my educated guess would be she's drinking heavily but hiding it well, so far."

Colby strolled in, closed the door and draped his long frame into the chair opposite her. "What makes you think so? She's like an institution around here. Been with Midwest longer than anyone."

"So she told me." Dionne opened her briefcase and began inserting papers. "Well, for one, she's reed thin, yet a sugar junkie. Chocolate candy and sweet soft drinks in the morning, not coffee."

"Maybe she's diabetic."

"I have her medical chart here and she's not. Alcoholics crave sweets, especially if they've had a considerable amount to drink the night before. They're also usually very thirsty. Her face is very pale and her hands tremble. Her eyes are cloudy, and she looks anywhere but directly at the person she's talking with. She gets defensive quickly, comes in late nearly daily and has made a few costly errors lately.''

''None of that's proof she's a boozer. Did you come right out and ask her?''

''Yes, I did. She says she has an occasional glass of wine. I believe it's more than that. I can't give you proof, only educated guesses. But we'll soon find out. She's agreed to let us begin blood testing on Monday morning.''

Colby whistled. ''No kidding! How'd you get her to agree to that?''

She shot him a quick smile, wishing he didn't look so damn appealing with that lock of blond hair falling onto his forehead. ''Professional secret.'' She snapped her briefcase shut. ''Actually, Theresa Abbott's not an unusual case. A spinster, caring for an ailing mother, starts taking a drink now and again to ease the loneliness. Before she's aware of what's happening, it takes more and more to make life tolerable, even for a little while.''

He frowned at her wording. A case. Theresa was a clinical case to Dionne, not a person with feelings. He hated medical terms. But, Colby chastised himself, was he any better, labeling them drunks and boozers instead of sick people as Dionne insisted they were?

''Then she's not sick, just using alcohol to get through the lonely times.'' That, he knew, would get a rise out of her. Why he wanted to, he wasn't certain. He'd missed sparring with her the past few days, oddly enough. He enjoyed her company and her quick mind, even when they were on opposite sides of an issue.

"She's still sick, reaching for a crutch instead of a cure for her loneliness. She could get out, make friends, join groups, take up a hobby, attend classes—anything that would prevent her from sitting at home nights and drinking herself to sleep. That solution only intensifies the problem."

"So why does my father drink, if we're to use your theory? Not out of loneliness, since he never lacks for pals—not when he's buying, that is. Maybe because he felt inadequate as a husband, a father, a provider. With good cause, I might add."

Dionne had guessed that that still bothered him. She chose her words carefully. "Not knowing him, it's difficult to say. He might have felt inadequate, perhaps had been made to feel that way as a child. He might have been one of thousands who lead lives of quiet desperation, as Mr. Thoreau pointed out, unable to honestly believe he could change his life for the better, so he stopped trying."

Colby braced an ankle on his knee, wondering why lately thoughts of his father kept nagging him. "I wish I knew what he wanted."

She shrugged. "Perhaps what we all want, peace of mind."

"From what?"

"From the demons that won't let him be. Don't you have any demons, Colby?"

His eyes narrowed as he stared at her. "More than you know." Sitting up taller, he deliberately shook off his introspective mood. "I've got a meeting this afternoon, but it'll be over by five. How about if I take you out to a nice quiet dinner somewhere?"

"Thanks, but I promised Dottie I'd go to a movie with her. Her husband's out of town." She hadn't exactly been dying to accept Dottie's unexpected invitation, but she'd thought it best to put some distance between herself and Colby.

He tried to hide his disappointment, but wasn't sure he managed. "Well, tomorrow then. Surely you're not planning to work on Saturday, too?"

"No, but I've made an all-day commitment. There's a little girl from St. Clair, one of my patients, who's visiting her grandparents in town." Quickly, she gave him a thumbnail sketch of Shelly Morgan's background and saw the sympathy jump into his eyes. "I think it'll do us both good to spend some time together."

"You *have* been working hard." Colby picked up a paperweight in the shape of a red apple and hefted it from hand to hand. "What are you and Shelly planning to do?"

Be careful here, Dionne warned herself. Straightening her desk unnecessarily, she kept her voice nonchalant. "Nothing spectacular. Dottie told me about a place not far from here, called Railroad Park. They've got a children's train and a couple of rides plus a picnic area. I thought I'd pick up a lunch somewhere and—"

"Aggie puts together a mean picnic basket. I've passed that park often—it's not far from my house. There are swings and slides. And we could take her to this puppet show they put on there most weekends. I've heard several people in the office talk about how much their kids like it." Dionne was sitting back, quietly looking at him, her expression unreadable. He set down the paperweight. "I'm sorry. I didn't mean to include myself like that, uninvited...."

The longing in his voice was unmistakable. How could she turn him down? "I didn't think you'd be interested in spending a day amusing a seven-year-old."

He leaned a hip against the edge of her desk and folded his arms across his chest. "I love kids, Dionne. Didn't I mention that?"

He hadn't had to. She cleared her throat. "Well, you're invited then."

Colby didn't bother to hide his pleasure as he smiled. "Great. I'll tell Aggie." He checked his watch. "I've got to get to my meeting. Are you finished for the day?"

"I want to try to reach Dan. I've set him up twice to go to AA and meet with someone there. He's missed both meetings."

"I'd guessed as much. Think he's a lost cause?"

"Of course not."

He stood. "You don't give up easily, do you?"

"No, but then, neither do you, I've noticed."

"Touché." He moved to the door. "What time do you want to start out in the morning?"

"I'll pick Shelly up about nine, then meet you at the house. We can go from there."

"Okay. Have a good time at the movies tonight." Hand on the knob, he couldn't resist asking, "Will you be late?"

Dionne frowned. He was pushing again. "Don't wait up, all right? I'm a big girl now." She watched him nod as he left.

She sat for several minutes, staring at the door and wondering if she'd just made a huge mistake.

Hair ruffling in a light breeze, Dionne sat in the second car of the children's train, her eyes on the engine. She wasn't sure just how he'd managed it, but Colby had talked the engineer into allowing Shelly and him to sit up front. He'd even persuaded the grandfatherly fellow into letting Shelly wear his blue-and-white striped cap. Much to her further surprise, shy and quiet Shelly was loving every minute of her ride.

To say that Colby was good with children was an understatement. She'd picked Shelly up promptly at nine and stayed for a cup of coffee with her grandparents. Concern for their hospitalized son was etched deeply on both their faces. They enjoyed having Shelly stay with them a few days, Mrs. Morgan had explained. But there wasn't much for the child to do in their small retirement home except watch television, which didn't interest her much. As Dionne and Shelly drove away, Dionne couldn't help noticing how relieved the two older people looked, and she hoped Shelly hadn't noticed.

But Shelly had brightened almost immediately at Colby's. Aggie's grumpiness, it seemed, was reserved for adults only. Aggie hugged Shelly, found a lollipop from somewhere for her and raved over Moppsy, the scruffy stuffed gray dog with one eye missing that went everywhere the child went. Colby presented her with a Detroit Tigers baseball cap that miraculously fit and showed her his elaborate tropical fish tank in the den. By the time they'd set out for the park, the wariness had left Shelly's eyes. This from a child who'd been timid around adults for months.

Now, Dionne smiled back as Shelly twisted in her seat to wave at her. Perhaps it was because both the man and the child were hungry for love and affection that they hit it off so well. Had that thought come from her training or her instincts? Dionne wondered. Maybe she should stop questioning things and be grateful they were enjoying each other.

The train chugged to a halt alongside the bright yellow station where another group of children and the adults with them waited to board for the next ride. Dionne stepped out.

Colby was already on the platform and reached his arms out to Shelly. "Here we go." She held on as he lifted her out. He noticed she left her hand in his as they strolled along the walkway leading to the picnic grounds. "Anyone hungry?"

"Not me." Shelly had spotted the playground. "Could we swing first?"

Colby's arm slid around Dionne's waist as naturally as if he'd been doing it for years. "Better *before* lunch than after, right?" Carrying the picnic basket, Dionne nodded.

Skipping ahead, Shelly found an empty swing and grabbed it. Pumping her legs, she had a little trouble getting started.

"Want me to push you?" Colby asked, walking to her.

"Yes, please."

Dionne set the basket on the ground and sat on a brick ledge that separated the playground from the wooded area where the picnic tables were scattered. She longed for a cigarette, but she'd been trying to cut down. Instead, she inhaled the clean fresh air, recognizing the hickory scent from the nearby cooking fires. It was a beautiful sunny day, jacket weather, but not chilly. The bright blue sky held no threat of rain. It was a perfect fall day, and she was glad she'd invited Colby.

Just watching him warmed her. He stood with his legs apart, giving Shelly an occasional push, chatting with a young mother who had three children on adjacent swings. As Dionne guessed he would, Colby was soon pushing one of the other children as well as Shelly and was chatting with all four children. The man was a natural, a born father. Turning aside, Dionne closed her eyes on the painful scene.

Why did this man have to come into her life? She'd been able to avoid caring, to evade intimacy for years. Suddenly, in what seemed like the blink of an eye, he was here, and nothing—*nothing*—was the same. He had her wanting things she'd schooled herself to do without, to not long for. Like children, family life, a home. Like love.

She swallowed hard, blinking back tears that threatened to reveal her turbulent emotions. She must never let Colby know how she felt. She couldn't bear to see on his face the expression Nathan had worn when he'd turned from her, when he'd made it abundantly clear that she was sadly lacking the things a complete woman could offer. Clearing her throat, Dionne swung her gaze back as Shelly called out. Forcing a smile, she waved.

As if sensing something amiss, she saw Colby whisper to Shelly, and then the two started toward her. Quickly, she stood and picked up the basket, turning to gaze toward the tables. "Ready for lunch?"

Colby helped Shelly scramble over the brick ledge, then took Dionne's hand. She'd been awfully quiet this morning, almost withdrawn. "You all right?"

To prove she was, she gave him a bright smile. "Fine. I hope you're hungry. Aggie must have thought she was feeding longshoremen when she packed our food."

They spread the cloth on the table, then set out the plates of cold chicken, chips, vegetable sticks, rolls and cold drinks. Munching on a drumstick, Colby used it to point to a shed with a striped awning off in the distance. "Is that an ice-cream stand?"

Shelly wiggled to get a better look, then turned back. "Yes, it is. I wonder if they have strawberry. That's my favorite."

She wasn't much of an eater, and he wasn't above bribery. "If you eat all your lunch, we can go see later." He glanced over at Dionne, who also was eating rather halfheartedly. "That goes for you, miss."

She looked up at him slowly. "Think you can bribe me, too?"

"I'm not against trying." A sound from the grassy area caught his attention. A man in his midtwenties, wearing a black T-shirt and tight black pants, was doing knee bends, running in place, working out.

Following Colby's gaze, Dionne watched the man pick up a jump rope and set it smoothly into motion, his muscles rippling as he moved gracefully.

"I never saw a man jump rope before," Shelly volunteered.

"Perhaps he's a prize fighter in training," Dionne suggested.

"I'd say he's a little obvious," Colby commented as several teenage girls moved closer to watch him.

Dionne caught his tone and couldn't resist teasing. "Oh, I don't know. I'd say he's quite a hunk."

Colby reached for another piece of chicken. "Why, Doctor, I thought you'd be drawn more to the cerebral type."

Lips twitching, she turned to him. "Did you? There's more to life than intellectual discussions, wouldn't you say?"

"Not for me. I choose brains over a luscious body every time."

Dionne laughed out loud and found it felt good. "Sure you do."

They finished lunch and packed away the remains. Colby suggested a lazy activity while they digested and produced a pack of cards after spreading the cloth on the grass. "Do you know how to play Crazy Eights, Shelly?"

"Grandpa taught me. I beat him all the time."

Colby dropped onto the blanket and folded his legs. "Let's see if you can beat me."

Sipping the remnants of her soft drink, Dionne watched them. There seemed no pretense to the man, which was probably why Shelly trusted him instinctively. She saw that he didn't let her win, but rather played honestly, forcing her to concentrate. Yet she seemed challenged and not frustrated.

Was she seeing what she wanted to see? Dionne asked herself. Hard to tell. After Nathan, she hadn't trusted her judgment of men for a long while. Perhaps she still didn't.

They played three games, then walked two long blocks over to the puppet show after stashing the basket in the truck. Dionne couldn't help but smile at the fact that Colby seemed to watch the puppets with the same intensity that Shelly did. Then she realized why.

He probably had missed out on all this as a kid. A young boy growing up poor, with a father prone to drinking and hitting, would hardly go on picnics, be pushed on swings and have anyone to take him to puppet shows. The realization made her doubly glad she'd asked him along. The heart she was trying so very hard to keep intact was splintering rapidly.

Afterward, they bought ice-cream cones and sat on a park bench to eat them, then walked over to the merry-go-round. Colby bought Shelly a ticket, settled her on a horse and asked if she wanted him to stay on board with her.

"No, I'm too big for that."

"Right." He pointed to where Dionne stood by the wrought-iron fence. "I'll be right over there with Dionne."

As he stepped down, a mother was trying to help her son climb up. The boy, about eight, had a cast on one leg from ankle to thigh and was having difficulty. "Can I help?" he asked her.

"Oh, yes, thank you." The woman stepped aside.

Colby picked up the boy easily and placed him on one of the horses, anchoring him well. "This okay?" The boy nodded as he gripped the pole. Once more, Colby stepped off as the woman again thanked him. Joining Dionne, he watched the ride begin.

His arm around her felt good. She squeezed his hand. "There's something to be said for cerebral combined with brawn, after all."

He smiled down at her. "So now it's my body you're after."

There was some truth to that. She'd thought him too handsome at first, cocky and conceited. But she saw character in his face she'd not noticed then, the all-important factor that had been missing in Nathan's countenance. Still, she wasn't about to let Colby know what she was thinking. "In your dreams, fella," she said with a smile.

"How did you know?" He had dreamed of her, restless, wide-awake dreams. Leaning on the fence, he watched Shelly go around and around. "She's a great little girl."

Dionne studied his profile. "What would you do if you couldn't have children?"

Colby looked into her serious eyes. "I can't imagine anything worse."

Nor could she. Keeping her expression even, Dionne swung her gaze back to Shelly. At last, the ride ended and the sunset began. Dionne pulled the zipper up on Shelly's jacket as they walked back to Colby's truck. It was time to take the child back to her grandparents and time to head for home. She'd learned more about Colby today, perhaps more than she'd bargained for.

"A perfect day, wouldn't you say?" Colby asked as he started the engine.

She stared at him a long moment over the top of Shelly's head. "Yes, perfect."

Chapter Five

Odd how Aggie was absent nearly every evening she and Colby decided to stay in, Dionne thought as she towel-dried her hair. They'd returned from taking Shelly home to find only one small lamp burning in the living room.

"Aggie must have decided to visit her sister," Colby had said.

Yes, but whose idea had that been? She wiped the steamy mirror and reached for her comb. She could have feigned fatigue and gone to her room. But he'd looked so boyish as he'd asked her to join him in front of the fire for a nightcap after her shower. As usual, she had had trouble turning him down.

Belting her robe, she left the bathroom.

Standing in the archway of the living room, she fought a smile. It was as if he'd set the scene. No lamps burning, only the flickering firelight. Soft music in the background and a brandy snifter waiting for her on the coffee table. Colby sat on the couch facing the fire, wearing corduroy slacks and a plaid shirt, his long legs stretched in front of him, his expression watchful as he looked over his shoulder at her.

She gave way to the grin. "'Step into my parlor, said the spider to the fly.'"

He smiled back. "Surely you don't think I'd stoop so low as to try to seduce you with such obvious trappings?"

Sitting down, she tucked the folds of her robe about her. "Of course not." From her pocket, she took out her cigarettes, then changed her mind. Self-discipline tonight might very well be in order. She tucked them away. Leaning forward, she picked up her glass and took a sip. "Mmm, that's good. Where's yours?"

He just shook his head and moved a bit closer, stretching his arm along the couch back.

The thing to do was to keep him talking, Dionne decided as she set her glass down. "I love a fire," she began. "One of these days, I'm going to have a house that has a fireplace."

Colby shifted his gaze into the flames. "I like them, too. When we lived in northern Michigan, up in the thumb area, we had a fire going nearly every night."

We? "Was that when you were married?"

Colby let out a sigh. "Yeah. We lived a lot of places— Chicago, Detroit, Florida for a while. Ariel worked for a large clothing-store chain, and they had her moving around a great deal. I followed her like a damn puppy, catching a job here, a job there. Finally, I got tired of that and moved back to Detroit, went to work for Zac and told her she could come or not. It was up to her."

"Ariel's a lovely name."

"A lovely name and a lovely woman, until you start examining the inside."

She hated to ask, but found she wanted to know. "What went wrong?"

He gave a short, bitter laugh. "What didn't? I was too young, Ariel too irresponsible. We ran through money as fast as we both could make it. She loved clothes and traveling, didn't take to cooking and cleaning. When the store made her head buyer for their imported lines, she was gone more than she was home."

"I would imagine that it's hard to keep a marriage alive when you're apart so much."

"You've got that right. I had enough of separations when I was growing up, my father always taking off for weeks at a time. I wanted a real home and children. I wanted us to be a family. Ariel had said she did, too. But once she tasted success and freedom, she wanted them more. We never should have married."

Dionne could hear the disappointment, the pain in his voice. Inexplicably wanting contact, she reached out and took his hand, lacing her fingers through his. "Some people aren't meant for marriage."

"I suppose. Or for motherhood. She came home one day after a particularly long buying trip and told me she'd had a miscarriage. I didn't even know she was pregnant."

Even though she'd been prepared for this, Dionne found herself unable to find the right words to say to him. She just clung to his hand.

Colby let out a shaky breath, wishing he didn't remember that day so vividly, even after all these years. "She didn't seem particularly upset, just stood there in this bright red dress, unpacking her bags as calm as you please, as if she'd lost her toothbrush instead of my child. *If* it was my child."

"Colby, you have to let it go."

"Yeah, I know. I think I could more easily if I knew for sure if she really lost it or if she...if she had an abortion."

Everything in Dionne cried out at the very thought. "You can't torture yourself with this, not after so long." Acting on instinct, she moved closer, embracing him. She smoothed his hair and held him as if he were the child that had been lost. How could Ariel have done such a thing to this man? she asked the silent night.

"Did you ever care for someone who disappointed you so deeply you wondered if you'd ever get over it? Someone who had this *little* character flaw that you refused to see until it was too late?" His voice was low, thick with emotion.

Dionne nodded. "Yes. I try not to think about that time in my life. It serves no real purpose."

He shifted until he was facing her, his breath warm on her face. "Yes, it does. A bitter memory like that keeps you from dropping your guard easily, makes you slow to trust and quick to doubt. It keeps you remembering how dangerous it can be to let yourself care for the wrong person."

She felt her heart thud in agreement, yet pound with sudden anticipation. "We would both do well to keep that in mind."

Colby moved his hand up to touch her silken cheek, then trail down the length of her throat. "I'm having trouble handling my feelings for you, Dionne. To be perfectly honest, my instincts tell me to keep my distance. But I can't seem to stop thinking of you, wanting you."

She tried to conjure up the cool, professional answer, the one she'd give if she were discussing this situation with a patient. But his touch had her trembling even as she searched for the right thing to say. "It's just isolation and firelight and chemistry—fleeting things. I think you should go with your instincts. We wouldn't be good together."

"Let's test that theory." His arm encircled her, drawing her close against the length of him as his mouth touched hers. He tasted hesitancy and a genuine effort to stay uninvolved. Angling his head, he took her deeper. Still, he sensed her inner turmoil as she struggled to keep from responding, her body almost rigid. Pressing, he inched his tongue into her mouth and heard at last her soft sigh of submission, felt her arms enfold him.

Now there was wholehearted participation as her tongue dueled with his, her mouth moved sensuously under his and her body softened. In moments, he was drowning in her, in drugging sensations, in desperate longings, in awakened passion.

He hadn't planned to kiss her, had meant every word about not dropping his guard and being slow to trust. But she'd all but issued him a challenge, one he couldn't resist. Only he was winding up learning a lesson, that one tiny taste of Dionne was not nearly enough.

She'd wanted this rush into madness, this battering of the senses, this loss of self. No man had ever made her feel like this, and the knowledge stunned her. It wasn't empathy for the story of his disastrous marriage that he'd shared with her, nor was it born of the comfort she'd instinctively offered him. It was need, pure and simple, that he was able to arouse in her in an instant. Desires she was good at backing away from. Passion was an infrequent visitor. But need for his hands touching her as they were now, need for his mouth making love to hers as it was doing, need for that lean, hard body wrapping around her own—that was something unfamiliar and unexpected.

She was losing control, letting his hands part her robe and close around the swelling flesh of her throbbing breasts. The pleasure she felt was only a small sample of the pleasure she knew he could give her if they continued. And, oh, she wanted it to go on and on.

But she knew it could not. Gently, she withdrew, dazed and shaken. His hands had stilled and she touched them with her own, brought them away from her breasts and pulled her robe closed. Her stomach muscles quivered with the effort to keep herself in check.

"Still think we wouldn't be good together?" Colby asked, sounding breathless.

"Good in bed isn't all there is to a relationship."

"It's not a bad beginning." He draped his arms loosely around her, not allowing her to retreat too far from him. He wasn't sure if he could put his thoughts into words, but he found himself wanting to try. "Something's happening here, Dionne. Something I don't believe either of us had counted on. It's not the firelight or the romantic music. And if it's chemistry, it's a damn potent variety."

Dionne drew in a deep breath she badly needed. Her heart rate still hadn't returned to normal, and her usually complacent body was taking far too long to calm down. She would admit to chemistry, but even giving in to that with this man was dangerous. She was beginning to admire him, to want him, to care too much. And that changed all the rules. She would have to discourage him without hurting him. If she could. She swallowed hard, uncomfortable with the story she'd have to sell him, though she knew she must.

"Yes, it is potent," she began. "But we're not teenagers, Colby. We've both been burned. Earlier, you said you wanted a home and family. That's the last thing I want. I don't know if you've noticed—though Aggie certainly has—that I'm a career woman, one who needs to be free. A lot like Ariel. You certainly don't want another go-around like that, do you?"

She heard his sharp intake of breath, felt his quick withdrawal. "I don't think you are. Could you lie to your husband, do away with your own child?"

Not that question, please. "Perhaps not in all things are we alike, but in being single-minded about our careers, I believe we are. My work, my job comes first."

He'd been wrong to think she was different. Would he never learn? "I can't believe a woman who comes from such a big, caring family as you've described wants to spend her life taking care of other people's kids."

With supreme effort, Dionne put a coolness into her voice. "Believe it."

He did, finally. He didn't have to be hit over the head twice with the evidence. "All right. I'm sorry I pushed."

"I hope you understand. I do like you—"

His voice was as chilly as the night air outside. "We'd better get some sleep." He rose and closed the fireplace screen. "Good night."

She'd hurt him. She wished she hadn't, but she'd had little choice. As she watched him walk away, Dionne sat perfectly still, as tears flowed freely down her cheeks.

She should never have come here, she thought. Her gut feeling had been to stay home, and she should have. The disturbing something she'd sensed between Colby and herself from the start had developed into longings she'd thought she'd successfully buried.

Colby didn't realize it now as he struggled with his hurt, but he was better off without her. He would make a wonderful husband for some special woman. Dionne had come to realize he was warm and compassionate, unselfish and devoted. And he could make her body hum and her blood sing at a mere touch, a gentle glance. But it was not to be.

Blinking, Dionne turned to stare out the patio windows into the inky sky, easily spotting the full moon. A lovers' moon. Only there would be no lover for her. Not now, not ever.

Silently, she brushed at her damp cheeks. She would finish her work and go back to St. Clair where she was on solid ground. She would put Colby Winters out of her thoughts, except where they concerned business, and go on with her life. If occasionally she remembered, she would remind herself of the day Nathan had walked away from her. She could not risk seeing that look on another man's face, could not bear another man's rejection, could not endure another man using her because of her body's imperfections.

She would go it alone, and she'd be fine. Taking another long sip of the warming brandy, she rose and headed for her room.

"I'm not surprised," Dionne said as she handed the letter back to Dottie Philips. "It's her way of avoiding the blood test."

Dottie shook her head as she stared at the signature on the letter. "But I know Theresa Abbott. She's only fifty-four. She can't afford to take early retirement."

"We need to prevent that, if possible."

"How?"

"Intervention. You know how it works. We need to get her to come to a friendly gathering of people who care about her. We need to let her know that we're aware of her problem, that we don't condemn her for it, that she must face this head-on and take steps to overcome it. We need to make sure she understands she's not being censured, but that this is done in a loving manner. For her good and the good of the company she's so proud of."

Dottie looked skeptical. "I don't know. Think it'll work?"

Dionne shrugged. "I wish I could say yes in all cases. But the failure rate is about fifty percent. Theresa has to *want* to be helped."

"She has so much pride."

"Yes, but she's losing some as she keeps on trying to hide her habit, and I believe she's smart enough to know it. Perhaps the angle of approach might be that we understand what a strain her mother's death was on her, that many women fall prey to relying on drinking after such a terrible shock. That kind of thing. What do you think?"

"That does sound right. She'd lived with her mother all her life. It was terribly hard on her, but I believe she began drinking before the death."

"Perhaps loneliness escalated things. Why don't you make a list of her closest friends and we can approach them individually and discuss how best to do this. You'll have to be very diplomatic."

Nodding, Dottie stood. "Will you be there, too? I think we need you on this one."

Monday morning. Dionne had hoped to start for home by Wednesday at the latest. This could mean another postponement. She'd talked with Hilary earlier and the practice was running smoothly. Yet Dionne longed to leave. Things had been strained between Colby and her since Saturday night. All yesterday, he'd kept a polite distance from her, his smiles few, his coolness bothering her more than she'd imagined. Yes, it was time to go. But she couldn't let Dottie handle a potentially explosive situation alone.

"I'll be there, but I'd like to schedule this meeting for as soon as possible. I need to get back to St. Clair by midweek."

"I'll start on the list right away."

The office door flew open and Colby rushed in. Not pausing to greet them, he stopped in front of Dionne's desk.

"There's been an accident. Terry fell from a second-floor loft where he was working this morning. It's pretty bad."

"Oh, God." Dionne reached to grab her purse as she stood. "Which hospital is he in?"

"I'll take you. My car's out front."

"I'll talk with you later, Dottie." Dionne hurried out the door, followed by a frowning Colby.

Terry looked very pale and very young as he lay on starched white sheets, his sandy hair the only hint of color on the hospital bed. Monitors whirred and beeped behind him. His heavily bandaged left arm rested on two pillows. It was four in the afternoon and the first time they'd been allowed to see him. Colby stood grim faced at the foot of the bed as Dionne moved closer to Terry's right side.

"Terry," she whispered in the stillness of the room, "can you hear me?" In the corridor minutes ago, she'd spoken with his mother and fiancée and had been told he was groggy but awake. She'd also talked with his doctor, who'd said that Terry had miraculously escaped internal injuries. However, the angle of the fall had all but severed his left arm. He'd been in surgery for hours and in recovery all afternoon. But it would be several days before he would know if the reattachment was successful. Or if Terry would lose his arm.

The doctor had also told her that when they'd brought Terry in at nine in the morning, his blood-alcohol level was .18.

Slowly Terry opened his eyes and blinked to clear his vision. "Hi, Doc," he murmured. He was groggy with medication but he tried a cocky grin. "You're lookin' good."

"You're not looking so good, Terry. What happened?"

"I fell, didn't you hear?"

"Yes, I heard. From the second story where you were laying the brick fireplace. Do you remember getting to work this morning, Terry?"

"Sort of," he answered vaguely.

"Dionne," Colby interjected, "do you think this is the time to get into all that?"

It was the best time, when Terry was semisedated and answering honestly. "Yes, I do. Terry, where were you last night, do you recall?"

He wrinkled his forehead, then gave a slight nod. "Preseason football game. Out at the Silverdome. The Lions won."

"And afterward, did you and your friends go out and celebrate?"

"Yeah. We had a great time, me and my buddies." He blinked heavily, trying to concentrate. "Boilermakers.

You ever drink those, Doc? Whew!" He frowned, remembering. "Jean's real mad at me. We had a big fight last night. She walked out and left me there."

"Left you where, at the bar?"

"Yeah. But she's not mad anymore. She was here... minute ago." A puzzled look crossed his pale features. "She was crying. Why was she crying, Doc?" He seemed to remember suddenly and raised his head to stare at his left arm. He swung eyes dazed with fear at her, his right hand reaching out. "My arm's in bad shape, right?"

Dionne swallowed hard and clasped his hand with trembling fingers. "Yes."

"Are they going to cut it off, Doc?"

"I don't know, Terry."

"Don't let 'em, please." He closed his eyes and squeezed her hand. "Colby, they can't take my arm. I won't drink anymore, honest." Two large tears slowly drifted down his cheeks. "I promise you, Jean."

A nurse tapped at the door, then entered. "Time's up. He needs to rest."

Colby moved to the head of the bed and wiped the tears from Terry's face. "Hang in there, Terry."

There was no response as sleep finally claimed Terry. Dionne laid his hand gently on the sheet, then turned and walked out.

Colby cleared his throat. He remembered another time, another hospital bed. His father had lain white and still as Colby's mother had sobbed and clutched her husband's hand. Harold Winters had totaled their only car, but managed to survive. Colby's mother had been grateful, but Colby had felt nothing. He'd been nine years old. Living with an alcoholic made him grow up fast. Feeling older than he should, Colby left the room.

Dionne was standing in the small alcove alongside a weary-looking woman with gray hair and a pale complexion. Seated next to Mrs. Hanson was Jean with her fluffy bangs and accusing blue eyes. Colby walked closer.

"Terry said he'd met with you just last week," Jean said to Dionne. "He said you spent a long time with him and said he wasn't an alcoholic, that he had his drinking under control. Why'd you tell him that, Dr. Keller?"

The truth would hurt this young girl, but she had to be told. "I didn't. I told him he was headed for trouble. I asked him to attend an AA meeting, to go and listen with an open mind. He refused."

Agitated, needing someone to blame, Jean jumped to her feet. "Why didn't you make him go, take him there? He's been drinking since grade school, just like his dad before him, like his brothers." She glanced at Mrs. Hanson, who nodded unhappily. "Terry needed help and he didn't get it from you. I thought doctors were supposed to help people."

Dionne felt the girl's pain, the mother's sorrow and her own failure. She rubbed at her forehead where a blockbuster of a headache had begun some time ago. "He's a grown man, Jean. I couldn't force him to go."

"You let him down, Doctor." She sobbed openly into a wadded tissue.

Struggling to stay calm, Dionne touched her hand. "I'm sorry." Turning, she nearly bumped into Colby. Moving around him, she headed for the elevators.

Confused that she didn't explain further, he let her go. For a few minutes, he talked with the two women, mentioning that he'd been there when Dionne had talked with Terry, that she'd tried to persuade him to seek help.

Finally, he left them to their grief and rushed after her. He caught up with her at his car.

They were inside and on the freeway before he spoke. "Why'd you leave like that? Why didn't you stay and explain?"

The late-afternoon sun was slowly sinking and traffic was already heavy with people rushing home from work. Dionne scarcely noticed as she tried to quiet her rolling stomach. "Because they weren't listening. They need someone to blame and I'm handy."

"So you just walk away?"

"There was nothing more I could say or do for them right now."

Colby gripped the wheel, his knuckles white. "So, another case closed. Didn't quite work out the way you'd hoped, but they can't all, can they? Tomorrow, you tackle Dan or maybe Theresa Abbott. You win some, you lose some. You can't expect to help them all, right, Doctor?"

She didn't need this right now. The many cups of bitter coffee she'd drunk all day threatened to reappear. She couldn't quite figure out why Colby was pounding away at her. Maybe if her head would stop hurting, she could sort it all out. She took a deep, steadying breath. "Look, could we discuss this later? I'm sorry if I didn't handle things the way you wanted me to. I've told you, the success ratio in my line of work is never guaranteed."

"Right, right." Anger rose in him, hot and swift. Not because she hadn't succeeded with Terry or even that she hadn't been able to calm Jean's fears. Her attitude aggravated the hell out of him. Yanking on the wheel, he zoomed up the off ramp.

By the time they entered his house, Dionne felt as if she were shattering into a million pieces. Blessedly, Aggie had gone to a movie. A note on the table told them she'd left cold cuts in the refrigerator. Dionne swallowed two aspirins and turned to Colby, who'd been dogging her steps. "Look, I'm not hungry. I think I'll lie down and see if I can get rid of this headache."

"Yeah, right." Colby poured himself a tall glass of iced tea with angry, jerky movements. He watched her head down the hallway and listened for the closing of her door before he drained half the glass. Times like this, he, too, wished for the oblivion that alcohol offered.

Wanting to hit something hard, he shoved open the patio door and walked outside. The sunset turned the sky to hazy orange, outlining the trees that were quickly losing their leaves. Tonight, he didn't appreciate their beauty. He started walking toward the back fence, needing to work off his angry energy.

Maybe it happened to them in med school, he mused. They walked in filled with notions of saving the world, took their oaths, then walked away without once thinking of each individual human being they treated. The social worker had treated his father like a case, one she'd been glad to cross off her list finally. Detached, she'd gone on to other cases.

Dionne, too, had been able to sit there and grill Terry when he faced the possibility of losing his arm, then walk away from his mother and Jean, untouched by their pain. She couldn't do anything more, she'd told him. Unaffected. Just as unaffected as she'd been when he'd wanted to make love to her Saturday night. They were wrong for each other, she claimed, so goodbye and farewell. Colby finished his drink and felt like hurling the glass against the fence.

Instead, he started slowly back. Maybe you had to stay detached from your cases or you'd go crazy empathizing with each one. Maybe. But how could you not? To hell with it, he thought as he came around the far side. She'd be gone soon and—

He stopped, listening. The sounds he heard were human and very much like weeping. They were coming from the direction of Dionne's room where the patio door was ajar, the screen in place. Colby stepped closer.

He stood there a moment. Great, gulping sobs, muffled but very real. Slowly, he slid open the screen and stepped through.

Only a small table lamp was lit. She was lying on the bed crosswise, still fully clothed. Her shoes had been abandoned near the closed door. Her face was buried in the spread and her slender shoulders shook with her weeping.

He'd thought her strong as a rock, cold as stone, unemotional except, perhaps, when she was kissing him. Even then, she always put on the brakes, unable to give up control completely. But here she was, giving herself up to a profound grief he recognized as real. And it had him rooted to the spot.

She had sought privacy and he should let her have it, he knew. Yet he'd never seen anything close to this in any of the women who'd been in his life, not even his mother. He was uncertain as to the best way to approach her. He didn't know if she'd turn from him, lash out at him or accept the comfort he longed to give.

Cautiously, he stepped closer and touched her shoulder.

Dionne's head whipped up and she blinked hot, burning tears from her eyes as a hiccup escaped her lips. What was he doing here? Couldn't he give her peace and privacy? Embarrassment had her already reddened cheeks flaming as she scooted away from him. "Please, just leave me alone."

"Dionne?"

She shook her head, unable to explain. Slowly she moved to the far side of the bed and ran a hand over her damp face. Her back to him, she hoped he'd leave.

He'd let her turn from him Saturday. But this was different; this needed an explanation. He walked over to stand before her. Gently, he cupped her chin and forced her to look at him. Her eyes were red-rimmed and vulnerable, her pale face streaked and swollen. She was hurting badly, and he didn't know how to help her, but knew he had to try. Wordlessly, he sat down and moved her onto his lap, cradling her against the warmth of his body as he leaned against the headboard.

Dionne stared for a long moment into the blue depths of his eyes, then she heard herself moan before she buried her face in his neck. She hung on to him, dry sobs taking her, clutching him to her as if clinging to a lifeline. And maybe he was.

He rocked her gently, swayed with her, murmured reassuring words, hoping to soothe, to calm. It took a long while before her breathing settled and she eased back. In her hand, she held something. Gently, he pried it from her fingers.

A snapshot. A younger Dionne stood smiling at a boy in his midteens with brown curly hair and a shy grin, his arm self-consciously resting on her shoulders. Colby looked at her, hoping for an explanation.

There was no way out but to tell him. Dionne straightened, wiping her eyes. "His name was Denny, and he set the scene to take this picture on his birthday with the camera I gave him. Denny didn't get too many gifts. His mother was into marrying, not into raising her son. Three marriages, three divorces, plus live-in boy-friends in between. She farmed him out to foster homes sometimes, too. Denny was in her way, and he felt it."

Was? Colby guessed what was coming, but he let her tell it in her own way. "He was your patient?"

"Yes, through the county medical program. He'd been an abused child, a neglected child, a problem child. But he tried so hard to straighten out, to hang on to a thread of self-esteem, to face each day. Until…until one day, he stopped trying. He climbed into his mother's car in his mother's closed garage, turned on the engine and ended his life. He was fifteen and a half." Fresh tears threatened, but she choked them back. "Such a fine young man who deserved to live, to be loved, to—"

"It wasn't your fault." He held her tighter.

She looked at him with a sad smile. "How easily you say that. Technically, no. But I failed Denny. So many people failed Denny. But that's not why I keep his picture with me always."

"Tell me why."

"Because I let myself forget with Denny that a doctor shouldn't get emotionally involved with her patients—not a surgeon or a GP or a psychologist. If they do, they make wrong decisions based on emotion instead of intellect and knowledge and training."

"You're not seriously blaming yourself for Denny's suicide?"

"Sometimes. Perhaps I could have approached his problem differently, sought a colleague's advice, turned him over to someone more experienced. This happened when I'd been in practice only two years." She pulled in a shaky breath. "I'm more experienced now, yet Shelly's become very important to me. And there's Terry, who snared me easily. I called him twice after that meeting in the trailer, you know. He chatted with me like a younger brother, swore he wasn't drinking and tried to charm me with his easy lies. Much as I wanted, I couldn't get him to acknowledge his problem, to seek help.'' She ran an unsteady hand through her untidy hair. ''Maybe I'm not cut out for this line of work.''

He searched for ways to ease her pain, truthful ways. ''I imagine everyone who was close to a suicide victim wishes they'd done something differently. As does every doctor when a patient doesn't listen or comes to them too late.''

The tears had dried on her face, and still she sat cradled in his arms. She so rarely let anyone comfort her or see the weak side of her. Yet it felt good, it felt right. And that worried her, too. She tried on a smile for his benefit. ''Maybe you do understand.''

''Maybe you'll find I do, if you'll trust me.''

Dionne let out a ragged sigh. ''There's another reason I keep Denny's picture with me. It's to remind myself that life is so very fleeting, so very fragile and precious. And so is trust. I've never, *ever* trusted anyone with the story of Denny—until now.''

He knew the small gift of trust had been hard won. ''We may not want such different things from life as I once thought, Dionne. Maybe we just go about getting them differently.''

She touched his face, running her hand along his strong jaw with its day's growth of beard. ''Don't go making more out of this than there is.''

Her cool approach to patients had bothered him. But he'd learned tonight that keeping her distance didn't mean she didn't care. And even that came with a high price tag. He touched his lips to her forehead, finding it cool. "I'm not making more than there is. But don't you make *less* than there is."

"All right, that's a deal." She extricated herself from his arms, surprised at how empty she felt the moment she did. She walked with him to the door and opened it. She hated anyone seeing her fall apart. But if someone had to, she was glad it had been Colby. "I trust you to keep this between us."

How had he known she'd ask? "Don't worry, lady. Your secret is safe with me."

She cleared her throat, a bit uncomfortable with that but given no choice. "Thanks. I appreciate it."

Leaning down, he brushed his lips across hers. He found hers soft and dewy and gently responsive. But this was not the night for further explorations. "I like having you here, Dionne Keller." With that, he turned and left her.

Chapter Six

It was about time something started going right, Dionne thought as she entered her office and sat behind her desk. Perhaps Terry's accident had spurred her on to try harder. Or perhaps the gods were ready to smile.

She took out Dan's file and opened it, still not sure if she'd caught him in a weak moment yesterday or if, in fact, he was ready to face his addiction. At any rate, when she'd finally tracked him down at lunchtime, he'd agreed to go with her to an Alcoholics Anonymous meeting last night, albeit reluctantly. And once there, he'd been pleasantly surprised that no one had exerted pressure on him.

Colby had gone with them, and they'd listened intently to men and woman from all walks of life tell their stories, some matter-of-factly, some quite emotionally. Several members had proudly announced they'd been sober for years, a few for a matter of months or weeks,

and others—like Dan—hadn't volunteered much beyond their names.

Still, it was a beginning, and Dionne felt that Dan was
giving serious thought to sobriety. One recovering
member's story—about finally facing his alcoholism the
day he'd nearly killed both his young son and himself
while driving under the influence—had really gotten to
Dan. Dionne was a firm believer that daily meetings
were necessary in the beginning for a recovering alcoholic and she'd gotten Dan to agree to go again tonight.
This time, she planned to trust him to go alone, and she
hoped he'd come through. Of course, she knew better
than to consider his turnaround a sure thing just yet.

Setting aside Dan's file, she picked up Theresa Abbott's. Dottie was close to finalizing arrangements for an
intervention meeting, and Dionne couldn't help wondering how Theresa would handle such a confrontation, gentle and loving though it would be. With a sigh,
Dionne rose and walked to look out the window.

Autumn was definitely in the air with crisp leaves
whirling around the parking lot, carried by a chilly September wind. In St. Clair, she imagined most of the
leaves had changed by now, offering a delightful array
of colors for the visitors that drove north every fall to
admire them. She wished she were going this very afternoon.

And maybe she would, but she needed to see Terry
first. She hoped that Jean would be there and be willing
to listen with an open mind. Whether Terry would be
able to keep his arm or not, he faced a rocky road. She
knew that alcoholics were tempted the most when things
looked darkest. Would Terry realize that his stubborn
refusal to admit that he had a problem that was out of
control had contributed to his accident, and therefore

give up drinking? Or would he wallow in self-pity and drink even more? Either way, Jean would not have an easy time of it, loving him as she did.

Raising her arms high, Dionne stretched, realizing her shoulder muscles were tense. Tension was part of her work, a part she'd never get used to. But this pressure had a different cause. She'd discovered the other evening that she was far more vulnerable than she'd suspected. A sympathetic ear, quiet understanding, a gentle touch, and she had dropped her defenses. She'd been vulnerable to a man once before, a man who'd used that defenselessness to hurt and humiliate her. She never wanted to go through that again.

Of course, Colby wasn't Nathan. Last evening, after a very long day of reviewing personnel files with all three department heads, she'd soaked in his hot tub before going to bed. And, as with the first time, he'd joined her.

Colby had been different lately. Friendlier, less challenging. He'd been around, but he hadn't pressed. And she'd caught him looking at her more often with eyes that were warm and affectionate.

As she'd sunk into the steaming water, he'd brought up her family again. They'd talked about her growing-up years, the good times with her family, their present relationship with her. He seemed hungry to hear about people who lived together and loved one another. Dionne fought the softening of her heart for the little boy inside Colby, the one who'd missed out on so much. She wanted him to have all that, but knew she couldn't be the one to give it to him.

He'd walked her to her door, and they'd stood there, dripping wet and beginning to shiver, their eyes locked together. It was Dionne who'd made the first move, reaching up on tiptoe for his kiss, needing again to experience that quick thrust of desire, that edgy passion that weakened her knees and turned her bones to liquid. She'd also been the one to break away, while she was still able. There was no denying the simple truth: she wanted this man desperately.

And she could not have him.

Turning from the window, she took off her glasses and picked up her cigarettes, studying the package. She'd cut down considerably, smoking only half a dozen a day. At first, she'd challenged herself to do it, then later, she'd struggled with her decision. Not easy. But perhaps she'd better understand what the addicts she worked with were going through. She tossed aside the pack and sat down.

Where was Colby? she wondered. He'd been gone when she awakened this morning, and Aggie hadn't seemed to know where. She glanced at her watch as the phone rang.

Moments later, she said goodbye to Hilary and hung up. Shelly Morgan's father had died, his body no longer able to fight the many injuries he'd received in the car accident that had taken the life of his wife months ago. He'd never come out of the coma. Her heart went out to the young girl as she pictured Shelly with her huge blue eyes and her sad little face. She was devastated, Hilary had told her, and was asking for Dionne.

She stood and quickly crammed her papers into her briefcase. She'd leave immediately. This shock just might reverse all the progress Shelly had made, send her back to her silent world where she trusted so very few. Dionne picked up the phone and checked with Marianne as to Colby's whereabouts.

But the secretary told her he hadn't checked in yet this morning. She couldn't take the time to hunt him down, Dionne decided as she grabbed her notepad. Hastily, she scribbled him a message explaining her sudden departure, then propped it on her desk by the phone.

Grabbing her briefcase and purse, Dionne hurried out the door. She'd leave her bag at Colby's and pick up the rest of her things later. Traffic shouldn't be too heavy at this time of day. With luck, she'd be in St. Clair by noon.

The sunset was beautiful from his back patio, though the air was nippy. Colby sat in his lawn chair, holding his coffee cup with both hands, watching the lowering sun tint the clouds orange and golden, while off to the north, the sky was streaked purple. Beautiful. And he had no one beside him to share the beauty.

Odd how that fact hadn't really bothered him until lately. Until a certain redhead had come into his life and pointed out the voids he'd somehow overlooked in the past. She'd done a number on him, which had certainly not been her intention. Or his, to let it happen.

Three days now she'd been gone, and though he fully understood her need to go to Shelly, he missed her. The weekend stretched before him, long and lonely. He knew of a dozen people he could call and get something going—a barbecue, a quiet dinner out, a football game. But he felt discontented with his usual forms of entertainment, unenthused about the people he'd been seeing. He found things lacking in the women he'd been dating that he hadn't noticed before, and therefore was reluctant to call them.

Sipping his coffee, he frowned. This wasn't supposed to be happening. He'd warned himself from the start that despite the undeniable attraction, Dionne Keller was wrong for him. A woman enmeshed in her career, involved with her patients though she knew better, seemingly complete without a relationship. Only was she?

Her response to his kisses was avid and instantaneous, though she fought the fact. Was the attraction merely physical, a normal woman reacting to a man she was suddenly spending time near? Could she satisfy that need eventually, yet turn from the more deeper need of sharing her thoughts, her feelings, herself with him. And was that what he wanted?

Rising, he began to stroll the yard thoughtfully. What did he want? Colby asked himself. A woman as different from Ariel as night was from day. A woman of warmth and depth who wanted to make a home, have a family, share a life with him for all time. At thirty-three, he felt he'd spent enough time alone, enough effort building for a future that he faced with mixed feelings. He had a lot to give, much to share, but he wanted no more mistakes. He was no longer a kid unable to see past the surface beauty of a woman. He needed substance and staying power.

The truth was, he hadn't spent enough time with Dionne to ascertain if she was made of the right stuff. She could make his heart race, his blood heat, but that was no longer enough. He wanted more, and he wouldn't settle for less. Reaching the fence, he stared off into the twilight of evening, seeing instead Dionne's face when she was spitfire angry, when she'd cried over not reaching Terry in time, when he'd lowered his head to kiss her and caught the quick spark of anticipation in her dark eyes.

Resolutely, Colby started back toward the house. Always, he'd been a man of action, not one who sat back and let life happen to him. He needed to see Dionne again in her environment, on her turf, so to speak. To see for himself if there was anything there. If he found it, he'd pursue her until she realized they belonged together. If not, he'd get her out of his system once and for all and get on with his life.

In his bedroom, he took down his bag from the closet. He'd spend tomorrow morning in the office, then phone Zac and tell him he was coming. A business trip to check on their building project in St. Clair, he would say. He did need to see how that was doing. And he hadn't seen Lainey since the wedding. But after all was said and done, he needed to see Dionne.

"I never saw two men put away more food at one lunch," Lainey Sinclair commented as she cleared the table. "If I ate like that, I wouldn't be able to get through the archway."

"You could stand to put on a few pounds," Zac said as his gray eyes swept over his wife's slender frame. "You don't have to be model thin anymore, remember?"

Returning to the table, she placed her hand on her husband's and gave him an impish smile. "You want me to be fat and sassy?"

"You're already sassy...."

Playfully, she cuffed him, then turned to Colby. "So tell the truth, why are you really here in the middle of a work day?"

Colby sat back with a smile. From the beginning, he'd liked Lainey, liked the honesty and down-to-earth ways she possessed despite her highly successful former career as a top New York model. Like Zac, he'd discovered that she was even more lovely inside than out, which was saying something. He looked into her dark violet eyes and found it hard not to tell her everything. "Just came up to see how our new building was coming along.

And to see if you've been taking good care of my buddy, here.''

Lainey nodded knowingly. "Sure you did." Rising, she glanced out the window toward the barn. "I've got a riding student due soon, so I'll leave you two." Gathering her black hair at the nape of her neck, she fastened it with a gold clip. Then she leaned down and touched her lips to Zac's, lightly yet lingeringly. "See you later." She turned to meet Colby's eyes. "Maybe you should tell Zac what's troubling you. Confession's good for the soul, I hear."

"Thanks, Dr, Freud," Colby answered.

"I'll leave the doctoring to Dionne," Lainey said as she opened the kitchen door, then skipped down the back-porch steps.

Colby saw Zac lean forward and watch her through the window, the love on his face something to see. Colby experienced a jolt of envy as strong as it was surprising. "I take it you two are happy." It wasn't a question.

Zac's gaze was still on Lainey as she greeted their handyman, who was leading a chestnut mare out into the corral. "Happier than I'd ever thought I'd be again." Turning, he shifted his attention to his friend.

"You've done wonders with this place," Colby said, glancing around the remodeled kitchen with its brick flooring, the new appliances, the wide bay window that looked out on the wooded acreage.

"Wait'll I show you the two new rooms I've added and the second bath. And I've extended the porch around two sides of the house. Evenings, we sit there in our rockers like two old folks and watch the deer drink from the stream down a ways. I'll bet you think that sounds like a boring life."

Colby thought of his own patio where he'd sat looking at the sunset last evening. "Maybe not so boring." Not if you had someone to share it with. He glanced at his friend, then quickly stood and spoke before Zac could comment. "So, you going to show me the building?"

Thoughtfully, Zac drained his coffee cup. "Sure, let's go."

An hour later, after walking the building site and talking with the job foreman, they strolled back toward Zac's truck. Getting behind the wheel, Zac frowned. "Well, what do you think?"

"Looks good. Jack seems to be a good man."

Zac swung out onto the road. "We haven't talked about how the employee-assistance program is coming along. I know you had your reservations from the start. Is Dionne making a difference?"

An understatement, to say the least. "Yeah, I think so."

"Are the department heads accepting her?"

"She's very professional, knows her stuff. She never backs down. I thought at first she was cool and dispassionate, you know. Like that social worker who used to come around when I was a kid. But Dionne's different. She cares about people."

Zac raised his eyebrows. "You seem a little out of sorts. Is there a new woman in your life messing up your head?"

"Hell, no." Colby tried a cocky grin. "Who needs women? You captured the only prize around, so why should I keep looking?"

"Because I don't figure you'll like the life of a monk."

"Love 'em and leave 'em, that's my motto. Don't let 'em get under your skin." The words sounded false to his own ears. Colby shifted his gaze to the buildings they were passing. "Isn't Dionne's office around here some-where?"

"We passed it a couple of blocks ago." Zac shot him an inquisitive glance. "Why? You thinking of calling her?"

Colby opted for nonchalance. "I might. Since I'm up here anyway. Did you and Lainey go to Shelly's father's funeral?"

"Yes. Shelly's one of Lainey's students. It was pretty bad. The child wouldn't leave Dionne's side."

"She has grandparents, an aunt and uncle. Yet she seems more attached to Dionne, right?"

Zac shrugged. "The grandparents are up in years, and Shelly hasn't been around them much until lately. She's staying with her aunt and uncle, but they've got their hands full with four children of their own. It's natural for the child to gravitate to someone as caring as Dionne, especially since she's helped her so much. I know Dionne's real worried about Shelly's long-term reaction to losing both her parents so tragically."

Colby propped an ankle on his knee. "She does get involved with her patients. You should have seen her with Terry." He told Zac the story, explaining the acci-dent and the scene at the hospital, but leaving out what had happened afterward, except to say that Dionne had been upset and blamed herself for not being able to do more sooner. Her revelations that night to him about Denny and the way she'd wept in his arms were too per-sonal to share, even with Zac.

"I'm not a bit surprised. I've seen Dionne with the children. And with Lainey when she was wrestling with a load of problems. She's a born doctor."

There was that career thing again. Colby angled on the seat toward Zac, trying to think how best to word his next question. "Does Lainey ever talk about when she and Dionne were growing up together, the guys they dated, stuff like that?"

Zac studiously swung the truck to the left to pass a slow-moving station wagon. "Well, I know Lainey spent a lot of time at the Keller house after her parents divorced because she felt welcome in the big family. Then the Kellers moved to Frankenmuth when Dionne was around seventeen or eighteen, about the time Lainey went to New York. She's never mentioned guys they dated. Why do you want to know?"

Colby shrugged. "Just nosey, I guess. Dionne told me about this man she'd known some time ago, somebody she'd cared for who'd hurt her. I just wondered who he was."

Zac pulled into his drive and stopped the truck near the barn door. Slowly, he turned to look at Colby. "You've fallen for her. That's got to be it."

Colby's face wrinkled into an incredulous frown. "Me? You think I'm crazy enough to get mixed up with another woman who loves her career?" He shook his head vehemently as he reached for the door handle. "Not me, partner." He hopped down. "Looks like Lainey's through with her lesson. How about showing me those new ponies you bought?" Colby slammed the door, hoping he hadn't overplayed his hand. Zac always had been able to see right through him.

* * *

Seven o'clock on a Saturday night, and the traffic was light on the road heading north. Colby wondered if he was making a mistake. Well, he would soon find out.

He'd called Dionne's office and gotten a recording saying they were closed, but giving out a number to be called in case of emergency. When he'd dialed that, a Dr. Hilary Drake had answered, telling him she was sorry, but Dr. Keller couldn't be reached right now, that she was off this weekend on a personal emergency. Not wanting to alert Dionne's partner, he hadn't pressed.

Next, he'd tried to look up Dionne's address in the phone book, only to find she was unlisted. He'd had no choice except to ask Lainey and Zac, who had exchanged a maddeningly knowing look. Trying to look casual, he'd turned down their invitation to stay the weekend, copied down Dionne's address and left, saying he just might drop in to say hello before heading home.

Lainey had hugged him goodbye, her eyes dark and curious. Zac had walked him to his truck, unable to resist a parting remark.

"Dionne's not as tough as she looks, Colby. Go easy."

He'd answered with a question of his own. "What makes you think I am?"

He hoped Lainey hadn't called her friend to warn her he was on his way. Colby liked to have the element of surprise on his side. Then again, he was taking a chance at finding her home.

The neighborhood he was driving through was full of winding streets and deep, wooded lots. Her apartment building was three-stories, vine-covered and secluded. She was in the back, on the second floor. Feeling only slightly foolish, he knocked twice rather firmly. He heard the television being turned down, then the door swung open.

She stood there wearing a pink sweatshirt, faded jeans and a surprised expression. Her hair was wind tossed, she wore no makeup and on her feet were furry Garfield slippers. It was all he could do to keep from pulling her into his arms.

"I was in the neighborhood," he said somewhat lamely.

Her mouth twitched. "I see. Well, since you're here, you might as well come in." She opened the door wider.

Not the warmest of welcomes, but she had asked him in. Then he saw Shelly seated in the corner of a pale green sofa, dressed exactly as Dionne was, right down to the furry cartoon-cat slippers. Her large eyes were a deep blue, the skin under them looking smudged with fatigue. She was holding her scruffy looking stuffed dog, which she dragged with her as she jumped up to give him a shy hug.

He hugged her back, feeling the fragility. "Are you all right?"

Shelly nodded into his chest. "I'm glad you came."

Such a sad little face, such a timid little voice. "Me, too." He released her, and she climbed back onto the couch.

Dionne indicated a box on the glass-topped coffee table in front of the couch. "We were just about to share a pizza. There's plenty if you haven't had dinner yet."

Colby shrugged out of his jacket. "I'd like that."

She placed three pieces on pale blue plates and handed them around. "We have milk or grape juice or root beer. What'll it be, folks?"

Everyone chose root beer, and after she'd set down their drinks and passed out napkins, Dionne seated her-

Get 4 Books FREE

SEE BACK OF CARD FOR DETAILS

FREE MYSTERY GIFT

We will be happy to send you a free bonus gift along with your free books! To request it, please check here and mail this reply card promptly!

Thank you!

DETACH ALONG DOTTED LINE AND MAIL TODAY! – DETACH ALONG DOTTED LINE AND MAIL TODAY! – DETACH ALONG DOTTED LINE AND MAIL TODAY!

self alongside Shelly. "So, you just happen to be in my neighborhood, eh?" she challenged Colby before taking a bite of pizza.

Chewing, he nodded. "Actually, I had lunch with Lainey and Zac, then spent the afternoon looking over our new building site. I was on my way home when I thought I'd stop by, see how you are."

"Mmm-hmm." Dionne knew Hilary wouldn't give out her address, so she guessed he must have coaxed it from Lainey. What story had he told them? she wondered. "I hated to leave so suddenly, but I had no choice. Is anything new? How's Terry?"

"Still no decision about his arm. Dan has attended two more meetings. And yesterday, Ed Donnelly from our drafting department came looking for you."

Dionne frowned. "I don't think I know him."

"Probably not, but he's heard of your program. I finally got it out of him that he's hooked on some prescription medication and worried about it. I made an appointment for him at Charter Hospital and told him you'd meet with him when you get back."

When she got back. When would that be? she wondered. "Keep me informed on him, will you?"

Colby nodded as he finished his piece. "That's good pizza."

"Help yourself," Dionne offered.

"I don't like pepperoni," Shelly said, still studying her piece as if it contained foreign matter.

"It's okay, sweetie," Dionne told her as she removed the small rounds. "We'll just take them off."

Colby winked at her. "I can't help but admire your matching slippers, ladies. Something new?"

Shelly wiggled her feet, breaking into a small, pleased smile. Looking at her, Dionne smiled, too. "Yes. We went shopping this afternoon. Shelly liked the Minnie Mouse ones, but I'm nuts about Garfield.''

"I should have come sooner," Colby commented as he took another piece. "Maybe I could have gotten a pair, too."

"We could go get you some tomorrow," Shelly offered.

"Oh, I think Colby wants to head for home before too long," Dionne answered because she was glad to see him. A little too glad.

"Can Colby stay and watch our movie with us?"

Finishing, Dionne set aside her plate. "I guess we'll have to ask him. We've rented a movie, Colby. *The Land Before Time.*"

"It's about dinosaurs, and it's very sad," Shelly added.

"Not exactly Bogie," Dionne said.

"I love movies. Sure, I'll stay."

She might have guessed. Rising, Dionne slipped the tape into the VCR, then turned back to the couch. Her eyebrows raised as she saw that Colby had moved to the other corner, leaving the middle seat for her.

He smiled up at her boyishly. "I thought I could see better from here."

"Of course." She sat down, taking Shelly's plate from her. She'd hardly eaten half a piece. Poor little thing hadn't had much of an appetite before, and now she was only nibbling. Slipping her arm behind the child, Dionne settled her into her side.

Colby's eyes were on the TV screen as the movie began, but his thoughts were on the woman beside him. The woman who said she had no interest in a family, in children. The woman snuggling a wounded little girl to her as if it were the most natural thing in the world. Why was it that her actions didn't match her words?

He leaned forward, catching Shelly's eye. "What's this movie about, Shelly? Have you seen it before?"

Shelly nodded. "Lots of times. This big earthquake comes, and Sara and Littlefoot are left all alone."

Dionne jumped in. "There are two kinds of dinosaurs represented, the three-horns, which is Sara's group, and the longnecks, which is what Littlefoot is. The earth splits and their parents are killed, so they go searching for the Great Valley."

"And why do they want to go to the Great Valley?"

"Because that's where the other dinosaurs are, the ones who will love them and look after them," Shelly answered. "There's lots to eat there, and no one gets mad at anyone."

Shifting closer to Dionne, Colby stretched his arm along the couch back until he touched her shoulder lightly. When she turned to look at him, he met her eyes. "I wouldn't mind finding the Great Valley myself."

In no time, he forgot it was a children's movie, finding himself engrossed in the simple story, watching the two young dinosaurs run into one obstacle after another as they searched for the land of their loved ones. He noticed Dionne was absorbed also, and despite its familiarity, Shelly seemed fascinated anew.

"Uh-oh," Colby commented, leaning around Dionne, "I think they're going in the wrong direction and they're lost, Shelly."

She shot him a knowing glance. "No. When you lose your way, you let your heart lead you," she told him.

Close alongside Dionne now, he took her hand into his. "I like that," he said, his voice soft and low. "Let your heart lead you. Something to think about."

Her own heart thudding, Dionne looked back. Sudden tears sprang to her eyes and she blinked them back. The arm circling Shelly tightened about the child who lay so trustingly against her. Colby's hand in hers felt warm and strong and so very welcome. This is how it could be, she thought, if only nature hadn't played a cruel trick on her years ago. She allowed the thought only a moment, then forced her attention back to the movie. She must not let Colby see how badly she wanted this simple, loving domestic scene to become a part of her life.

A trap. If she revealed her growing feelings for Colby, he would be trapped. He cared, she knew, but she could not chain him to a woman who couldn't meet his needs for the family life he all but cried out for. Even busy as she'd been these last few days with Shelly and her grief, Dionne had thought about Colby, missed Colby, wanted Colby.

Somehow, she would have to get over him, to let him go.

The narrator was wrapping up the story. Colby half listened, feeling a deep contentment seep into his very pores. This is what life should be, he thought. He empathized with the little girl who'd suddenly lost the magical closeness of a family unit. He knew Dionne had known something similar in her youth. He would find a way to convince her that they could have this between them and still enjoy their work.

Somehow he would get through to her.

The singer could be heard as the two little creatures, having found the Great Valley and their loved ones, romped and played in the serenity of their families. Dreams see us through to forever, the song went on. Colby couldn't have agreed more.

Composed again, Dionne cleared her throat and looked down at Shelly. "She's asleep," she whispered to Colby. "Poor little thing hasn't had much rest lately."

"Is she staying with you?"

"Just until Monday. She wanted to, and I thought her being here would give her family a chance to recover." There was no need to add how much pleasure she found in having Shelly with her.

"I thought you weren't going to get involved again with one of your patients?"

"Yes, I thought that, too." Dionne let out a ragged sigh. "I seem to be a little short in the willpower department."

"I'm delighted to hear it," he said, smiling as he rose. "Let me carry her to her bed." He scooped the sleeping child and her stuffed animal into his arms, inhaling the sweet childish fragrance as he followed Dionne to the guest bedroom.

She pulled back the covers of the twin bed against the wall. "I've been sleeping in here, in the other bed, so I can be near her. She awakens at night crying. It's enough to break your heart."

He laid Shelly down, then watched Dionne tug off the child's jeans and slippers and tuck her and her dog in. As Dionne bent down to brush back the damp blond curls, placing a kiss on the soft cheek, Colby felt something inside him shift. Impulsively, he leaned down to touch his lips to Shelly's hair. Swallowing past a lump, he trailed after Dionne, leaving the door slightly ajar.

She needed to keep busy and she needed him to leave before she broke down in front of him again. Quickly, Dionne gathered up their dinner remnants and moved to the kitchen. It had been a trying, emotional few days, and now this. What had happened to her marvelous control?

Colby stood in the doorway and spoke to her back. "I should go." She made no comment, just loaded plates and glasses into the dishwasher. He checked his watch. "Of course, it *is* late. The traffic on a Saturday night going toward Detroit can be—"

"All right." She closed the dishwasher and swung about. "You can stay. But I have to tell you, I'm really beat. I want to take a shower and go to sleep."

He faked a yawn. "I have no problem with that. Tomorrow morning, maybe I can take you two out to breakfast."

"We'll see." Walking past him, she stopped at the linen closet, pulled out fresh towels and handed them to him. "I just changed my bed. You'll have to use my room."

"Fine." In her room, among her things, and her on the other side of the wall. Colby almost groaned. "I have a bag in the truck."

She folded her arms across her chest and nodded. "Always prepared, like the marines."

"I'd intended to stay with Zac and Lainey. They asked me, but I wanted to see you." He took a step nearer, reached out and touched the ends of her hair. "Dionne, I—"

She took his hand in her own and brought it down. "Colby, I can't cope with this right now. Honestly, I can't."

He stepped back with an understanding nod. "I'll go get my bag."

Feeling whipped, she let out a deep breath. "I'm going to take a shower. See you in the morning."

"Right." He returned quickly, locked up and turned off the lights. The homey little nighttime ritual mocked him. Would Dionne ever want to share a home with him, open to him, come to him willingly? She was exhausted and he understood that. Why wouldn't she allow him to comfort her, to hold her, if only for a little while? Wasn't that what caring was about?

Slipping off his shoes, he lay down on her bed, waiting for her to finish in the bathroom.

Maybe she should have turned the water to cold, Dionne thought as she dried herself off. Instead of relaxing her, the hot shower had her skin humming and her blood warming. Or was it the man in the room across the hall?

Mixed emotions churned in her as she rubbed lotion on her arms and legs. She wanted him to go; she wanted him to stay. She wanted him in her life; she never wanted to see him again. Oh, Lord, this kind of vacillation from a doctor who'd been trained to advise others. Annoyed with herself, Dionne reached for her nightshirt and robe.

The hallway light cast dim shadows as she left the bath and went to the guest room. The door to her own bedroom was ajar and, as she slipped between the sheets, she heard Colby moving around. In moments, the shower was turned on. Shelly was lying on her back, snoring lightly. Dionne tried to relax.

And she almost made it. But then the radio came on with a loud rock song. She leapt out of bed and was in the hallway before she was aware she'd moved. The bathroom door opened and Colby stood there next to the open window, a puzzled frown on his face.

"It was steamy in here, so I opened the window and—"

"I forgot to tell you," Dionne said, brushing in past him. Stooping, she craned her neck, looking for the button. "Ah, here it is." She shoved it in and instantly, the music stopped.

Sighing, Dionne stood, glad Shelly hadn't awakened. "An electrician rented this apartment before me and he rigged up this alarm system. When any of the windows are opened, the radio kicks on. That button's the only way to turn it off. He was away a great deal and he wanted to protect his wife and daughter so he..."

She stopped, knowing she was babbling. Her pulse beat erratically as her eyes traveled up the long, lean length of him. He had a towel wrapped around his middle and the curly hairs on his chest were still damp. His eyes were smoky blue and aware. Dionne stood rooted to the spot.

She wore only a thin nightshirt that came to just above her knees. Her bottom lip trembled slightly as her dark eyes held his. Afterward, he wasn't sure who moved first, but suddenly his arms were around her, his mouth devouring hers as her small hands roamed his back restlessly.

Colby dragged her closer, feeling her soft breasts press against his chest, feeling his heart pound. His tongue entered, searching out private tastes, her special flavors. He felt his body harden in response as he sought her welcoming warmth.

Lost. She was lost to him again, flying on the wings of a passion so compelling she could no longer fight it. On tiptoe, she eased her hands into his hair, pulling his head down to her, her body reacting shamelessly to the answering desire she felt through the thin material separating them. She drew in the dark masculine scent of him and tasted his need with her exploring tongue as it mated with his.

Her breasts ached with the need for his touch and, as if he knew, his hands moved between them. Dionne swallowed a sigh as his fingers closed about her flesh and his lips trailed a heated path down her throat. She moved her own hands to caress the soft hair of his chest, feeling the hard muscles tense as he fought for control.

It would be so easy, he thought hazily, so mindlessly easy to drop to the rug with her right here. Or to pick her up and carry her to the bed. So easy to drop his towel and pull off the flimsy layer of silk she wore and bury himself inside her. Her body was pressing against his, eager and aroused.

But a voice in the back of his head reminded him that only last night he'd decided that sex wouldn't be enough. Not with this woman. He could take her now and she wouldn't fight him. But what about the morning after? Desire appeased, would she then want him gone, out of her life?

Colby already knew he wanted more. He wanted Dionne to come to him, not accidentally as had happened just now. But on purpose, after careful thought and consideration, knowing full well that when they came together, they would be sharing more than their bodies.

Drawing on a slim slice of control still remaining, he stepped back from her, the hardest step he'd ever taken. Breathing hard, he watched her dazed eyes focus on his, saw the quick confusion, the disbelief.

Straightening her nightshirt, Dionne pulled in a deep breath. She'd almost lost it there, almost given in to the aching need that she knew would keep her restlessly awake much of the night. She could see in Colby's eyes the reluctant control that had had him pulling back when she knew it cost him greatly. What had stopped him? she wondered as she ran a shaky hand through her damp hair.

Colby tightened the towel about his waist, then raised a hand and touched the silk of her cheek. He needed to explain so she would understand. "I want you more than I've ever wanted another woman," he said, his voice thick. "But not like this. Do you know what I'm saying?"

She searched his eyes, then dropped her gaze as she nodded. "I wish with all my heart that I could be all that you need," she whispered. She placed a soft kiss in the palm of his hand, then walked quickly out of the bath.

Colby heard the bedroom door close behind her and went to lie down. He knew sleep would not come easily this night. He knew also that most would think him foolish for what he'd walked away from just now. But he felt differently.

He was going for the gold this time. Dionne was a woman to be cherished, not one to be plundered on a bathroom floor. He wanted all of her and he was prepared to wait.

Stretching his restive body, Colby prayed he had the courage of his convictions.

Chapter Seven

The fish were biting. Colby reeled in his first catfish, a wiggly little thing that looked to be less than half a pound. Rising from the end of the wooden dock, he held his catch up for Shelly to admire.

She made a face. "It's ugly. Why do they call it a catfish?"

"Because of these long whiskers." Colby touched the gaping mouth and brushed at the whiskers. The fish gave one last lurch. Deftly, he removed the hook and dropped the fish into the bucket of water. "Who's going to catch the second one?"

"I will, if you'll help me bait my hook," Shelly offered.

"You got it." Picking up the smaller pole he'd bought her earlier, Colby bent to his task. It was a beautiful day at the end of September, sunny and warm. At breakfast, he'd suggested they all three go fishing and, to his surprise, Shelly had shown a spark of enthusiasm. Not one to let that go, Dionne had agreed that fishing sounded like a wonderful idea.

Perhaps, but she hadn't stuck her line in the water yet, he noticed. Sitting at the end of the weathered dock, Dionne leaned against a thick post and threw scraps of bread into the lake, halfheartedly attempting to lure the fish near the surface. In her solemn way, Shelly had watched him silently until he'd caught that first fish. Now he was pleased that she wanted to try. Finished baiting the hook, he handed her the pole.

"You can sit next to Dionne and drop your line into the water." He showed her how, then scrunched down beside her. As if she could conjure up a fish by merely concentrating, Shelly stared intently at the bobber that told her where her sinker had dropped. Smiling at the child's intensity, he glanced over at Dionne.

She had on a gray sweatshirt with matching pants, and her eyes were hidden behind huge sunglasses. But he could tell she was watching him. She'd been quiet and subdued all day, offering very little in the way of conversation to him, not doing much better with Shelly. He'd shaken her last night, though unintentionally. He'd explained his unusual behavior so she wouldn't take his reluctance to make love to her as rejection. And he didn't think she had. She knew exactly what he was after. And the thought obviously scared her to death.

"Penny for your thoughts," he offered.

Dionne just shook her head, angling her body and shifting her gaze toward the middle of the quiet lake. She'd always liked it out here, though she'd never fished at this spot. Half a dozen little inlets wove in and out of the shoreline where aging docks snaked toward the center, built years ago by residents long gone. Just sitting and fishing and letting your thoughts drift along with the slow movements of the water was a popular pastime and one Dionne enjoyed. But not today.

Perhaps because her thoughts were in a jumble, heavy, disturbing. She'd wanted to make love with Colby last night, wanted to experience the soul-shattering release she knew he could give her. Then, maybe then, she could have turned from him, sent him from her life and begun to forget him.

How had he seen through her and guessed, when even she hadn't known her intentions? He'd tossed the ball right back in her court. He was a man who wanted forever, and he was gambling that he'd get it. Only he'd picked the wrong woman. She'd never reacted well to pressure, subtle or otherwise.

"Something's pulling on my line, Colby," Shelly said, her voice rising in her excitement.

"Hold tight, honey," he told her. "I'm here if you need me."

"It's pulling *real* hard."

Scooting behind her, he brought her into the V of his legs and placed his hands over hers on the rod. "Together, we won't lose him." Colby looked toward Dionne, who had turned back to watch them. "Together, we can do things that one of us alone can't do." He watched Dionne finger her hair, then avert her gaze as her eyes followed a rising bird.

Not one to miss an opportunity to make a point for his side, was he? Dionne thought. It was time to score a few for her side. She'd have to do a good acting job, convince him that she was dying to get back to work tomorrow, to her career. She would smile, say it's been fun and send him on his way. Unbidden, the memory of how he'd looked when she tried the same tack on him the night in front of his fireplace returned full force. How could she do that to Colby again? How could she hurt him?

"Look at that!" Helping her only a little, he watched Shelly yank up the line and grin at the fish dangling on the end. "You did it."

Looking proud, Shelly stood and held the fish out for Dionne to admire. "Look, Dionne."

"It's beautiful," Dionne answered, rising. She'd have to set aside her concerns for Shelly's sake. "Looks like I'm the only one who hasn't caught her dinner yet." As Colby removed Shelly's fish and added it to the bucket, Dionne picked up her pole. "Okay, here goes."

They fished the afternoon away, and Colby was pleased that Dionne had finally brightened. She chattered away with Shelly, drawing the child out, even getting her to laugh with a crazy story about an elephant who wore pink booties. But he knew it was only temporary, for he'd caught her sending him long looks as if hoping she could find the answers to her questions in his eyes. Then Shelly would say something and Dionne would slip on a smile. After dinner, they'd be dropping Shelly back at her aunt's. Maybe then they could talk and get things out in the open.

By five, the sun was heading down and the air was turning cooler. Colby counted six fish in the bucket, none very large, but a nice day's catch. "There's this place not far from here where they clean and fry your fish for you, and even throw in fries and cole slaw. Ever stop at Fishhead Charlie's?"

"Never heard of it," Dionne answered, rinsing off her hands. She would go anywhere where she wouldn't have to fix the fish herself. "We can sure try it, right, Shelly?"

"Are we really going to eat the very same fish we caught?"

"Better than eating some strange fish." Colby held out his hand, pleased when she took it. "Ready, gang? Let's go."

Fishhead Charlie's was out on the wharf, with windows all around, boat lanterns for lighting and oilcloth on the tables. They sat in a dim corner booth and waited for their fish dinners, sipping on frosted glasses of lemonade. Colby dug out several quarters, and Shelly took them to the thrumming jukebox.

"I want to thank you for coming along, for giving Shelly this fun day," Dionne told him.

"I should be thanking you for letting me join you. She's a lovely child."

Dionne nodded, wondering how Shelly would cope with returning to school next week. "She's got a ways to go, but she's doing quite well."

"She's lucky to have you." Close beside her in the booth, he took her hand in his. "And I'm lucky to have you."

Dionne took a deep breath. Now or never. "No one *has* me, Colby. I'm my own person. I think you should know that."

"I do and I agree."

"To a point, you agree. But you want more. More than I can give." She held on to his hand, to take the edge from her words. "Do you remember when we talked, the night I told you about Denny?" He nodded, and she went on. "I told you I also kept his picture to remind me that life is so very fragile, so often fleeting."

"And I agree with you. That's why I don't want to waste a minute of it."

He wasn't seeing, though he thought he did. "You see that child over there? She could have died with her parents in that terrible accident. But she didn't. She's here. We have to live today, enjoy *today*. I care about you, Colby, and I want to be with you. But for today. I can't make future plans. I won't. If you want that, you'll be disappointed in me. I promise you nothing, but today. My work, my patients, come first with me. All my energies, my commitment, my time are devoted to them. I've never lied to you. I told you that right from the start. And now there's this . . . this . . ."

"Minor attraction?" He fought back the anger, knowing it would only cloud his thinking.

Dionne released an uneven sigh. "All right, so it's not so minor. But major or minor, I have precious little left over for *any* relationship. If you want to see me occasionally on that basis, fine. If not, I feel you should look for someone else." The words stung, they hurt, but they had to be said. And even the ones she'd said weren't as strong as they should have been.

He cupped her chin, forcing her to face him. "You. I want you, not someone else."

And I want you! But she dare not say it. "On my terms?"

For now. He needed time to wear her down, to make her see. For now, he would be patient, he would go along. "Looks like they're the only game in town." Dipping his head, he touched his lips to hers, briefly, gently.

He raised an eyebrow. "It's even better if you help."

"You want me to kiss you, *really kiss you,* here in this public place?"

"No. I want to take you home and I want you to kiss me then, when we're all alone and behind closed doors. And I want you to make love with me."

Just the thought and she felt her palms grow damp, but she held his gaze. "I want that, too. Just don't ask for promises, declarations, words I'm unwilling to say."

It wasn't what he wanted, but it was what he'd have to settle for, for the time being. Otherwise, he'd lose her before he had her. "All right. No promises, no declarations." He took an impatient swallow of his lemonade, wishing their dinners would arrive. Suddenly, he was a man who wanted the evening to end and the night to begin.

She didn't cry. The closer they got to her aunt's house, the sadder Shelly's little face became, but she didn't cry. It was as if she'd used up all her tears over the last year. Colby's heart turned over at the sight of her taking his hand and climbing down from his truck. Her lower lip quivered only slightly as she looked up at Dionne.

"When will you be back?"

"Soon, honey. Don't forget your riding lesson tomorrow after school at Lainey's. I'll bet Trixie's missed you." She hugged the child tightly for a long, heartstopping moment. "I'll call you, too, and we can tell each other what kind of day we had, okay?"

Shelly nodded solemnly.

"I have a present for you," Colby said, handing her a paper bag.

Ever so briefly, her eyes lit up as she opened the sack. She pulled out a bright yellow fishing hat with a variety of small lures attached. Her name was written on the brim in navy blue. "I can keep it?"

"You bet." He'd ordered it from the counter at Fishhead Charlie's as a surprise for her, and he was glad he had. He set the hat on her head at a jaunty angle. "Do I get a hug?"

Shyly, she hugged him. "Maybe we'll fish again one day."

"It's a date." Colby leaned against his truck as Dionne put her arm around Shelly and strolled down the walk with her. He saw the door open and a blond woman smilingly welcome the child home. Home. She didn't seem terribly anxious to return to what would now be her permanent home, and he wondered what was wrong.

"She's been an only child," Dionne explained when they were once more on their way. "She was used to individual attention from her parents, and her aunt simply doesn't have much time, especially for a troubled child."

"Are you still seeing her professionally?"

"Not in the office, if that's what you mean. I often take her to Lainey's and stay while she rides, then drive her home. And we talk in the car or when we stop for a bite to eat. She's lonely and lost, and I wish I could do more for her." She sent him a warning glance. "And if you tell me I'm getting overly involved with one of my patients again, I'll punch your lights out."

He sought to lighten the mood. "I'll bet you're the tough broad who could do it, too. You must weigh all of a hundred five."

"A hundred three, but I've been known to wrestle one of my brothers and beat him at it, too."

He shot her a look of pure disbelief. "Your brothers must be really puny, or they let you win."

"They're all bigger than you, except Werner, and they do *not* let me win." She punched his arm, grateful for a little horseplay to lift her spirits. "Take that back."

"Tell you what. When we get to your place and I stop this truck, I'll take you on, two out of three falls. And may the best man win."

Dionne felt a rush of emotion, a feeling of rightness as overwhelming as it was unexpected. Giving in to a need for contact, she laid her head on his shoulder. "*You* are the best man, the best I know."

Colby pressed down on the gas pedal.

"I'm sorry I didn't call earlier, Hilary," Dionne said, speaking into her kitchen phone. "You're sure there's nothing that needs my attention?"

Listening to her partner, she watched Colby shove the leftover fish the restaurant had insisted they take home into the refrigerator. Next, he put on a kettle of water, searched through her cupboards for a teapot and bags, making himself at home. She couldn't help but smile at how quickly he'd acclimated to her environment. But then, she couldn't think of a place where Colby wouldn't fit in.

There was a long pause on the other end of the line, then Hilary asked if Dionne was all right. "Of course, I'm all right. Why do you ask?"

It would seem she'd missed a question or two. "What was that again?" Dionne rubbed her neck and turned aside, tearing her eyes from the distracting sight of Colby unbuttoning his shirt. "Oh, yes. I remember the DeYoung boy. I'll meet with his parents tomorrow at two, as you said. Anything else?"

Relieved when Hilary said no, she quickly said good-bye and hung up. Swiveling about, she nearly collided with Colby who was very near, the top half of him un- dressed. His arms slid around her and drew her closer, burying his face in her hair.

"I'm making some tea, to warm you."

Closing her eyes, Dionne gave herself up to sensa- tion. For tonight, this man was hers. Perhaps for only this one night, so she would make it count. Heart beat- ing in anticipation, she sighed softly. "Do you honestly think I need tea to warm me when you're here?"

Reaching over, he flipped off the stove. "Okay, we dispense with the preliminaries." Bending, he scooped her into his arms as easily as if she were a child and started toward her bedroom. "The lady wants no rom- ancing."

Laughing, she shook her head. "The lady didn't ex- actly say that."

He stopped in the hallway in midstride. "The lady changes her mind." Quickly, he set her on her feet. "Wait here." He left her staring after him as he disap- peared into her room. Moments later, he appeared in the doorway and beckoned her.

He'd lit both candles she'd had on her nightstand, and the air was ripe with the pungent aroma of vanilla. The stereo in the far corner was on, something low and bluesy. He'd slanted the wooden window blinds, and moonlight poured in on the big four-poster bed. Dionne smiled up at him. "Looks like you've found everything you need."

Colby moved her into the circle of his arms, holding her lightly. "A room tells a lot about a person, espe- cially a bedroom."

Prolonging the pleasure, letting her need build slowly, she ran her hands along the smooth skin of his back and looked up at him. "Tell me what you learned about me from my room."

"That you like soft lighting and low music, delicate scents." He pointed to her open closet with a nod of his head. "And you prefer silken fabrics, vibrant colors and satin to sleep in." He indicated the books on the nightstand shelf. "You range from Robert Frost's poetry to Robert Ludlum's mysteries in books, your taste in magazines extends from gourmet food to trendy *Lear's*. Poetry, mystery, food and fashion."

"Seems like you've done this a time or two."

He aligned their bodies more perfectly, more intimately and watched her eyes go smoky. "Not lately. Your perfume I can't figure. It's very light, yet very memorable, but no label on the bottle."

She smiled. "A chemist friend makes it up for me. He's very talented."

There was that quick flare of jealousy. "And he is..."

"Out of my life."

"And all other men?"

Despite what he'd promised, he still needed the words. She would give him a few. "Also out of my life. I never could concentrate on more than one thing at a time. Is that what you wanted to hear?"

He drew her closer, where she could feel his rising need. "It is what I wanted to hear. What do you want to hear?"

His hands were under her shirt, caressing her skin. Her breathing grew shallow. "You're doing just fine without my coaching."

"Women have fantasies, too."

"A few. I'd rather hear the truth, how you really see me, not what you think I want to hear."

"The truth in the bedroom? You are unusual. Okay, the truth according to Colby Winters." He nuzzled her neck with his mouth and felt her shiver. "You're lovely, a very feminine woman. You have the most incredible eyes, so expressive."

"They're too close together."

"Your hair is—"

"An awful color, I know, but I . . ."

He pulled back and gave her a mock frown. "Hey! This is *my* vision here. Don't interrupt and don't contradict." He moved closer, nibbling her ear.

She laughed at his playful reprimand, enjoying this. She felt him shift, his tongue touching her lips, skimming the surface from corner to corner, then back again, the journey very slow, very seductive. Suddenly, her laughter stilled. She didn't, couldn't seem to move, to breathe. She felt the shock of sensation ricochet through her, her mouth trembling where his tongue glided.

Colby drew back, looking into her flushed face, seeing the stunned passion in her eyes. A slow climb up the mountain was always more exhilarating then a frantic rush. He wanted to coax her along until she was edgy and eager. He thought about her beauty, the sweetness of it, the wonder. He thought about the people who were filled with doubts, with remembered pain and the temporary cures they sought to free them. And he thought about how short, how precious life was—and how fortunate a man he was to have Dionne Keller in his arms.

Dionne touched a shaky hand to his chest as she caught her breath. He made her feel more alive than she'd felt in . . . in so long that she couldn't put a time frame on it. There was a hint of danger in his eyes, shadowy in the moonlight, and she found that oddly exciting. That he could make her tremble so readily surprised her, even though he'd been doing it for some weeks now.

Suddenly, he pulled her into position and heard her quick gasp. "May I have this dance?" His thighs in tight denim were close against hers in loose cotton, the gentle friction of their movements causing his blood to heat.

She heard the sweet moan of a saxophone and melted in his arms, swaying with him to the dark rhythm, her head on his shoulder. She felt him ease back a moment, pull her sweatshirt off and fling it onto a chair, then press her to his firm chest. Her breasts yielded softly as he rubbed against her, and her head began to spin. Eyes closed, she felt the candlelight flicker against her warming skin. Her limbs were comfortably heavy as she moved with him, drugged in pleasure.

"You dance well," he whispered into her ear. He slid his hands along her spine, then settled at her waist as his lips tasted her neck. She didn't answer, just gave out a low sound and thrust her hands into his hair.

Aroused, Dionne's mouth sought his, and when his tongue slipped between her parted lips, she welcomed it. She made a muffled sound as his hands slid beneath the waistband of her jogging pants. Inside, they cupped her soft flesh, to press her intimately against the hard evidence of his desire.

His touch was unhurried, a lazy seduction that held her prisoner nonetheless. She pressed closer to the mouth that caressed her own, to the magical feel of his body against hers. Her hands ran along his shoulders and touched the muscles of his arms, feeling his strength. Dreamily, she let him lead her.

Moonlight turned her pale skin creamy. He found her impossibly soft, unbearably sweet tasting as his mouth moved to kiss the tender spot behind her ear. He felt her knees begin to buckle as she shuddered briefly.

Stepping back, Colby guided them to the bed, then pulled back the spread. "I have protection with me. Do we need it or are you on the pill?"

She hated the question and hated the lie she would give. Why was it so hard to say, after all these years. "No, we won't need it," she said quietly.

Something in her expression had him searching her face, but she averted her eyes. Dismissing the thought as nerves, he guided her down onto her back. For a long moment, he knelt beside her, taking in her beauty.

Dionne struggled with her emotions and the irrational urge to cover herself, suddenly uncomfortable under his dark-eyed gaze. Instead, she reached a hand to his belt buckle. "Can I help you with this?"

He needed more time. "In a moment." He trailed his fingertips along the underside of her breasts and saw the peaks harden at his touch. Lowering himself to her, he cupped both breasts in hands that weren't quite steady, then met her eyes watching him in the gentle light of the candles. "Do you know how long I've wanted you like this, just you and me locked away in a quiet room somewhere, with the whole night ahead of us?"

"No, tell me."

His fingers molded her swelling flesh. "A long time. Maybe forever."

There was that word again. Languid, she heard it nonetheless. "Tonight, Colby. We're together tonight. Let's not talk about forever." She watched his head dip down, his tongue glide over her breasts, and she swallowed a gasp. "I'm *not* interested in forever, and I'm not getting involved with you, Colby."

"Mmm-hmm, I know."

Expertly, he moved down her, trailing kisses over her flat stomach. In a quick movement, he pulled off her pants, taking the small swatch of silk with it, and threw them both aside. Before she could react, his mouth was on hers.

He was lingering, yet demanding a response from her that she was helpless to withhold. In moments, he took her from dreamy to desperate, his mouth devouring, his fingers seeking. She could no longer lie still beneath him, her fitful body arching as he ran his hands up the inside of her thighs.

Restless needs inside Colby fought for dominance. The need to make her wild, to make her want as much as he did, to make her his consumed him. Desire was a rush of sound in his ears, the feel of her skin teasing his senses. He slipped his fingers inside her and felt her dig her nails into his shoulders.

A rush of heat, and she crested quickly, then fought for breath only to find he was driving her up again. Mindlessly, she struggled to keep up. Suddenly, she experienced a stunned release that had her moaning low in her throat. Dazed, she opened her eyes to find him watching her.

"Are you involved yet, Dionne?" Colby asked, unfastening his belt and shoving off his jeans. Naked as she, he came back to her, framing her face with his hands. As she struggled to slow her breathing, he kissed closed her eyes. Let her deny what she was feeling, he thought. He knew, and he knew there was more. Much more.

Nothing, no man, she admitted to herself, had ever made her feel like this, her every nerve end sensitive to his touch, his feel. She was glowing yet reaching for him again, but he evaded her hands as his mouth moved hungrily to her breast. Restlessly she shifted beneath him, her hands clutching his shoulders as he wandered lower.

She whispered his name and he felt the sound rocket through him. Her hands on him were no longer timid, no longer patient as they sought to give, to touch, to learn him as he was learning her. Her desire fueled him further, taking him to the swift edge of reason as he returned to crush her mouth with his.

Passion ripped through Dionne as she answered his demands ravenously. The control she valued so deeply had long since fled, and she only dimly realized she'd handed it over to this man who'd stripped away that final barrier. Even in the bedroom, she'd somehow managed always to cling to some remnants of control. But that was before she'd known this unbridled need, before she'd discovered this desperate yearning, before she'd reached out greedily for total fulfillment.

Overwhelmed by her responsiveness, he softened the kiss, moved to tenderness. He'd guessed there was passion in her, kept carefully in check, but he had not dreamed how much. Nor had he thought how deeply it would touch him. She had allowed him to see her vulnerability and he would do no less. Drawing back from her slightly, he let her restive hands find him, then guide him inside of her.

He wanted to watch her climb, watch her soar, his own completion suspended by the joy of her response. Her eyes were open and on his, her skin damp with passion, her mouth a breath away from his. There was an aching pleasure on her face as she reached for the stars. And then he gave them to her.

From the bed, Colby watched the moon, through the window, slide behind a cloud, but the candles burned still, sending dancing light flickering over Dionne's pale skin as she lay curled into his side. Her breathing was level once more and she was awake, her lashes grazing his chest where her head lay. But she was quiet, alone with her thoughts, as he was.

The moment of truth, he thought, drifting down from the height of passion. New and different with each partner, especially the first time. The moment when the mind clears and assesses the situation, decides whether to go or stay. And he wanted badly to stay.

Dionne. From the first, she'd piqued his interest with her feistiness, then her seeming indifference. She'd moved him with her tender vulnerability, touched him with her caring ways, intrigued him with hints of passion hidden deep inside. He hadn't felt certain he could awaken the sleeping giant. Yet, now he knew he had.

Abandoned. She'd been totally abandoned in his arms, something Dionne had never experienced before. Had she been too young before, too self-involved, too inhibited? How had he found the magic key to making her feel so wonderfully alive, so completely a woman? Had she known he would, she might have avoided this. For how could she walk away from him when already her body, so long without, was aching for a rematch?

"I knew when we first met that one day we'd be here like this," Colby said, nestling her closer. He threaded his fingers lightly through her hair.

"I had no intention of letting this happen when we first met." She sighed, a trembling sound.

His fingers stilled, his heart lurched. "Then you're sorry?"

She frowned. "Sorry?" She shifted so she could look into his eyes. "No, not sorry. Disappointed in myself, in giving in." She tangled her fingers in his soft chest hair, loving the crisp feel. "You're a weakness I have."

"And you'd like to get over this so-called weakness?" He didn't know whether to laugh or get angry.

"It would help."

He opted for anger. Rolling over, he pinned her beneath him. "It would have been nice for you if making love with me had been a big dud, wouldn't it? Then you could send me packing more easily, your weakness conquered, your vow to stay uninvolved still unbroken, right?"

She understood his anger and knew he was right. Again, he'd seen right through her. But she would not answer in kind, for the feelings she had were quite opposite. "Yes, but it didn't work." She raised a steady hand to touch his face, the face her heart now recognized as the dearest on earth. "I've never felt like you make me feel, Colby. Never."

She took the wind out of his sails. Gentling, he relaxed, but his eyes were still challenging. "So you'll stick around a while for the sex?"

She supposed she deserved that. Emotions in a turmoil, she caressed his cheek, still unable to be angry. "What we had just now was much more than merely sex. I'll stick around a while... for the loving."

That stopped him. Wanting to believe, he aligned their bodies more perfectly. "Be careful with that word. I might grow used to the sound."

She felt the pain then, the self-imposed pain that just being with him now would bring. Love. Yes, she rather liked the sound, too. If only she had the right to say it freely. "Talking about love can only lead to problems." She kissed him lightly, then did her best to put on a teasing smile. "But making love? That's another story."

Her hand on his neck brought his head closer, his lips to hers.

She tasted the residual of his anger, then the hunger, the fierce demand. Her own mouth was eager again, moving again, needing again. She felt his hands stroke her body, felt the fire rising just under her skin. When he slipped between her thighs, she arched in welcome, moaned in delight.

Closing her eyes, Dionne let him take her to a place where no problems existed for the moment, where love was more than a word and reality slid out of focus.

Chapter Eight

He awoke to the sound of the shower across the hall. The sky had been wispy with dawn when he'd finally allowed her to sleep and rested himself. Like a man coming upon water after having been lost in the desert, he had not been able to get his fill. Yet she'd matched him stroke for stroke, her mouth weakly protesting even as her arms reached for him.

Hearing the water turn off, Colby rose and tugged on his jeans, wondering at her morning mood. He knocked once, then opened the bathroom door and was met with a cloud of rolling steam. Through the mist, he saw her standing on the rug, quickly winding a towel about her body. He smiled at the belated modesty.

Walking in, he took her in his arms, marveling at the feeling of rightness that came over him as soon as he touched her. "Going somewhere?" he asked, kissing the top of her wet head.

She should be resentful at this invasion of privacy, shouldn't she? Dionne wondered. Sharing an apartment with Nathan years ago, they'd always respected each other's space. But Colby was different. He assumed she'd be glad to see him, and she was shocked to discover that she was. For a moment longer, she let herself savor the pleasure of being held by him, then she drew back. "Work. I have to get back to work. I'm so far behind."

Leaning forward, he nuzzled her neck. "Then one more day won't matter. Play hooky with me."

Tempted. She was so very tempted. Even his stubbly growth of beard excited her. This was definitely getting out of hand. She pulled back a second time, searching for a diplomatic exit line. "I'd love to, you know that. But I have appointments, people depending on me."

He swallowed the urge to coax her. He would not beg. "Right."

She saw the quick disappointment he tried to hide. She looked up at him and smiled. "I have time for coffee though. Want some?"

"Sure. I'll shave while it's perking."

In the kitchen, she measured coffee. She felt pleasantly achy in the afterglow of a night she would long remember. It had been a miscalculation to think she could easily dismiss Colby Winters from her mind once she'd made love with him. Yet it would be a disaster to continue.

Plugging in the pot, she then opened the blinds. Early-morning sunlight trickled in, a bright fall day. That was the thing about mornings, they made you aware of your flawed thinking of the night before. She picked up her cigarettes from the counter. Four whole days without one, and she felt the need screaming in every pore. Feeling foolish, she held the pack to her nose and inhaled slowly. Feeling dumb, she threw the pack down and reached into the cupboard for coffee mugs.

The thing to do was to look at this rationally, in the cool light of day. She was a modern woman of today. She found Colby attractive and so she'd made love with him. End of story. Off they would go to their separate worlds and . . . damn!

Sighing, Dionne picked up the three pieces of broken mug and tossed them into the wastebasket. Okay, so she wasn't comfortable with that version of what had happened. Bracing her hands on the sink, she let herself remember, for just a moment, the wonder of being in Colby's arms last night. Of his eyes on hers, his heart beating against her own, his body moving within her. No, that had been no cool decision on her part. She had talked a good game, but only one reason reeked of the truth.

Love. Love had taken her where she'd gone last night. Dear God, how had she allowed this to happen, and how would she be able to keep him from knowing?

She should have known better than to let him into her apartment that first night. On the drive from Detroit to St. Clair days ago, one part of her mind had been on the child who needed her. The other had been on Colby, on running from him and the love she knew had already begun forming in her heart for him.

Years ago, she'd vowed to steer clear of love for the sake of the man and for the sake of her sanity. She had so little to offer Colby. If he'd married a woman who later discovered she couldn't give him a child, that would've been the luck of the draw. But to deliberately choose to do so would eventually cause resentment and regret. Not to tell him was unthinkable. Feeling noble, he might accept her anyway, but she wanted no man to sacrifice for her, to settle for second best when he could have it all.

No choices left. She would have to be convincing, to send him away, to distance herself gradually because he was persistent. But how, for he also had this incredible insight into her thoughts, a vaguely disturbing, all-too-frequent occurrence? As she chewed on her lower lip, trying to think of a solution, the phone rang. Distractedly, she answered it.

"Hi, Dionne," Lainey Sinclair greeted her. "Hope I didn't wake you."

"No, not at all." Dionne whipped the towel from her head and dabbed at her damp hair. There was an odd note in her friend's voice. "Is anything the matter?"

"I don't think so, but I have a rather awkward question to ask you." Lainey paused. "Zac just heard from his Detroit office. Something's come up and they need Colby. He left there Friday noonish and spent the afternoon with us, but they haven't heard from him. His housekeeper hasn't seen him, either. When he left here that evening, he asked for your address and so we thought maybe you'd seen him."

Oh, God! A flash of guilt mingled with an unexpected wave of embarrassment washed over Dionne. So much for being the cool, controlled woman of today. She cleared her throat, realizing the silence was lengthening. She would face Lainey and her questions later. "Yes, he's here. Just a minute."

Laying down the phone, she went to the bathroom and knocked once. She couldn't meet his eyes when the door opened. "There's a call for you." Turning, she went into her bedroom and closed the door.

She was seated at her dressing table, blow-drying her hair minutes later when he opened the door and walked in. Meeting his eyes in the mirror, she saw he was scowling. She turned off the dryer. "I hope nothing's wrong at your office."

He noticed she'd changed into a short cotton robe. Her calm voice irritated him further. "Not at the office, but something's wrong, all right. Are you upset that Lainey and Zac found me here with you?"

"No, of course not." She pulled the brush through her hair. He was wearing only a towel and she wished he'd get dressed.

"Then what is it?"

"Nothing. Coffee's probably ready."

"Forget the coffee." He pulled her to her feet, whirling her about and bringing her close up against his chest. "Tell me the truth. Are you ashamed of our relationship?"

Put that way, the question shocked her. "No. I just don't like people to know my private business. I'm a doctor and—"

"Sacrosanct, is that it? You get to listen to everyone's problems, all their secrets. But you don't have any. You're above all that."

She let her voice cool. "*I* don't have a problem. Do you?"

"Yes, I do, and her name is Dionne Keller." Even a cold shower hadn't depleted his earlier exasperation, and the furtive way she'd called him to the phone had fueled it further. It seemed she was able to arouse his displeasure almost as quickly as his pleasure. It was obvious, despite last night, that she wanted him out of here this morning. She'd probably been in the kitchen rehearsing the goodbye speech, one she would serve with the coffee. Since meeting her, he'd felt himself teetering on a high wire and was damn fed up with it. He would go, but he would leave her with a memory she wouldn't soon forget.

"When are you going to admit you're human, Doctor, just like the rest of us? When are you going to concede that you need someone in your life? And that that someone just might be me." He pulled her closer, one hand low on her spine, the other on the back of her head. "When?"

"Wait—"

"I'm not waiting." He bent his head.

"Colby—"

Hungrily, he ground his mouth on hers, the need roaring inside him savage, fierce. Throughout their lovemaking last night, he'd held on to that thread of control that kept him civilized. Now, he felt on the verge of losing it. His touch was not rough, but it wasn't gentle.

His hand moved between them and he opened her robe, pushing it off her, his mouth still locked to hers. She curved into him, moaning low in her throat, her hands clutching his arms. The need to be skin to skin with her raced through him and he yanked off his towel as he backed her toward the unmade bed. Together, they fell onto it, their passion mounting.

Drawing back, breathing hard, Colby gazed down into eyes, dark brown and smoky with unspoken needs. "Now. Tell me now you don't want me and I walk out that door."

Her heart beating wildly, Dionne stared back, her chest rising and falling against his. "I want you," she murmured. "I *do* want you, Colby." And she reached out for him.

Suddenly, his mouth was everywhere, skimming her heated flesh, pausing to taste her breasts, returning to ravage her mouth. Dionne could fight him no longer, nor did she wish to. Truth be known, it was herself she'd been fighting in denying this shimmering need, this incredible passion. Over and over on the bed he rolled with her till they threatened to topple to the floor, yet he held on. Pliant under his hands, fluid beneath his lips, she clung to him.

He entered her quickly and she welcomed his urgency, moaning his name as he began to move. Unaware, she shivered and buried her face in his throat. Wrapped around her, his labored breath puffed into her ear. Racing, racing, she closed her eyes and saw a rainbow of colors burst inside her head. With a shuddering breath, she went limp in his arms.

Passion spent, Colby felt a new emotion rising inside him. Drawing back, he let his eyes let her know what he dared not say as he cupped her chin and looked at him.

Blinking, she studied his face, then closed her eyes and pressed her cheek against his. "Oh, Colby," she whispered, rocking him gently. What was she going to do about Colby? She was afraid of what she'd glimpsed in his eyes.

He rolled them over so she lay atop him, then brushed her hair back from her face. "You make me crazy, lady. And now I've made you late."

She took in a calming breath. "It's all right. Is it important, at the office?"

"Theresa Abbott left word she has to see me right away."

Dionne frowned. "I hope she's not quitting, not running from her problem. Call me later if you need me."

He sobered, his fingers on her cheek. "The problem is, I'm beginning to need you far too much."

She could relate only too well. What she couldn't do was come up with a solution. She eased back. "I'm heavy on you."

"Hardly. I'm sorry if I pushed. You have a way of getting me worked up."

She smiled then. "Getting you worked up has its rewards." Quickly, she kissed him, then slid from him and stood. Squinting at the clock, she saw it was past nine. Hilary would be shocked; Dionne always arrived ahead of her partner. And Lainey would undoubtedly be calling later. "I've got to get going."

Colby lay watching her walk away, wishing he wouldn't have to leave, wishing he could take her with him.

At the doorway, she paused and looked back. What the hell! Late was late. "Wanna share a quick shower?"

A slow smile forming, Colby rose. She laughed, turned and hurried across the hall. Quickly, he followed her.

Indian summer. Colby stood looking out his office window at the red-and-yellow leaves on the maple tree at the far corner of the parking lot. October first, and they were having a spurt of warm weather that was confusing the trees. The air drifting in through the screen was tangy with the smell of burning leaves from a nearby fire. Autumn was a season he usually enjoyed, and yet this year he felt a restless yearning.

Turning back to his desk, he glanced at a report he'd read earlier. Their building projects were going along well, with their winter schedule lining up nicely. The shell of the office building in St. Clair was up and insulated, ready to be bricked next week, Zac had told him only yesterday. And the employee-assistant program was making progress.

He'd returned last Monday after his weekend with Dionne to meet with Theresa Abbott, a surprising visit. Eyes moving all around her office, never lighting on him, she'd told Colby she'd checked herself into a spa in New England and was leaving the next day. It was an expensive treatment center, but came highly recommended and used primarily by people like her, she'd gone on to explain. Not really addicts. "Inadvertent dependency" her doctor had labeled her problem.

Colby had heard her out without comment, listening to her tell of a strong cough she'd developed last June and of the cough syrup her doctor had recommended. Throughout the long summer, she'd taken her medicine dutifully, the cough slow in disappearing, only to realize that when she tried to stop, her body craved alcohol. Looking into her eyes finally, he knew she'd made up the story to save face, and he'd allowed her that.

The point, after all, was to seek and get help, to admit there was a problem. At the treatment center, they'd help Theresa face her denial. He'd gone a step further because of her many years of service to Midwest Construction by granting her a leave of absence with pay and assuring her that the company would take care of any bills that her insurance didn't cover. He'd seen tears in her eyes when he'd shaken her hand, and he'd felt a mixture of sadness and accomplishment when he'd left her.

Colby had called Dionne that night to tell her the story, and he had been pleased at her reaction to the way he'd handled the dignified bookkeeper. That had been six days ago, and he'd talked with Dionne every evening since, finding himself looking forward to discussing the details of his day with her. And of hearing about her cases, especially Shelly, who'd asked again when he'd be returning. Today, if he had his way, Colby thought with a grimace. Sharing things by phone wasn't enough for him. He wondered if it was wearing thin with Dionne.

She was friendly when they talked, always interested in what he had to say, but reserved. When he tried to press her about a return visit, she came up with a dozen reasons that he thought of as excuses. He had tried to entice, but he would not plead. The memory of her hot and ready, reaching for him, of her husky voice telling him she wanted him kept his nights restive and his body hungry. Was she feeling the strain, as well? Colby wondered. She cared for him, he was sure of it. But something was keeping her from coming to him completely, and he doubted if it was her work. What, then?

Marianne pressed the intercom button, interrupting his thoughts. The doctor who was treating Terry was on the line, wanting a word with him. Minutes later, Colby was grim faced as he hung up. This was not the way he'd envisioned Dionne being drawn back to them. Yet, picking up the receiver and dialing, he was sure now she would come.

The receptionist put him through almost immediately. He wasted little time on the preliminaries. "I have some bad news. The reattachment of Terry's arm didn't take. Tomorrow he goes in to surgery at ten to have it permanently removed."

"Dear God," Dionne murmured. She was a doctor and therefore accustomed to the harsh realities of life and death. Yet each time, the shock struck anew. She took a deep breath, mentally rearranging her schedule.

"I'll tie things up here today and drive in early in the morning."

"My place is on the way to the hospital. Do you want to pick me up, or shall I meet you there?"

"I'll pick you up around eight. How is Terry, do you know?"

"No, but I'm going over now. Maybe I can catch Jean or his mother."

"Damn, I wish I could have talked to Jean earlier." Dionne felt the frustration of being needed in two places at the same time. She fondled her rumpled pack of cigarettes. Maybe one. Just one. Disgusted with the insistent craving, she flung the pack into a drawer and brought her attention back to Colby. "Thank you for letting me know."

"I thought you'd want to be here."

"Yes, I do."

"Would it be unseemly of me to say that I'm glad you're coming for my sake, as well?"

She let out a heartfelt sigh, like an admission of defeat. Or was it victory? "If it is, then I'm guilty, too." Was there a greater aphrodisiac in the world than someone you cared for wanting you with him? Dionne checked her watch. "I'll see you in about eighteen hours."

"I was so terrible to you," Jean said, her eyes awash in tears. "Can you forgive me?"

"You needed someone to blame." Alone with her in a corner of the waiting room, Dionne squeezed her hand. "It's all right, really. I wish I hadn't had to leave, that we could have talked again sooner."

Jean balled a tissue in her other hand, obviously agitated. "I—I don't know how to say this, except to say it out loud. I figure you're the only one who'll understand. I'm sorry Terry's losing his arm, but I think if it takes something like this to wake him up, maybe it's not all bad." She looked up at Dionne, expecting censure and found only understanding. "I mean, he lost an arm, but if he keeps on drinking, he'll lose more. Like maybe his life, our future. You know what I mean?"

The girl had grown up overnight. It was a shame she had had to this harshly, Dionne thought. But thank goodness that she had. She would need all the maturity she could muster. "Yes, I know, Jean. And you're right. Terry has his whole life before him and much he can do despite losing an arm."

"I'd like to think this will change him, but I have to be realistic. It's too soon to tell."

Dionne agreed, knowing how many promises were made and broken by alcoholics. Still, Terry had a strong woman who loved him and believed in him. He had a fighting chance, if only he would take it.

The nurse came around the corner, announcing they could all go in for a minute before they took Terry up to surgery. Mrs. Hanson took Jean's hand and Dionne found herself reaching for Colby's. Some pillar of strength she was, she acknowledged. Yet oddly felt not in the least compromised by her need for his touch.

They stood back, letting Terry's mother and Jean lean close and assure him of their love. Foggy though he was from medication, Terry spotted them and motioned them closer with his good hand.

"I've been wrong, Doctor," he said, his eyes on Dionne. "I lied to you and to Jean." He blinked rapidly a moment. "Drinking's fun, you know. Makes you feel ten feet tall, king of the hill. When you're a little guy, like me, kind of a nobody, you need that sometimes." He shook his head sadly. "Wish I hadn't." He sniffed, then tried a smile. "No more, though. I know that to Jean, I'm *somebody,* even when I don't drink." He turned to look into her eyes. "Even when I screw up. Drinking wears off. The way she makes me feel doesn't."

Dionne watched Jean lean down to embrace him, her eyes moist. She gripped his hand, offering her encouragement. "You've learned an expensive lesson, Terry."

"Yeah," Mrs. Hanson said. "I only wish his father had lived to see this. Maybe we could have saved him." She shook her head wearily.

Fathers and sons, Colby thought. Always a problem. He moved to the other side of Terry. "You've got a job with us, Terry. Jean tells me you like working with figures. There's always openings in our accounting department. You could go to night school, any number of things."

Terry nodded, somewhat vaguely. "Thanks, Colby. Couple of weeks and I'll be knockin' on your door."

Dionne reached for Colby's hand and led him toward the door, thinking the two women needed a few private moments with Terry. In the hallway, she let out a shaky breath.

"It went better than I'd hoped," Colby said.

She looked up at him. "I've left word for the doctors to call us when Terry's out of surgery. Do you need to get to the office?"

"I really should."

"I'll go with you and check on a few pending cases."

Colby slid his arm around her as they walked toward the elevators. It felt good having her back.

The message came around three in the afternoon. Colby'd been out in the yard talking with one of his foremen and had found his secretary's note on his desk. Sitting down, he stared at the phone memo. Harold Winters. Urgent. And an eastside phone number. Leaning back, he closed his eyes.

His father. Easily two years since he'd heard from him last. He'd wrecked his car that time as he had several times before, wrapped himself and his junk heap around a tree trunk, drunk as usual. He'd wound up in the hospital but, again as usual, he'd escaped with fairly minor injuries. It had cost Colby a bundle since Harold carried no insurance. Colby had bailed his father out, paid his bills, stuffed a couple hundred in the pocket of his cheap pants and wished to hell he'd stay out of his life.

Now, here he was again, needing something undoubtedly, stirring up memories Colby would just as soon have let stay buried. Of course, he could ignore the message. Kathy was free of Harold, happy in Iowa with her family, and Colby wanted to keep it that way. Were she here, would she rush to their father's aid? Probably, Colby acknowledged. His sister feared their father and disliked him, yet she'd probably go to him. The bonding of blood lines, Colby supposed. A hard one to turn away from.

Cursing himself for a fool, he picked up the phone and dialed the number. The conversation was short and not so sweet. Pocketing his checkbook with a frown on his face, Colby stood as Dionne walked through the door to his office that had been left ajar.

Seeing his stormy face, she stopped. "Am I catching you at a bad time?"

Relaxing his features, he walked around the desk and placed his hands on her arms. He felt better just looking at her. "Do you know how glad I am that you're here?" Pulling her closer, he buried his face in her hair. "So glad."

Something was wrong. She could feel the tension in him. After a moment, she drew back. "What happened?"

Colby stepped away, shoving his hands into his pants pockets. "I just talked with my father. He wants to see me."

"Oh." She followed him to the window where he stopped to gaze out. "Is he all right?"

His laugh was bitter. "Probably. He's got nine lives, you know. He's used up a few, but he's still here. More than likely, he's in another jam and needs money."

And he would give it to him, though he'd been dealing with the hurt for years. She touched his arm, sensing his anger warring with the loyalty he would deny. "Do you want me to go with you?"

He was tempted. But he hated to have her see the pitiful wreck his father had become. Swinging to her, he shook his head. "No, but I thank you for offering. This is something I have to do alone." The smile he gave her felt false on his face. "Why don't you go to the house when you're finished here, and I'll be there as soon as I can. This shouldn't take long."

She touched his face, hoping he wouldn't transfer his irritation to her. But some things had to be said. "If you could just keep in mind that he's sick—"

"Yeah, so you've said." A muscle twitched in his jaw as Colby struggled to keep his emotions level.

Dionne sensed that words weren't reaching him. There were other ways. "Would you kiss me before you go?"

It started off gently, but heated quickly as she molded her body to his. This wasn't wise, Dionne knew, in his office in the middle of a workday with the door ajar. But he needed her now as she'd not seen him need her before. And that need drew her in as little else could.

Colby heard a sob and realized it had come from him as he gathered her closer. This is what he wanted, to lose himself in her, to let her make the world go away for him. She was soft, feminine—giving, nurturing. She was peace for his restive soul, salvation for his self-doubt, warmth for all the cold places inside him. She was love.

Coming down from tiptoe, Dionne moved only fractionally from him as she met his eyes. They were not untroubled, but the light was back in them. Stunned that she could do that for him, she just stared.

Colby smiled. "Thank you." Reluctantly, he released her. Picking up his keys from the desk, he walked with her to the door, his arm draped across her shoulders. "Why don't you ask Aggie if she'd like to visit her sister tonight?"

Dionne smiled back. "What a good idea."

Harold Winters was not yet sixty, yet he looked easily ten years older. His hair, once as blond as Colby's, was sparse and streaked with gray. The blue eyes were pale and watery, his complexion sallow with broken capillaries about the nose and cheeks. He'd never been tall, a good six inches shorter than his son even on his best day, yet he seemed to have shrunk even more since their last visit. Seated across the scarred wooden table from him in the shabby kitchen of his second-floor apartment, Colby watched his father swallow iced tea, his hand on the glass surprisingly steady.

"Your mom used to like tea, you remember, Boyo?" Harold smiled at the son he barely knew, but the smile was a little off center.

Colby had always hated the nickname his father had given him, maybe because it had never been said with affection but rather with a taunting edge. Colby shifted on the hard chair impatiently. "I remember a lot of things. What is it that you wanted to see me about that's so important?"

The rheumy eyes narrowed resignedly. "I see you still don't have much use for your dad." Harold wiped his mouth with the back of his hand. "That's all right. I let you down and you can't let it go." He stared down at the melting ice cubes.

Self-pity. Colby wasn't in the mood for it. "Yeah, you did. Let's get to the point. What do you need?"

Slowly, Harold raised his head. "Another chance."

Colby stared at him for a long moment, then rose and walked to the dirt-streaked window. He stared out unseeingly, breathing in the lingering smell of sweat and beer. He fought the urge to run out the door and never come back. "I'm fresh out. You need some money?"

"You never understood, did you, Boyo?" The whiskey voice was thick with regret.

Colby swirled, calling on the anger never far from the surface. "Understand what? That you broke my arm not once, but twice in your drunken rages? That you hit Kathy so hard once she can't hear out of one ear? That you poured every penny you made down your damn throat while we didn't have shoes that fit or food on the table? No, I guess I'm not a very understanding fellow." Suddenly aware his hands were balled tightly into fists, he forced himself to relax, to take a deep breath and sit back down.

"Your mom understood. She knew why I drank."

"Don't talk about her. You don't have the right."

Harold's hand shot out, the thin fingers surprisingly strong as they settled on Colby's arm and squeezed. "Watch yourself, Boyo. She was the best thing ever happened to me."

"And you sent her to an early grave." Yanking his arm free, Colby reached for his checkbook and slammed it onto the table. "What trouble did you get yourself into this time and how much do you need?"

Harold sat taller, reaching for a small scrap of dignity. "I don't need your money. I got me a job. Night watchman at this small factory on Jefferson. And I'm off the drink, four months and ten days now." He almost smiled at the surprise on Colby's face as he gestured toward the cupboards. "Go ahead, have a look. You won't find a drop."

He'd heard it before, though not in years. The fervent promises, the pleas for forgiveness. He hadn't believed him then, and he didn't believe him now. "What brought this about?"

Trying not to grimace, Harold angled sideways and pressed a fist into his belly. "You've become a hard man," he commented.

"It's a hard world out there." How would his father know? He'd anesthetized himself against harsh realities with booze. "All right, so you're dry and you're working. What did you want?"

"I just wanted you to know. I wrote to Kathy, too."

"How'd you know where she lives?"

"She writes me every Christmas."

He might have known. Colby stood. "Okay, so now I know. Is there anything else?"

Harold drained the glass, gulping down the tea. He looked up at his son's stoney face. "Just one more thing.

I wanted to tell you I'm sorry. I know you don't believe me, but..." His voice trailed off wearily.

Colby looked down at the scuffed linoleum. This was one he hadn't figured on. He tried to harden his heart, tried not to look at the broken old man who'd given him life. Dionne's words drifted back. *He's sick, remember.* "You said that mother understood why you drank. Make me understand."

Harold's eyes were on his hands clasped together on the tabletop. "Because I knew I was nothing, knew I'd never be anything better. I'm a weak man, Boyo. Not like you. Oh, no, not like you. The drink made me feel strong, powerful."

Colby stood looking down at him, remembering Terry's young voice only that morning. *Drinking makes me feel ten feet tall.* If he hadn't gotten hurt, would Terry have wound up like this thirty years down the pike? What a terrible thing to have eating away at you always, the need for a drink or a snort of drugs, just to feel good about yourself. A pervading sickness that ate away at the victim, tore apart the fabric of the family and affected each of them.

Maybe you don't want to understand, Dionne had said to him earlier. *Because if you admit your father is a sick man and not just a drunk, you'll have to forgive him.*

Colby shifted his keys from one hand to the other, studying his father's unhealthy pallor, the hopeless look in his eyes, the defeated slump to his shoulders. All these years, and this is the first conversation they'd shared beyond a sentence or two. A wasted life, he thought with no small amount of regret. *You'll have to forgive him.* Maybe. Someday.

Yet he was sorry, too. Sorry for so damn much. Stepping closer, he held out his hand. It was all he could offer for now. "Good luck on your job, Dad."

Eyes nearly overflowing, Harold shook his son's hand as he nodded, unable to speak.

Colby left then, closing the door with the peeling paint behind him. The hallway smelled of garbage and broken dreams. A nearby radio was playing heavy metal, and a baby across the way was crying. He walked down the rickety stairs, his step somehow lighter. Outside, he breathed in the cool evening air.

More than anything, he wanted to see Dionne, to just hold her.

She'd never been in a water bed. Dionne waited for the water to settle as Colby got in with her, then moved to take her in his arms. The soft swaying added to the sensual feel of his satin sheets. Earlier, he'd confessed he'd gotten them for her. Every day, she was learning more about his complexities. Getting in deeper. Would she ever be able to get out?

Gently, he brushed a lock of hair off her face and gathered her to him. Dionne listened to the erratic beat of his heart under her ear. He was still upset, still churning inside after visiting his father.

She'd sent Aggie to her sister's as he'd requested, and the older woman had left reluctantly, muttering under her breath. Dionne had then thawed a couple of steaks, made a salad, but when he'd walked in, he hadn't been hungry. Not for dinner.

He'd made love to her in front of a roaring fire, slowly, drawing out the moment, the pleasure. Together, they'd soared to the sweet place they'd created for themselves alone, then afterward, lain together in the quiet afterglow. Colby had hardly spoken, hardly moved, just held her, lightly caressing her hair, her skin.

Dionne hadn't pressed him then, thinking he needed to sort things out in his own mind. Even now, with her head on his chest, listening to his rhythmic breathing, she wondered if he was ready to talk.

Shifting, she rose on an elbow and looked into his face, shadowed in the dim light of the bedside lamp. Trailing her fingers along his jaw, she waited until his eyes met hers. "Do you want to tell me what happened?"

He let out a shuddering breath. "You were right. He's a sick old man, sitting there in this shabby place, left with the remnants of all his broken dreams. He had them once, I imagine, like we all do. He blew it, and he knows it."

"That's something, at least. A start."

His eyes bored into hers, fierce with need. "Oh, God, Dionne, I don't want to wind up like my father."

Feeling her heart turn over, she pulled his head to her breast and held him close. "You won't, Colby. You won't."

Chapter Nine

"It's like withdrawal, you know." The young man seated in Dionne's office fidgeted in his chair as he stretched his hands out in front of him. They were obviously trembling. "You see what I mean?"

Dionne nodded. "It's not easy, is it? But then, you knew that when you went to Charter Hospital for assistance, didn't you?"

Ed Donnelly wiped the perspiration from his thin face with a damp handkerchief. "Yes, I did. But no one knows how bad it is until they have to go through it. They think it's only pills—not really drugs. But they're just as addictive."

Only twenty-six, she saw as she glanced at his chart, and admitting being hooked on a strong painkiller for four years. She was glad Ed had had the strength to face his addiction and that he'd enrolled in the hospital's outpatient program. She looked up as the young draftsman gave her an ironic smile.

"You know, before my back injury, I rarely even took an aspirin." He shook his head ruefully. "How easily things get out of hand."

Dionne closed his file and folded her hands over it. "Ed, you should be very proud of yourself. The process may be slow, but you're regaining control of your life."

A bit shakily, he stood. "Thanks. I just wanted you to know how it was going. Colby said you'd be interested."

She rose, as well. "I am. Anytime you need to talk, please feel free to call me." She handed him her card listing her number in St. Clair.

Studying it, Ed frowned. "St. Clair? I thought you were going to be a permanent fixture around here. Colby sort of hinted . . ."

Had he really? Dionne shook her head. "No, my practice is there. I'm here on a temporary consulting basis only."

Ed shoved the card into his shirt pocket and reached out his hand. "Thanks, Doctor. I appreciate your time."

She shook his hand and watched him quietly leave her office. A shy, introverted man, she hoped he'd have the fortitude to lick his problem. Straightening the papers on her desk, she picked up the messages from that morning when she'd been counseling at one of the building sites.

Dan had been one of the men she'd talked with, and she had been pleased at what she'd heard. He'd not only been attending AA meetings, but he'd asked his ex-wife to go to Al-Anon. The affiliate support system just might help Dan's wife to cope with his addiction, a necessity since they shared a son. Browsing through the pink slips, she saw that Hilary had called but that all she'd had to report was that Dionne's mother had phoned looking for her.

A smile formed as Dionne thought of Bertha Keller, the strong woman who'd borne five children, yet was still tall and slender, her blond hair showing only traces of white strands. Dialing quickly, Dionne swiveled her chair around so she could look out the window and waited for her mother to answer.

"Liebchen," Bertha said warmly. "It's good to hear your voice." The German accent wasn't as strong as her mother's before her, but still evident. "You're working too hard again, I can tell. We don't see you, we don't hear from you nearly a month now."

A month when she'd been working with patients in two cities and working around an attraction that had all but consumed her. "The life of a doctor, Mama. What can I say? How is everyone?"

"Good, good. Papa and Konrad finished glassing in the porch, just in time to sit and look at the leaves turn colors. John is head cook now in this fancy restaurant. Karl's Lisa, she's going to have another baby next spring."

"That would be four, right?"

"Four, yes. Lisa already told Karl, even if he don't get a son this time, no more. She's got her hands full, that girl."

Four children and Lisa wasn't thirty yet. Dionne didn't know whether to envy her or sympathize. "What about Werner?" Her youngest brother had always held a special spot in her heart.

"Ah, Werner. Like you, no wedding bells for Werner yet. Girls today don't want to settle down, he tells me. Is that right, Dionne?"

She sighed, bracing herself for the rehashing of an old discussion, one her mother never tired of. "That's right, Mama. Some women enjoy their work and love their independence." Hearing a sound behind her, she swung her chair about and looked into Colby's blue eyes. She smiled in welcome, though she noticed he'd overheard her last remark and it didn't sit well with him. Maybe she should get in the habit of closing her office door.

Bertha made a disapproving sound. "Some women have much to offer some lucky man, if they just let go of the past. You can't cuddle up to a job on a cold night, *liebchen.*"

"Yes, Mama." She groped for a change of subject. "I got a nice note from Emma. She tells me she's getting straight A's." Konrad's eight-year-old Emma was Dionne's oldest godchild. Last year, she'd announced that she was going to be a doctor like her Aunt Dionne, pleasing her no end. "Tell her I'm proud of her, will you?"

She watched Colby nonchalantly stroll closer, lean against her desk and bend down to brush his lips across hers. Startled, she colored slightly, as if her mother could see through the wire.

"You can tell her yourself on the weekend. You didn't forget?"

Trying to concentrate, Dionne searched her memory for birth dates in October or special anniversaries, but came up with none. "I guess I did. What's happening on the weekend?" Colby's fingers touched the ends of her hair, making her shiver. She sent him a warning glance and angled her head out of his reach.

"*Oktoberfest,* that's what." Bertha chuckled. "Papa's favorite time."

How could she have forgotten the famous German celebration, always a big deal in Frankenmuth? "Of course," she said into the phone. Colby had moved around back of her, his hands on her shoulders massaging the tense muscles. Distracted, Dionne murmured something incoherent.

"That's a yes? Good. Papa will be pleased and so will the boys. We'll make a big dinner Saturday night and..."

"Wait, Mama." The conversation had somehow gotten away from her. "I didn't say I could go. I'm really very busy right now."

Go where? Colby mouthed to her as he swung her chair to face him.

"Yes, I know *Oktoberfest* is important to the family," she said when her mother used her most persuasive tone.

Colby's eyebrow shot up and he nodded as he grinned. Quickly, he scribbled a note and held it up to her. She read it and her heart skipped a beat. "Tell her we'll go." Never had she taken a man home to Frankenmuth. The thought both excited and unnerved her.

"The little ones are growing so quickly," Bertha went on. "You haven't been home since June. You should make time to be with family, those who love you."

Dionne pictured the big house her folks had never left, even after the children had all moved out, a two story white frame set on a sloping lawn leading to the lake. Thick-trunked weeping willow trees, geraniums thriving in circular flower beds, the children swimming, playing tag, tossing a ball around after Sunday dinner. The smell of her mother's cooking and Papa's pipe.

"Well, I suppose I could come, just for the weekend." She glanced up at Colby's face, the challenge in his eyes daring her to include him. She saw the hunger, too, for the family he yearned for. But could she handle having him there among her memories? "Maybe even bring someone along," she heard herself say.

"Sure, sure." Sounding pleased that she'd convinced her stubborn daughter, Bertha's voice lightened. "That young doctor who works with you?"

Dionne swung her chair about, avoiding Colby's victory smile. "Uh, no. His name is Colby Winters. We've been working together on a special project." The long moment of silence that followed told Dionne that her mother was adjusting to the shock of her mentioning a man. Lord, did she think she never even dated? "If that's inconvenient..."

"No, no," Bertha hurriedly jumped in. "You know any friend of yours is always welcome here." She cleared her throat. "You know this man a long time?"

Her mother didn't know Colby was in the same room, but Dionne was acutely aware of his presence. "Not so long."

"He's a doctor, too?"

"No, he owns a construction company." She glanced over and saw Colby's smile at her mother's obvious interest. "Mama, you want his social-security number, too?"

Bertha sighed. "Four nice boys I have, and a daughter with a sassy mouth. You bring this man. I put clean sheets on Karl's bed. His old room is big and sunny."

She frowned, hearing the hope in her voice. "Don't let's get carried away, okay?"

"You just come. Tell your young man Papa has homemade beer."

Her young man. "He doesn't drink. Can we bring something?"

"No, we have everything. Just bring your construction man. He and Papa, they talk about building."

Dionne rubbed her forehead, wondering already if she'd just made a grave error. "All right, Mama. We'll see you Saturday."

"You drive careful in that fast car, you hear me?"

She smiled at the familiar warning. "Yes. I love you, Mama." Hanging up, she heard Colby's pleased laugh, then let him draw her up and into his arms. "You may regret this," she said.

"I'll take my chances. I haven't been to an *Oktoberfest* in years. Does your family make their own sausage and sauerkraut and all that good stuff?"

"Yes, enough food to feed an army. Fortunately, you like to eat. But do you like to be questioned? My mother wrote the book on how to learn all your secrets in one weekend."

"I look forward to it."

She felt a need to minimize the importance of the trip. "Colby, this is no big deal, you know. It's just this thing my mother has for entertaining half the free world at the slightest excuse."

"Uh-huh." He locked his fingers behind her back, feeling the ripple of tension. "I take it you don't drag too many male friends home to the family compound for inspection."

She needed to keep it light. "I wouldn't say that. Last summer, there was this balding banker with a nice smile and a great portfolio, but he didn't like my mother's *Wiener schnitzel,* so he wasn't asked back. And before that, there was this chap with a bushy red mustache who drove a snazzy Porsche, but he snored louder than my father, so he struck out."

Colby rubbed against her lightly, stirring them both. "Mmm-hmm. How do you know he snored?"

"Not from sleeping with him, if that's what you mean. Mama puts all gentlemen guests in my brother Karl's old room." On impulse, she kissed his chin.

"Is your old room nearby?"

"Right across the hall." She waited for the devilish smile. "Next to Mama and Papa's." She laughed when his face fell.

"Guess I'll have to ravish you before we leave." He checked his watch. "What do you say to a long lunch hour? I know this little inn not far from here."

Each day, she wanted him more, needed him more. How could that be? Feeling her blood heat, Dionne grabbed her purse. "I thought you'd never ask."

She surprised him by driving sensibly, well within the speed limit, her eyes hidden behind huge sunglasses. She'd been quiet since they'd started out, seemingly concentrating on the heavy traffic of a Saturday afternoon. Yet he could see tension in the way she gripped the wheel, in the set of her shoulders.

"Is this how you drove your race car?" he questioned, trying to get a rise out of her. He couldn't help wondering if she was regretting having invited him along.

She ignored the challenge. "Not exactly. That was in my misspent youth and it wasn't on a highway."

He patted the Corvette's dash in admiration. "I'll bet this baby can leave 'em all in its dust."

Dionne checked all three mirrors, her eyes intent, then shot him a quick glance as she felt her adrenaline rise. "You want me to show you?"

Colby grinned. "Yeah, I do."

Outwardly calm, Dionne pushed on the pedal and angled around a van as she whipped into the left lane and watched the needle hit eighty. She kept it steady a long moment, dodged around a BMW, rushed past a lumbering pickup and shot in front of a New Yorker already straining on the slight upgrade. Noticing nothing in front of her for a long ways, she saw she was close to ninety. Heart racing, she let the Corvette glide. "Enough?"

"Not bad. Get many tickets?"

Coasting down to the speed limit, she eased her hold on the wheel. "Not anymore. I'm a sedate, small-town doctor these days."

He laughed at that as he angled his body more comfortably in the bucket seat. The windows were up to keep out the noise and to lock in the intimacy. He wanted to get her talking, get her relaxing. "Did you say your father's retired?"

"Yes, he retired some years ago after thirty years as a plumber. He putzes now. He redid the cupboards, enclosed the porch, built a rose trellis for Mama. And he makes his own beer, very dark and strong, sort of bitter."

"I heard you mention that I don't drink."

"I've never seen you take a drink."

"You probably won't. I drank enough before I was twenty-five to last a lifetime."

"Was it hard quitting?"

He took a moment to consider her question. "It was a way of life, you know. My buddies and I were young, a little wild, a lot stupid. My marriage had gone sour and I didn't much give a damn about anything."

She'd never head this story. She found she wanted to. "What made you decide to quit?"

"One night, my friend Robby and I were out barhopping. He'd been going with the same girl for years, since high school, and she'd just dumped him. We were determined to get blotto." Suddenly he was back there, watching Robby climb behind the wheel of his souped-up VW and pop open another can as Colby jumped in beside him, both of them swaggering with that invincible feeling drinking always gave them. "There was a crash, a bad one. They had to pry Robby out. I didn't have a scratch."

Her hand closed over his. "Colby," she whispered.

He squeezed her fingers, brought himself back to the present. "I figured I'd been given a second chance and maybe I shouldn't blow it." Like his father had. Maybe this time, Harold would make it, too, he thought remembering their last visit.

Dionne's eyes were once more on the road, but her thoughts were on Colby. "And you haven't had a drink since?"

"I couldn't. Every time I thought about it, I could see what was left of Robby, all tangled up in metal and broken glass." He stared at her profile. "We don't often get second chances."

"No, not often."

"Has it been hard, giving up smoking?"

She wasn't aware he'd even noticed. She should have known better for he noticed everything. "Yes, very."

"But you feel better, don't you?"

She found a smile. "I'll let you know in a year or so." She hit the turn signal, eased into the right lane and headed for the off ramp. "Brace yourself, Mr. Winters. You're about to meet the Keller clan. Don't say I didn't warn you."

Wondering why she felt it necessary to warn him, he merely smiled as she turned onto a winding country road.

The Keller living room was a comfortable clash of colors and prints that somehow managed to appear charming. The floral wallpaper was slightly faded, the patterned carpeting worn. But the mahogany furniture was polished to a high luster, the dining room table draped with a delicately embroidered cloth, and the welcoming smiles were most genuine.

Otto Keller, tall and robust, his head bald but his mustache full, embraced his only daughter and kissed her roundly. "*Liebchen,* I've missed you."

"Me, too, Papa." She moved next to her mother, while Otto shook hands with Colby.

"Welcome to our home," Bertha said next, giving Colby a hug that was as natural to her as breathing.

"Thank you for having me." She was exactly as he'd pictured her from Dionne's description, right down to the apron. He felt Otto's hand on his elbow.

"You like beer? I just opened a new keg."

"Papa," Dionne interjected, "Colby doesn't drink."

He shot her a look of disbelief. "Come to the kitchen. You see my beer, you maybe change your mind."

Colby let himself be led, then was swallowed up in a sea of introductions as Kellers, large and small, swarmed about the kitchen—chopping, stirring, fetching. Shaking hands and nodding, he tried to sort them out. The eldest, Karl, was a younger version of his father with thinning blond hair. John's eyes were dark like Bertha's and his hair was thick. Or was that Konrad?

Then there were the wives and the children, ranging from twelve all the way to baby Nina, a mere four months. Sipping the iced tea he'd managed to get after turning down three glasses of beer, Colby glanced through the doorway into the dining room and caught Dionne's eye as she helped set the table. She sent him an I-told-you-so smile, but he just grinned. He was having the time of his life.

"He fits in, your blond friend," Bertha told Dionne as she handed her more silverware.

Running a hand through her red hair, Dionne smiled up at her mother. "More than I do."

"Ah, but if Grandma Klinger was here, the two of you would stand out."

Dionne smiled, remembering the little lady whose hair had once been as red as her own. "You still miss her."

"How can anyone stop missing a mother?"

How, indeed. Impulsively, Dionne hugged her own mother, vowing to visit more often. She seemed to need this warm outpouring of love more than she used to. Releasing her, Dionne glanced into the kitchen and saw Colby deep in conversation with her brother Karl. Yes, he did fit in. Deliberately pulling her eyes away, she turned back to the table. She would need to keep a firm grip on her emotions during these two days.

"Hey, big sister," came a voice from behind her. Bending down from his height of five-eleven, Werner gathered her into a bear hug and swung her about. "Thought you forgot about us hicks up here."

An electronics whiz in charge of a computer lab at GM and just turned twenty-five, she couldn't imagine anyone less of a hick than Werner. She smiled up into his lean poet's face and touched his cheek. "I've missed you."

"You could come more often," he suggested.

"The road goes both ways." She held up a hand before he could protest. "I know, I know. The boy genius is hard at work."

He slipped his arm around her, led her to the couch. "And what about the lady doctor? Still shrinking heads?"

"On occasion." She sat with him, comfortable, the hominess drifting over her.

Some time later, someone put on an oompah-pah recording, the thrumming beat all but shaking the floorboards. Colby eased out of the kitchen and found Dionne in a serious discussion with what had to be the youngest brother. He wandered over.

She spotted him, introduced them and made room for Colby beside her.

"Midwest Construction," Werner stated. "That's a big outfit." His voice was softer than the others, filled with respect at the moment. "You run it?"

"I have a partner. We've opened a branch in St. Clair."

Werner looked from Colby to Dionne. "Convenient. But you live in Detroit?"

"A westside suburb. You ever get into the city?"

Werner shook his head. "Nah, I hate big cities. So does Dionne." He looked at her then, long and hard. "Or used to."

Time to cut him off at the pass. "Werner, don't steal Papa's thunder. He's the one that gets to ask the what-are-your-intentions questions."

Grinning, Werner stood and clapped his hand on Colby's shoulder briefly. "Just thought I'd give you a preview, old man." He sauntered toward the kitchen.

Colby glanced around. Three children were seated in front of the television, several more were out on the lawn, and the baby lay sound asleep in a playpen beside the couch. The adults were scattered throughout the dining room, the kitchen and the large enclosed porch. He turned to Dionne and leaned close to her ear.

"Where would a guy take a girl around here if he wanted to be alone with her for, say, five minutes?"

Grabbing his hand, she led him through several rooms and down a dim hallway that ended at a closed door. "It's fairly private here," she whispered as she stopped and turned into his arms. "That leads to the attic." Her face in his neck, she inhaled his familiar scent and shivered.

"Cold?" Colby asked, though it was warm in the house, almost stuffy in the kitchen. She wore wool slacks and a short-sleeved sweater, so he rubbed her arms as he held her close, warming her. "That better?"

"Much." She drew back and searched his eyes. "Are they all too much for you?"

"They're wonderful. Your father went into a lengthy story on how beer really doesn't harm you like hard liquor, especially his. Your mother discovered I love sausage and keeps slipping me samples of dinner. Karl asked me to play horseshoes later, and Konrad wants to talk carpentry with me. I like them."

She'd known he'd take to them like a duck to water. They weren't perfect, but they were close. She hoped he wouldn't get too attached. "Yes, they are," she said, but eased back from him.

"You must have had a great childhood. Did you see those kids on the lawn tossing a football around? They don't know how lucky they are."

"Maybe they do. I always did."

His expression was puzzled. "Yet you don't want the same life for yourself."

Dionne took a step back, hoping she could carry this off. "I grew up with all this and although I loved my childhood, I want something different now. My work, helping people, it's what I was trained to do. What I *want* to do."

"Why can't you have both, a career and a family?"

Why did they always come back to this? "Some people can handle dividing themselves down the middle. I can't." She brushed her hair back, hating the need to defend the lies. "Are we going to keep having this discussion?"

Colby swallowed his disappointment. "No, I'm sorry. I don't want to upset you." He moved her back into his arms. "I wish I could make you happy."

She felt the tears behind her eyes and hoped he couldn't see them in the dim light. "You can make me happy right now. Stop talking and kiss me."

It was a cop-out, but she didn't care. She closed her eyes as his mouth touched hers, twining her arms around him. Her need for this man overwhelmed her, fired her, drained her. When would it dry up and blow away like the rustling leaves whirling around on the front walk? What morning would she awaken and be able to say she no longer wanted, no longer cared? When would his taste no longer excite her, his touch no longer thrill her?

There was something desperate in her kiss, Colby decided. It seemed as if she deliberately kept herself from loving him completely. As he moved his mouth over hers, as his tongue tangled with hers and his arms brought her closer, he wondered how he could discover why that was so. Didn't she know, couldn't she tell the depth of his feelings? What could he do to make her trust him?

She should pull back, move away, let him go. Not just now, but forever. She was so strong, such a controlled woman, in everything but this. With everyone but Colby. Just looking at him across a room sometimes, her lips ached to feel his, her hands trembled to clasp his, her body quivered to join with his. Yet she must not....

A nearby footstep, a creaking floorboard and they drew apart, startled. Dionne met her mother's surprised gaze.

"I'm sorry. I need something from the attic." Bertha recovered, her look speculative.

Her face heating, Dionne adjusted her sweater. "What do you need, Mama?"

"The blue serving platters. They're up in the attic closet."

Taking in a steadying breath, Dionne grabbed the doorknob. "I'll get them." Leaving Colby and Bertha both looking a little nonplussed, she hurried up the stairs.

Attics were supposed to smell musty, she told herself as she switched on the light and climbed. But this one never did. The faint odor of moth balls drifted down, and the unmistakable smell of floor wax. Even up here, her mother kept a spotless house.

Odd how quickly one could feel like a teenager again around a parent. Nearly thirty, Dionne need not apologize for being seen kissing a man, yet foolishly, she felt like she should. But it wasn't the embarrassment that bothered her as much as the flash of hope she'd seen spring into her mother's eyes. For years, Bertha had been preaching marriage to Dionne, telling her it was unnatural for a woman to want to live her life alone. Not every man wanted children, Mama had stated emphatically. Her rotten luck, Dionne thought, to fall for a man who not only wanted children, but craved them.

Stepping around an old wooden table and chairs, she walked past two heavy trunks, wondering what they held that Bertha hadn't been able to part with. Moving to the largest storage closet, she opened the door and pulled the chain that turned on the light.

"Oh!" Hand to her mouth, she stepped back as if burned. Her mother had obviously forgotten this was here, as she had. Shakily, Dionne walked closer and touched the soft white netting, then pulled it back.

The bassinet had been used for all the Keller children, and several of the first grandchildren. She remembered when the family had moved to Frankenmuth from Detroit, remembered being a teenager helping her mother store the dainty little bed up here. "One day, your little ones will sleep in here," Bertha had told her. That was the year before Dionne's world had fallen apart.

Throat clogged, Dionne felt her eyes fill as she gazed down at the tiny satin pillow her mother had hand stitched so many years ago, the beautifully crocheted receiving blanket, the full white skirt that circled the bed and fell softly to the floor. "No, Mama," she whispered. "I will have no little ones sleep in here." On a sob, she turned aside, swiping at the tears she suddenly couldn't prevent.

Why today? she asked herself. Why did she have to remember, to relive and regret all over again? The nostalgia that coming home always resurrected, she supposed. The emotion that being with Colby the last month had brought about. She was doctor enough to know she'd set herself up for just this reaction, and woman enough to realize she couldn't prevent these occasional recurrences.

Gently, she replaced the netting, hating anew the circumstances that had robbed her of a child of her own. Taking a deep breath, she found a tissue and wiped her cheeks. She would get past this, as she had many times before and would again. Dionne blew her nose, then turned when she heard a sound behind her.

"Your mother sent me to find you," Colby said, walking over. "Are you all right?"

Hands shaking, she hurried into the closet. "Of course." Scanning the shelves, she found the two platters and grabbed them, then snapped off the light. She turned and nearly bumped into him.

"You look upset, Dionne. What's wrong?"

"Nothing." She sniffed exaggeratedly. "I think I'm coming down with a cold, that's all." She moved around him quickly. "Mama's waiting for these." She skipped down the stairs.

Hands on his hips, Colby stood staring after her a long moment. He never would claim to be an expert on women. But one thing he was sure of: the reason for Dionne's red eyes and damp cheeks wasn't a cold.

She'd been crying, up here alone, and he needed to know why.

Chapter Ten

Had he ever seen so much food on one table? Colby asked himself. He doubted it. The fragrances mingled and mixed, making his mouth water. Heaping plates of sausages, sauerkraut, apple pancakes as light as air, sweet-and-sour cabbage, hot potato salad with bacon, and chunks of dark bread. He indulged his appetite sinfully.

Mrs. Keller never sat down, just hovered around the table, urging another helping on someone, cutting a youngster's meat, pouring coffee. Smiling, her hand lingering on a cheek here, touching a shoulder affectionately there, she patrolled her table and accepted the praise deservedly lavished on her. Clearly this was her finest hour, feeding her family generous portions of food and love.

Colby listened to the comfortable conversations, the affectionate ribbing of one brother by another, the unconscious deference to the father when he joined in from the head of the table, the laughter and teasing of the children. He'd experienced the warmth of family meals at Zac's house when he'd lived there during his teens, but nothing to match this. This he absorbed, this he digested as much as the food he ate, this he immersed himself in.

Passing the butter, he looked across the table at Dionne seated alongside an animated little girl named Emma, whom he'd met earlier. Emma had confided to him that she wanted to be a doctor like her aunt and clearly she adored Dionne. She chattered away at Dionne, who listened intently, adding a word occasionally and smiling at the child frequently. Yet he noticed that Dionne was quieter than usual, her eyes looking haunted since she'd returned from the attic.

His cheeks ruddy from the wind and Papa's beer, Karl lifted his stein for a toast. "To *Oktoberfest,* a wonderful occasion because it brings us all together. To Mama's food and Papa's beer, to happy times and to our family and friends, healthy and safe under one roof. *Gesundheit!*"

Glasses clinked around the table, children giggled, the oompah band rang out from the stereo and Colby held his glass high, saluting Dionne across the space dividing them. Though she smiled, her expression was thoughtful, contemplative. As he pondered her mood, Karl tapped him on the shoulder.

"Come on, Colby. The horseshoes are waiting. Let's see how good you are."

Colby stood. "Maybe we should stay and help clean up."

Karl laughed heartily. "Not on holidays. The ladies won't let us, right, Mama?"

Bertha smiled at her eldest son indulgently. "Go, go. Outside, you two. I got plenty of help right here."

Konrad drained his beer stein and got up to go with them. John and his father rose, as well. Colby sent Dionne a questioning look, but she just nodded. He didn't particularly want to leave, but he didn't see how he could refuse. The men and boys and the younger girls spilled out onto the lawn. Except Werner, who kissed his mother's cheek, whispered something in Dionne's ear, then dashed out an opposite door and made for his car.

Like old times, Dionne thought as she helped clear the table. If she had a nickel for every boisterous family meal she'd shared around this table, she'd surely have a piggy bank full. Carrying a stack of dishes into the kitchen, she noticed Gwen eyeing her. John's wife had always been a little shy, causing her to stand out in the noisy Keller crowd.

"I sure wish I knew how you stay so thin," Gwen commented with an envious sigh as she loaded the dishwasher.

"So do I," added Lisa, not yet showing from her pregnancy but aware it wouldn't be long.

"And I wish I had long blond hair like yours," Dionne told Gwen honestly as she touched her own short curls. "It's so limiting, having curly hair."

"Throw me in that briar patch," Lisa said with a laugh.

"We always want what we can't have," Bertha interjected as she scooped leftovers into storage dishes. "Tina," she went on, including Konrad's wife, "your *spaetzle* is better than mine."

They laughed, then one by one, the women followed the men outdoors, grabbing a sweater against the cool evening air. Left alone with her mother, Dionne sprinkled cleanser in the sink and began to scrub.

Bertha peered out the kitchen window. "Papa likes your young man. You see how they talk, over by the rose trellis?"

Glancing up, Dionne saw that Colby and her father were deep in conversation. "They have construction work in common, I suppose."

"No, *liebchen*. They have *you* in common. I think your man cares for you, no?"

Somehow, Dionne had been certain they'd be having this conversation before the weekend was over. "It would seem so."

Bertha ran a towel around a pot too large for the dishwasher. "And you, how do you feel about him?"

"I've known him a month, Mama."

"You already told me on the phone. I saw your face when you kiss him. Maybe a month is long enough."

Dionne released a sigh as she rinsed the suds from the sink. "He doesn't know everything about me. If he did, he wouldn't be here." Her eyes moved to the window again. Colby was bending low, showing John's oldest boy how best to grip a horseshoe before pitching it. "Look at him with Curt, Mama." She shut off the water with an unsteady hand. "He wants children. How can I tell him?"

Bertha turned her daughter into the circle of her arms, her expression troubled as she held her close. "Don't, *liebchen*." She smoothed the fine hair, patted the slender back. "I read all the time in the papers, so many children waiting to be adopted. Why you don't look into that, Dionne?"

"Because it wouldn't be fair to Colby. He can have children of his own. Why should he settle for someone else's?"

Bertha drew back, gazing into eyes filled with an old pain. "You look at him and see Nathan, am I right?"

Dionne shook her head. "Colby's nothing like Nathan. He's kind, thoughtful, considerate." She thought about the way he'd taken in Aggie, his concern over Terry, his gentleness with Shelly. "He genuinely cares about people. I can't let him settle for second best."

Impatiently, her mother shook her shoulders. "Don't you say that, not ever. *You* are the best. He would be lucky to have you."

Her heart aching, Dionne moved back into her mother's embrace. "Oh, Mama, why did I have to fall in love with a man whose needs I can't satisfy?"

"You are judging without knowing. Tell him, Dionne. I don't think he is fool enough to let you go."

She closed her eyes, wanting desperately to believe, yet knowing that this time, her mother was wrong.

The lake water sloshed against the rocky shore as they followed it lazily, Colby's arm about her shoulders. Behind them, the lights on the glassed-in porch glowed warmly. The others had left, each small family unit returning to their own homes, the men shaking Colby's hand as they left as if meeting him had been a genuine pleasure. Bertha and Otto, sitting in matching chairs, were watching television, and Werner wasn't home yet. The fall night air was crisp as Colby pulled Dionne closer, wanting to share the heat of his body as they strolled.

"Does Emma remind you of Shelly?" he asked, wondering if that was why she seemed drawn more to that particular child.

The comparison had not escaped Dionne. "Yes. The way Shelly could be if life hadn't treated her so unfairly."

Colby thought of his own sister, her early years marred by unhappiness. "Life treats us all unfairly at times, Dionne. You can't live and not be touched by problems."

Tell him now, a voice inside her urged. But she couldn't form the words. Wordlessly, she held on tighter, her arm circled about his waist.

He gazed up at a sliver of moon and streaks of clouds in an inky sky. A few hardy crickets serenaded. The air was so pure and clean this far from the city. "I could get used to this," he commented casually.

"And here I thought you were a city boy."

"Did you? It's where my work is, but it's not necessarily where I want to be. I envy Zac living in St. Clair." He envied his best friend a lot.

"I guess if you're unhappy, the thing to do is move to a place where you'll be contented."

They came to a large willow tree, its leaves still intact, and he took both her hands as he turned her to face him. "Is that the doctor speaking, or the woman?"

"That's just common sense."

"Why were you crying up in the attic earlier?"

She'd known he'd ask and had her answer ready. "Oh, I get all sentimental and nostalgic when I come home."

He didn't believe her. Perhaps the best thing would be if he told her how he felt about her. Maybe then she'd trust him. "I guess what I want to do is move to wherever you are—St. Clair, here, Detroit. The moon, if that's your choice. I love you, Dionne."

Abruptly, she let go of his hands and began walking again. For a moment, he'd seen something flare in her eyes, a flash of hope, of intense emotion. But it was quickly replaced by a heartbreaking sadness before she turned away. He followed, catching up with her easily. "I've upset you again."

"I'm not upset. I'm just not... interested in a serious relationship."

Annoyed, he caught her wrist, swung her around. "I'm not talking relationships here. I'm talking love as in marriage, a family, a home." He pointed toward the house. "I want what those two good people in there have, a life together, sharing things, memories. And I want it with you."

She hadn't thought the hurt could go deeper, but she'd been wrong. She steeled herself for what had to be said. "For a marriage to work, two people have to want the same things. I don't want what you want." There, the lie was out, and she was surprised the words hadn't clogged her throat.

Angry now, he pulled her close to his body, as if physical contact could change her mind. "That's a lie."

She forced a coolness into her voice. "You can kiss me, make me want you. You've done it before. But you want more than that. And I can't give more to you."

There was moisture in her eyes and something else, something resembling utter hopelessness. He frowned, searching their brown depths. She was holding something back, something that was eating away at her. "You don't trust me enough to give me explanations, reasons."

He was getting too close. Again, she shook free of his hands. "From the beginning, I told you I wanted no complications, no changes in my life. If I've led you on, I'm sorry. I never wanted to hurt you."

He took a deep breath to give himself time to think. Someone in the past had hurt her, so was she now afraid of being hurt again? Had that man betrayed her trust so now she was unwilling to trust him? What was it she was afraid of, unwilling to share with him?

He knew her well enough to know it wasn't minor. He could be patient if he wanted something badly enough. And he wanted her badly, not just in his bed, but in his life. So he would chip away at the wall she'd built around her emotions, her defenses. And he would prove to her there was nothing they couldn't overcome together.

"I believe you. I know you don't want me to care about you, but it's too late. There were days I didn't want to feel it, either. You can't stop loving someone just because you want to."

Yes, you can, she thought. She'd stopped loving Nathan after he'd hurt her then left her. She didn't want to hurt Colby, so she would have to leave him and leave him for good. Then he would stop caring and get on with his life. She brushed a lock of hair from her face as she met his eyes. "I won't change my mind, Colby."

"All right," he said, sliding his arm about her and leading them back toward the house. "Let's just take it one day at a time."

She knew he didn't believe her. Walking with him, Dionne began to make plans.

It would seem she would have to hurt him after all.

The woman who sat at the opposite end of the couch shredding a tissue in her trembling hands was upset and angry. Amy Prentice, Dan's ex-wife, looked at Dionne through red-rimmed eyes. "It wouldn't be so bad if I didn't still love him," she said. "I only divorced him because I didn't want to stay and watch him destroy himself. And because I didn't want our son to live day-in and day-out with an alcoholic father."

"He's promised to stop before?" Dionne asked quietly.

"Oh, sure. Lots of times. When he came to me and told me he'd been going to AA meetings with you, I wondered how long that would last. He asked me to go to Al-Anon and I went. I'd do anything if it would help." She choked back a sob. "But he always goes back to drinking. He doesn't think he's an alcoholic because he isn't falling down drunk every night. But he is, Doctor. He is an alcoholic."

Dionne thought so, too. She'd suspected from the beginning that Dan had given in too easily. She'd had too much experience listening to drinkers swear they were through, to fall for yet another lie they themselves believed. She'd sat there, at that first AA meeting, watching Dan's face as he'd listened to another victim tell of nearly killing his own son while driving drunk. She'd seen the shock, the determination. Yet it hadn't been enough. "I know it's difficult for you to not give up on him."

"I have." The words were said forcefully. "This time, I have. Dan's a drunk, and that's all there is to it."

Dionne moved closer, touching the distraught woman's shoulder. "No, Amy. He's sick. He needs to check himself into a hospital, to admit he's got a problem he can't lick alone, to *want* to overcome his addiction. Even then, he's got a long, difficult road to travel. But he needs you to believe in him."

Amy brushed light brown hair back from her thin face. "I can't anymore, Doctor. You don't know what it's been like, waiting for him to come home nights, wondering every time the phone rang if he'd killed himself or someone else. Then after I left him and we divorced, I worried about Kevin when Dan picked him up occasionally. Dan vowed he'd never drink when he had Kevin, but I can't trust him. He lies, he promises and later, he doesn't even remember."

"Of course, you need to protect your son first and foremost."

"Last night, he came over, swaggering and singing. He wanted to take Kevin to a movie." She gave a harsh laugh. "A movie! He could hardly walk. I told him he was drunk, and he said he'd had only two beers. More like ten, probably." Her eyes were pleading, demanding answers. "Why do they do it, Doctor? Do they have a death wish? Make me understand."

"I wish I could." She thought of her cigarettes, still in their unopened package across the room in her desk drawer. "Addictions of all kinds are hard to admit to, and even harder to conquer."

"Dan never misses a day of work, so no one thinks he has a drinking problem."

"A common misconception, but we know better. So what are you going to do?"

Amy dabbed at her eyes. "I don't know."

"Do you want me to talk with Dan again?"

The thin woman stood, looking older than her twenty-eight years. "I don't think it'll do any good. I'm calling my attorney and rescinding his visitation rights. I know that'll hurt Dan, but..." She made a helpless gesture with her hand, then offered it to Dionne. "Thanks, Doctor, for trying."

Dionne rose and shook her hand. "I'm sorry I couldn't do more, Amy." Dionne watched the woman walk out of the office, struggling with the regret. When Colby appeared in the doorway, she waved him in. "Dan Prentice's wife was just here. He's drinking again."

"Damn! I could have sworn..." He studied Dionne. "You're not surprised."

"No. Dan's simply not ready to admit he has a problem, and until he does, there isn't much we can do."

"I'll tell his foreman to keep an eye on him. The slightest infraction and we'll put him on probation. I'm not about to have another accident." He rubbed the back of his neck, feeling drained. "How do you stand it?"

Seated at her desk, Dionne folded her hands atop Dan's file. "As I've said, the failure rate in this line of work is disappointingly high. A fact of life you have to get used to."

He eased a hip onto the edge of the desk and touched the ends of her hair lightly. It had rained yesterday, and one of their work sites was ankle deep in mud. The wiring hadn't arrived for the office complex going up near Northland, which would undoubtedly put them behind schedule. And now this thing with Dan. He didn't want to think about problems right now. He wanted some time alone with Dionne.

At her parents' house, he'd been able to steal a few kisses and not much more. On the drive home, she'd been withdrawn and quiet, then when they arrived at his house, she'd told him she had a migraine and had gone to her own room. Today, they'd both been busy with their separate commitments and this was the first free minute he'd had.

"I've missed being alone with you," he told her honestly.

She raised her eyes to his, saw the love he no longer bothered to hide. "I've missed that, too." More than she'd thought possible. But she'd used the time wisely, knowing what she had to do. Now, as she prayed for the courage to carry out her plan, she smiled at him. One more night in his arms. Was it so much to ask when it would have to do her for all time?

He saw the sadness in her eyes, but he saw the willingness, too. He touched her cheek, ran a finger along the smooth column of her throat. "I'll tell Aggie we won't need her. We'll have a light dinner by the fire. And make love in my water bed."

Dionne's smile slipped, and she swallowed to strengthen her voice. "I'd like that."

"Good." He touched his lips to her cool forehead, then moved to the door. "Ready to leave in half an hour?"

She nodded, then waited for the door to close. Hurriedly, she stuffed everything she'd brought into her briefcase, snapped it shut and went to stand by the window. Shadows were lengthening, though it was only late afternoon. The sky was gray and forbidding.

Soon, winter's hand would turn everything white and bring with it the unrelenting cold. Halloween would lead to Thanksgiving, then the Christmas season would be upon them, and another year would be over. The years slid by so quickly, it seemed. This next one might not, however. She would have to keep busy and school herself to forget, as she had had to do once before.

But this was Colby, not Nathan. Swallowing a low moan, she wondered if she had the courage to forget Colby.

* * *

The flames danced and crackled, sending waves of heat to envelop them. Colby watched the fire turn Dionne's hair a golden red, her skin to honey. Picking up the wine, he topped off her glass, then set the bottle on the fireplace ledge.

"Are you trying to get me tipsy, sir?" she teased.

"Yes, so I can ravish you."

She leaned against the ledge and twined her fingers with his. "You don't need wine for that."

He moved closer. "How is it I don't tire of you? Why do you excite me more than any woman I've ever known, and you don't even try?"

She would let him sweet talk her, then let him love her. He needed this, and perhaps she did, too. For tonight, only for tonight. "Maybe I've cast a spell over you."

He trailed his fingers along her bare arms, watching her shiver. "I thought witches had black hair."

"Only the old ones, the ones with warts on the end of their noses. And when the prince comes along and kisses the witch, all her imperfections disappear like magic."

"You don't have any imperfections."

She kept her voice light. "Perhaps I've just fooled you into not noticing them." Shifting, she knelt beside him, then drew him up until they were thigh to thigh. Lovingly, she touched his face, his hair, finally resting her hands on his shoulders. "Let's not talk about imperfections or witches or problems tonight. Let's not talk at all. Let's just touch and feel and love one another."

Their mouths met dreamily, lazily, a slow searching out of familiar tastes. For Dionne, passion tonight was mellow, haunting, tempered by the knowledge that she might never again feel this way. She sighed as his lips trailed down her throat, and she let her head fall back. His hands on her were light, almost breezy, unhurried.

Her fingers on the buttons of his shirt were steady, her touch on his skin easy when she pushed the material from him. She knew his body nearly as well as she knew her own now, and she lingered over the layers of muscles of his back, then shifted to caress the strong wall of his chest. She inhaled the masculine scent of him, put her lips to his throat and tasted the rich, dark flavors she'd come to love. When her hands moved low on his flat stomach and unsnapped his jeans, she heard his breath catch, and she laughed softly into his ear.

She watched the firelight flicker over him, highlighting his hair, shadowing his face. She pressed her mouth to the pulse in his throat, felt it pounding hard and fast for her. Only for her. Leaning into him, she paused to brush her lips along his bristly cheeks, his temples, each corner of his mouth, and finally, she sampled the dimple that fascinated her so.

For him, she was every fantasy he'd ever had, so giving, so patient. Colby touched the hem of her sweater, pulled it from her and met her eyes. Reaching behind her, he unfastened her bra, slowly slid it down her arms and tossed it aside. Still kneeling with her, he inched closer, closer. The sweet friction of her breasts brushing his chest had him breathless, had him trembling.

He raised his hands to frame her face, the delicate features that haunted his dreams. He rained kisses on every inch, watched her eyes darken as they half closed. She swayed with him, grew weak and shaky with him. His mouth claimed hers then, a long lingering kiss, while needs built and blood heated.

Lowering her onto the thick rug, his lips skimmed along her throat, then lower, closing over a swelling peak. She arched as a soft moan escaped from her. Her hands in his hair drew him nearer as her restless body shifted. Impatient with obstacles, he removed the rest of her clothes and then his own, eager to be flesh to flesh with her. A log shifted in the grate but he scarcely heard it as his mouth journeyed down her body, sleek and damp with desire.

Shuddering, she clung to him. "Now, Colby," she whispered, her voice hoarse in the quiet room. But he ignored her as his hands roamed, touching everywhere his mouth strayed, tasting everything.

Before Colby, she had not believed she could be seduced, for she was a woman always in control—yet he seduced her. She had not thought she could be enticed, made mindless with longing, for she was a woman in command of her emotions—yet he enticed her. She had not felt she could be captivated, delirious with need, begging for release, for she was a woman in charge of her own body—yet he captivated her. On a quavering sigh, she let him lead her.

Tormenting them both, he nipped and suckled and kissed, and felt her muscles go lax. Utterly responsive, she flowed like rich wine beneath his hands. Her scent captured him, tangling his already aroused senses. He was relentless, seeking out each secret place—the throbbing pulse behind a knee, the sweet underside of a breast, the tender skin in the crook of her arm. His breath was a fire in his lungs, flaming out of control, raw and powerful as the desire that whipped through him.

She was the stuff dreams were made of, his dreams. She was the woman books were written about, songs were composed over, poems were created for. She was a challenge to his restless soul, the love he'd been longing for. She was hot, she was here, she was his. Half mad with his need for her, he stared into the simmering depth of her eyes.

All her life, it seemed, she'd dreamed of passion like this, of love so strong, of desire so consuming. She'd not believed—truly believed—it could ever be, but she'd imagined, she'd fantasized. He raised himself over her and she saw that the reality was better than the dream.

"You're so beautiful," she whispered, touching his face.

He struggled for control, the arms holding his weight quivering with tension. "That's my line." Aligning their bodies, he leaned closer. "Never before has it been like this." He needed her to know, to believe. "Never again, with anyone else, can it be like this."

She believed. "I know. Only with you."

He touched his palms to hers, erotically sliding along her skin, then watched her eyes as he filled her. A soft sigh slipped from her as she welcomed him home. He began to move within her as a slow flush spread along the silken curve of her throat. His breath rushed from him as he picked up the pace.

She could think of nothing but Colby, no one but Colby. Her heart raced and her blood rushed for Colby. Her body moved in rhythm with his, her pulse pounded against his, her mouth accepted his.

Heart to heart, hands to hands, they flew higher and higher, then shattered together in an endless sky.

The ringing of the phone broke the drowsy mood of the afterglow. Languidly, Colby lifted his head and saw that it was only eight in the evening. No building sites open; nothing of importance, he was sure. "Let it ring," he murmured, and gathered Dionne closer.

But she could not. Rising from him, she reached for his shirt. "I can't. I'm a doctor. A ringing phone could be an emergency." Shrugging into the shirt, she crossed the room, dragged the instrument to him and held it out. "It's your house."

Grudgingly, he sat up and said hello. Listening, he frowned, certain this wasn't good news. "It's for you, your partner," he said, handing her the phone.

"Yes, Hilary." Dionne's mind was already racing, considering possibilities. What she heard had her heart pounding. "Oh, no. How long has she been gone?...I see.... Where have they looked?...No, she wouldn't do that."

Gathering her scattered clothes with her free hand, Dionne came to a decision. "Yes, all right. I'll leave right away. Where will you be?...Fine, I'll see you there. Thanks for letting me know so quickly. Bye."

Hanging up, Dionne looked up into Colby's concerned face. "Shelly's run away from home. She never arrived on the school bus. Her aunt found a note and...and she's been gone nearly five hours." Her voice trembled, shaky with fear. "I've got to go."

"I'll go with you."

She was already on her way to her room. "No. I can do this faster on my own. I know Shelly, where she likes to go, what she likes to do." In the bedroom, her eyes flew to the window. It was already dark out, so very dark. A small child alone in the dark. *Dear God! Not Shelly. She couldn't lose another one.*

Dionne rushed to pull on her clothes, trying to block out the terrible scenarios that came to mind.

Behind her, Colby zipped up his jeans. "You're in no condition to drive. I'll go with you."

She stopped, fear and fury making her voice loud. "No. Please, just let me go. I'll be fine. I need to do this myself."

"Quit being so damn stubborn. You don't need to be a tower of strength alone. Let me help you."

Grabbing her suitcase, she flung it onto the bed. "I don't want your help or your company right now." Why couldn't he understand? she wondered as she pulled clothes off hangers and crammed them into her bag. "Shelly's my problem, not yours. I solve my own problems."

He stood in the doorway, only his tightly clenched fists revealing his mood. "The invincible Dr. Keller, right? She needs no one, wants no one. She stands alone." Two strides and he was up close to her, pulling her to face him. "I love you, dammit. Why are you turning from me?"

She saw red. A little girl was out somewhere, frightened and alone, and Colby was preventing her from rushing to find her. She glared up at him, feeling her temper rise. "I didn't ask you to love me. I didn't ask you for anything. My patient needs me. Let me go."

He tried to simmer down, to realize a doctor's first obligation was to patients. Taking a deep breath, he stepped aside, watching her slam shut her bag. "All right. I understand. When will you be back?"

"I don't know." She picked up her suitcase and flung the strap of her purse onto her shoulder. "My work here is pretty much finished." She left the room, walking toward the front door. "I'll keep in touch with you by phone about the couple of cases still unsettled. And the department heads can call me anytime." She opened the door.

"Wait." His hand touched her arm. "I'm not talking about your work here. What about us?"

She couldn't meet his eyes. It was killing her to say the words, but she had to. "There is no *us*, Colby. There never was." Turning, she hurried down the steps.

In disbelief, he watched her pile her things into the car and get in. In moments, she was moving down the driveway.

Out of his yard. Out of his life.

Chapter Eleven

"Moppsy's cold," Shelly said, hugging the floppy-eared stuffed dog to her.

"We'd better cover him up then," Dionne said, tucking the blanket under the animal's chin as well as under the child's. She sat on the edge of the bed and smoothed back the pale blond hair. "Are you warm enough?" When she nodded, Dionne smiled and leaned down to kiss her good-night.

Shelly's eyes misted, and her small arms reached out as she swallowed a sob, her face in Dionne's neck. "You aren't going away, are you?"

Dionne felt her heart wrench. "No, I'll be right in the next room. I promise you. And I'll leave this lamp on low, all right?" Shelly eased back, and Dionne rearranged the covers again.

"You're not mad at me, are you, Dionne?"

"Of course not." She patted the soft cheek. "Now you go to sleep, and don't worry. We're going to work things out." At the doorway, she turned back to see those huge blue eyes watching her. "Sweet dreams." Leaving the door ajar, Dionne walked to the kitchen.

Her movements automatic, she put water on for tea and glanced out the window as she waited for it to boil. Cold and rainy, the wind picking up. She shivered involuntarily. The digital clock on the coffeemaker read eight o'clock. It had been a hellish twenty-four hours, and she'd had only snatches of sleep since the phone call last evening telling her of Shelly's disappearance.

She'd put the scene of her departure from Colby's house aside as she'd raced toward St. Clair, twice almost catching the eye of the state police, but managing to slow in time. Her thoughts had focused entirely on Shelly, where she could have gone, why she'd felt the need to leave.

Arriving in town, she'd met Hilary at the Morgan home, finding Shelly's aunt and uncle pale and pacing from the strain. A police officer had been with them, explaining that the child's description had been broadcast every hour and that men on foot and in cars were out searching. Dionne had had some ideas of her own and left then, saying she'd be back or call in.

The whistling kettle caught her attention and she poured steaming water into her cup. Stirring idly, she drifted back again—could it have been only last night? Like a lifetime ago, it seemed. She'd circled the wharf area where she and Shelly liked to feed the fish and the birds, then take long, chatty walks. It had grown cold, and she'd been relieved when she'd found no sign of Shelly in that dark, deserted area.

Next, she'd tried Lainey's, knowing how much Shelly loved the horses. Enlisting Zac's aid, they'd searched the barn and the wooded area close by, but came up empty-handed. Zac had immediately joined the searchers while Dionne had gone off alone, over her friends' objections. The police, she knew, were scouring the school and grounds, Shelly's classmates' homes. Dionne could think of only one other place Shelly might have gone.

She'd found Shelly asleep under the curved stairwell of her second-floor apartment building. Dionne had awakened the little girl and held her tight, rocking her. Shelly had cried then, harder than she had at her father's funeral, pouring out her heart.

Dionne sipped her tea, wondering if she'd handled the emotional scene as well as she could have. She'd phoned the Morgan house and told the relieved relatives that Shelly was safe. The hardest part had been informing them that she didn't want to go back. While Hilary stayed with their children, Shelly's aunt and uncle had come here. Dionne had bathed and put the child to bed by then, and the three adults sat and talked for a long while over coffee.

Taking her teacup into the living room, Dionne curled up on the couch, asking herself if she'd acted in everyone's best interest. She prayed she had. Some hard decisions had had to be made. Tilting her chin, she vowed she would have no regrets. Always, she tried to act impersonally and professionally on behalf of her patients. This had been a decision of the heart.

Shelly's guardians had left, and she'd caught a few winks, then had gone to work, setting her plan in motion. Once she knew she had the Morgans' blessing, she felt free to act. There was a judge she knew, a fair man and a good friend. She'd enlisted his aid and been pleased at his cooperation. There were more details to be taken care of, but she would manage.

Now, with the knowledge that Shelly was safe, Dionne swallowed more tea and allowed herself to think of other matters. Her counseling sessions back in Detroit were in various stages of progression. Theresa Abbott was at her expensive treatment center, hopefully overcoming her dependence on alcohol. Maybe when she returned, she would be willing to enroll in one of the after-care programs to strengthen her recovery.

Ed Donnelly was attending his meetings at Charter Hospital. And once Terry recovered from surgery, hopefully Jean could persuade him to enter counseling.

The one outstanding failure so far was Dan Prentice. It would seem he had not yet lost enough or fallen low enough to want to climb back up. Dionne knew she'd need to keep in touch with the three department heads regarding all these patients' progress. If Colby would allow her to after the way she'd left him.

Colby. Shelly's timely gambit had given Dionne the impetus to leave him, as she'd known she had to. Though she hadn't meant to be so abrupt, so cruel, she'd had little choice when he'd pressed her in the midst of her fears. She'd hurt him, but stringing out their relationship when it had nowhere to go would have hurt him more.

A clean break. That was always the best way. She would have to take business calls from him, but she would make them brief and discuss only her patients who worked for him. She would not give him false hope, but rather set him free. Free to find a woman who could love him wholly and give him all he needed, all he deserved.

Tears welled up as Dionne closed her tired eyes and leaned her head wearily against the couch back. A few short weeks ago, Colby Winters had been someone she'd met twice, a man she'd stood up in a wedding with. How could you come to need someone, to love someone so quickly? Already, he seemed like the other half of her. Without him, she knew she'd always feel incomplete. Yet she had to let him go, let him forget her. Though she knew she would never forget him, she felt she was doing the right thing.

For some, happily ever after was never meant to be.

"I don't give a damn about your delivery schedules being screwed up," Colby barked into the phone. "I'm too busy worrying about my own problems.... No, *you* look here. I was promised that pipe shipment three days ago, and here it is four o'clock of the fourth day and it still hasn't shown up. You guys don't seem to realize that we can't complete our preliminary plumbing until that delivery arrives. I've got inspectors scheduled for next week. Plus men standing around with nothing to do, men I have to pay by the hour while you whine about a new girl who messed up."

Colby frowned as Frenchy came into the trailer, a stiff wind following him inside. Tossing his hard hat aside, Frenchy went to the stove and poured Colby a cup of coffee, setting it within reach, then backing off. Everyone on site knew that Colby didn't let his temper loose often, but when he did, it was best to steer clear of him. And he'd really been on a roll the last few days, shouting orders, yelling at each small infraction, his nerves frayed. Frenchy thought he knew what had set Colby off, but he wasn't about to risk the man's wrath by mentioning it.

"All right, all right," Colby said impatiently. "Tomorrow before noon or I'm coming down there breathing fire, buddy." He slammed the phone down and tasted the coffee. Hot and bitter, like he was. He turned to Frenchy. "Those plaster guys ever show up on Unit Six?"

Picking up his clipboard, Frenchy checked. "Yesterday. They got one more day's work and they're finished."

"How about the painters over on One and Two?"

"They're one guy short, but they're working."

"Short? Again?" Shoving aside a rolled blueprint, Colby swore under his breath. "What's with these guys that they can't show up for work?"

Frenchy looked up from his schedule. "It's Dominic Franco. His wife had their first baby today. He thought he ought to be with her." There was the merest trace of censure in his voice.

Colby glared, but he simmered down. So he was out of line on that one. He raised his mug, then changed his mind and walked back to pour the rest down the sink. "This stuff tastes like mud." Wearily, he ran his hand over his face. He was bone tired and cross as a bear with a splinter in his paw. But it wasn't Frenchy's fault.

He laid a hand on the older man's shoulder. They'd worked together six years. No one was more loyal or more tolerant than Frenchy. "I'm sorry. I've got a lot on my mind."

Frenchy relaxed. "Yeah, I know."

Colby turned, cramming his hands in his jeans pockets. "No, you don't know."

"Sure I do. No man as quiet as you gets to yelling and cursing except for one reason. Woman trouble. That doctor lady, right?"

Colby swiveled. "How'd you know?"

Frenchy chuckled. "News goes like wildfire in all companies, boss. You don't want people to know your business, you shouldn't be kissing women out there in the rain with a dozen guys watching."

Yeah, that had been an error in judgment, Colby thought, turning toward the window. But she'd made him so damn mad that day. She'd done that quite often, at least at first. He sighed. Yet the good times had overshadowed their few skirmishes. Except maybe the last one.

Bracing his hands on the counter, he leaned forward. She'd left him, just like that. Made love with him on his fireplace rug, slowly, beautifully. Then duty beckoned and she was out the door. Not only leaving, but telling him they had nothing together.

He hadn't wanted to believe it, had felt she'd call the next day, tell him they'd found Shelly and then apologize for her hysterical behavior. But she hadn't. The call had come from Zac, saying Shelly was safe, but that he didn't know too many of the details. So Colby had waited.

The fourth day now and still no word. He'd picked up the phone a dozen times, but couldn't make himself dial. No, not this time. If she didn't want him, so be it. Maybe he had pushed. Maybe he had pressed. Maybe he had rushed her. He'd thought himself patient, but discovered he wasn't even close. He'd told her he loved her, wanted to marry her. And still, she'd left.

"It's quitting time, boss," Frenchy said from behind him. Grabbing his hard hat, he stepped to the door. "See you tomorrow?"

"Yeah, probably."

"Take it easy. Women, they give us trouble all our lives. You got to learn to live with it."

The door slammed shut, and Colby grimaced. Learn to live with it, hell! He was not going to run after her, beg or plead, ask her back. She knew where to find him. This time, she would have to come to him.

Still fuming, Colby left the trailer.

"I've made notations on all the files you gave me as to the status of these patients," Dionne said, handing Hilary a stack of manila folders. "And here's a list of pending appointments and what needs to be done with each. Only three can't be put off. The rest I've rescheduled for next week."

"Fine," Hilary said as she scanned the top sheet. "So you leave in the morning and you'll be back Monday, right?"

"I plan on returning Sunday sometime, which is only four days away." She was beginning to feel guilty about all this time she needed Hilary to do double duty for her.

"What if...well, what if Colby Winters calls?" Hilary looked a little uneasy having to ask.

"He won't." A full week and he hadn't. She'd been both relieved and surprised. Evidently, Colby had accepted her departure from his life more easily than she'd dared hope. She should be pleased. She'd been too busy to give it much thought, except at night as she tried to get to sleep. She'd hurt him and he was backing off. It was what she'd wanted, yet it was still hard to live with. "On the off chance he does, just tell him I'm away and be sort of vague."

"Sure, no problem. I know it's an important trip, but I hope you get a chance to relax a little. You look like you could use a weekend of R and R."

Dionne removed her glasses and rubbed the bridge of her nose. "Well, this should end it. I hope to settle down when I get back. I know you've been putting in a lot of hours. Why don't you plan on taking a vacation after next week?"

"I would if Jim could get some time off and go with me, but I hate to go alone. He completes his residency in January. Maybe then we can get away for a week." Hilary smiled dreamily. "A week together sounds like such a luxury."

"Such is the life of doctors." Dionne checked her watch, then turned off the Tiffany lamp on her desk. "Got to go. You've got the number where I'm staying?"

"Yes, but I won't use it unless I really need to."

She hugged Hilary briefly, feeling grateful for her uncomplaining assistance. She'd make it up to her when she returned, Dionne vowed silently. "I'm off. See you Monday."

"Right. Don't worry about a thing."

Easier said than done, Dionne thought as she hurried to her car.

It was drizzling, a chilly fall rain with accompanying winds disturbing damp leaves clustered on the dying grass. Colby stood with the collar of his raincoat pulled up, his hair absorbing the steady moisture. He didn't notice as, hands thrust into his pockets, he gazed at the fresh mound of earth. Gazed at the final resting place of Harold Winters.

His father's landlord had called to tell Colby that he'd found Harold dead in his bed. Colby had gone back to the shabby apartment then and found two letters written in a shaky hand. Reading his, he'd learned that

Harold had known for some time that he was dying. Certainly he'd known the last day they'd talked. Colby stood wondering why Harold hadn't mentioned it.

The truth, when it came, didn't sit comfortably with him. Perhaps because he hadn't exactly been cordial that day they'd talked in Harold's kitchen. Oh, sure, he'd wished him well on his job and shaken hands. Big deal. But he hadn't invited confidences or deathbed conversations. And now, his father was gone.

Hunching into the wind, Colby turned and walked slowly down the slight embankment. He'd called Kathy in Iowa and told her. She'd sounded odd, as if she'd been expecting his call. She didn't think she would fly in for the funeral. It would serve no purpose, she'd told him, and he'd agreed. In her way, she'd said goodbye to their father a long time ago, she'd explained.

Colby had mailed Kathy Harold's letter, told no one else and set about burying his father.

On foot, Colby passed his car and continued walking along the winding road, needing to keep moving for a while yet. For years, he'd been expecting a call from someone saying that Harold had died—in a car accident, in a brawl or from falling down a flight of stairs. Yet when the news had come, it had startled him. Had he really put such store in the fact that Harold had a job and had quit drinking? Not really. Then why was he unnerved now?

Because he'd begun to understand. Not understand his father, perhaps. But understand, at least a little, why Harold had drunk so much. And because, with Dionne's guidance, Colby had begun to forgive Harold for the things he'd done—and the things he hadn't. Perhaps he even felt a little cheated that they hadn't had a chance to begin again. His fault, of course. He hadn't called Harold even once since that afternoon, had made no attempt to build from that tenuous moment.

Pausing, he glanced up at gray clouds, feeling as leaden and dismal as the sky. If his father had blown dozens of chances to change, to win the love of his children, perhaps Colby himself had blown a few, too. He'd blown a biggie in his youth when he'd taken his wounded pride and left his wife without trying harder to understand her. One person was seldom the cause of a marriage breakup. More recently, he'd blown the chance to nourish a fledgling friendship with his father before it was too late. Was he also blowing his chance for happiness by not going after Dionne?

Pride. He supposed there were times when it was a good thing. But mostly, it was, as they said, the first deadly sin. Something to think about there. Turning, he strolled back to the car.

For some time now, he'd felt there was something Dionne wasn't telling him, some part of her life she wasn't willing to share with him. It had to be very important to her or she wouldn't have walked away from what they had together. He was experienced enough to know that no woman could fake the emotions, the tenderness, the physical responses that she'd shown him. She was— as a woman, as a daughter, as a doctor—a warm and caring human being. She touched people, reached out to her family, her patients and to him. Why, then, did she say that they had nothing together, that she didn't want him in her life?

Something didn't add up. Getting behind the wheel, he sat for a moment, wiping the moisture from his face with a handkerchief. There had to be a reason, a good and valid reason. Maybe if he learned what it was, if he understood, he could live with the explanation.

He started the engine and turned on the windshield wipers. Her family was obviously close and very protective, so they'd be no help. But there was someone who might know, who might be willing to assist him. Her friend Lainey. He would call and wangle an invitation on some pretext or other. Then he'd go there, talk with Lainey, then with Dionne, and not give up until he learned what he needed to know.

With a last glance at his father's grave, he shifted the car into drive. With a purpose in mind at last and an outlet for his restless energy, he drove out of the cemetery.

"A baby? That's wonderful!" Colby smiled at Zac's proud grin and hugged Lainey. "I'm really happy for you both. When's the big event due?"

"In the spring. You're the first person we've told." Lainey couldn't keep the smile from her face as she laced her fingers with Zac's. She got up to pour more coffee around the kitchen table where they'd just finished dinner. "So, godfather-to-be, you can mark it on your calendar."

"I wouldn't miss it. Does this mean you've stopped riding, Lainey?"

Sitting back down, she shook her head. "The doctor says as long as I don't overdo, I'm fine."

"The lessons go on hold for the winter months anyhow," Zac said. "And Lainey's been training a college girl who helps out."

"Debbie's good with the kids and with the horses. In the spring, I'll probably just supervise until after the baby's born and let Debbie do all the physical stuff." She touched her stomach where the tiny life was growing, feeling the tenderness swell deep inside her. It was the miracle she'd once thought she'd never experience. She turned her soft gaze to the man who'd made all her dreams come true. "And Zac'll be here, bossing me around, as usual."

"I don't boss. I just . . . oversee."

"Right." She laughed as he took her hand. "I do have a tendency to overdo."

"I'll say," Zac piped in. "She's got fourteen students now, and most of them come twice a week."

"No kidding," Colby commented. "They're not all Dionne's referrals, are they?" He'd been sitting and listening, trying to be patient until he could insert Dionne's name into the conversation without looking too obvious.

"No. A friend of hers, Dr. Martin from Port Huron, has recommended several." Zac frowned thoughtfully. "And what's that judge's name?"

"Judge Tobias," Lainey answered. "He's sent a couple over, through Friend of the Court."

Colby nodded, impressed. "I see. But you do still have a couple of Dionne's patients?"

"Oh, sure. Shelly, of course. And about four others. Dionne's the only clinical psychologist in the area who specializes in children. And besides, everyone knows how good she is with her patients, how concerned with their welfare."

Colby toyed with his napkin. "Yeah, everyone knows that."

Zac shot a questioning look at his wife. Straightening, he leaned forward. "Is something the matter, Colby, some problem between you and Dionne?"

"You could say that. I asked her to marry me and she walked away a week ago, telling me it would never work between us."

After a somewhat hooded glance toward Zac, Lainey let out a long breath. "I think I'll put on more coffee."

Colby shoved aside his cup. "Do you two have any idea why she should feel that way?"

"I didn't know you and Dionne had progressed so far in your relationship, although I know Lainey suspected as much." Zac looked concerned. "Do you want to tell me what happened?"

"I wish I knew. We sort of waltzed around each other when she first came to Detroit, you know. Neither of us too crazy about working with the other. I thought she was just another do-gooder, like some of those social workers who used to come around when I was young."

Lainey returned, listening carefully. "Go on."

"There was this attraction between us that was pretty hard to deny. But she kept pulling back."

"You went to her place that night after you left here, as I recall," Lainey interjected. "When I phoned that next morning looking for you, Dionne seemed a little embarrassed that we'd discovered you'd spent the night."

Colby nodded. "She was, but she got over it." He almost smiled at that, remembering.

"I thought then that Dionne cared a great deal for you," Lainey went on. "We never talked about it, but I know she's not one to allow a man to get close to her unless she cares. In the year since I moved back from New York, I've not known her to date anyone around here. Have you, Zac?"

"No. She never mentions men in connection with herself."

"She told me about this guy in college who really did a number on her, I guess," Colby said. "She never really told me why they broke off, only that he hurt her badly. Do you know why?''

Lainey shifted in her chair. "Yes, but Dionne told me in confidence years ago. I can't betray that, Colby. I hope you understand. I've never even told Zac.''

"I understand." He ran a hand through his hair as he sat back and stretched out his legs. "I just don't know what to think.''

"Have you tried calling her or seeing her since she left?'' Zac asked.

"Last night, before I called you, but Hilary's taking her messages. All she would tell me is that Dionne's on an important trip and she'll be gone for several days. When did you see her last?''

"The night she came here looking for Shelly.'' Zac turned to his wife. "Have you heard from her since?''

"I called her the day after she'd found Shelly hiding in her apartment stairwell. She sounded so relieved that the child was all right that we talked of little else. I haven't heard from Dionne since, but that's not unusual. Sometimes we don't talk for a week or more at a time.''

Colby felt his frustration mount. "And she didn't mention going on a trip?''

"No, sorry. We could check with her parents.''

"Not there. Hilary specifically told me.'' He hated to ask, but remembered his vow to himself to swallow his pride. Leaning forward, he took Lainey's hand. "Lainey, I love Dionne and I believe we could have a good life together. I'm not asking you to betray a friend's confidence. But please, just answer one question for me. This reason that she broke up with that guy so many years ago, could it still be affecting her? Could it be why she left me?''

Lainey studied his eyes. "Yes, I think it's something that is still affecting her. It's also probably why we've never seen her with a man or heard of one she's dating."

Colby had guessed as much. "She told me she's dedicated to her work and that she can't divide herself in half, that marriage and a family are not for her. I don't buy it." Exasperated, he stood and began to pace the kitchen. "I know she cares about me. And I saw her there in Frankenmuth with her family. She cares about all of them, her folks, her brothers, the kids. How can work satisfy all the needs of a woman like that?"

"I don't know." Lainey shook her head. "As soon as she returns, you can go to her. Maybe she'll tell you her reasons."

"Yeah, maybe," Colby said with little conviction.

Lainey rose. "Meanwhile, how about some dessert, guys?"

"Not for me," Colby answered. "You two go ahead. I think I'll turn in. Thanks for listening. See you in the morning."

Before Lainey could insist he stay, he left the room.

He was about ready to climb the walls. He'd arrived Friday, and here it was Sunday and Dionne still hadn't returned. He'd made such a pest of himself that Hilary was having trouble being civil to him. He was having a problem being civil himself.

He'd spent hours in the barn cleaning stalls and then painting the third bedroom recently added to the house, working alongside Zac. They'd talked about everything, and finally Colby had told his old friend about his father's death and about his last visit with him. It had been therapeutic and healing to be able to put his past to rest, to put his disturbing relationship with his father in perspective.

He'd ridden the horses, then groomed them, anything to tire himself physically so he could sleep at night. It had worked only minimally. His body was weary, but he couldn't seem to turn off his roving mind as it tried to come up with solutions, possibilities.

Had Colby ever doubted the depth of his feelings for Dionne, this weekend had convinced him he loved her. Though he realized that might change nothing for her, it changed everything for him.

He'd driven the streets, gone past Dionne's office, even been to her apartment several times. Nothing. Thank goodness Zac and Lainey were understanding friends, for they left him alone, more or less. He was driving everyone, including himself, crazy. He'd all but lost his appetite, picking at his dinner tonight. Giving Lainey and Zac a break for a while, he got into his truck and decided to take another circle tour.

The lights were on in her apartment. It took him a moment to realize it wasn't just wishful thinking that made him see a warm, inviting glow coming from the second-floor corner apartment. Taking a deep breath, he parked the truck and climbed the stairs. Pausing at the door, he heard the muffled sound of a voice inside. She was really there.

He would be reasonable, Colby told himself. He would gently ask a few questions, listen politely, discuss their situation without losing his temper. And never,

never let her know what he'd been through these last miserable days. He knocked twice and waited.

She stood in the doorway wearing a long, peach-colored robe, her eyes dark and guarded. He lost it.

"Where the hell have you been?" he asked.

Chapter Twelve

Dionne was outwardly calm, but her eyes narrowed, and she glanced over her shoulder before answering him. "I would thank you to watch your language."

Colby saw Shelly sitting on the couch, her huge blue eyes watching them. Shuffling his feet, he rubbed the back of his neck. "I'm sorry. It's just that I've been worried." His eyes met her wary ones. "You don't seem surprised to see me."

Hardly that. She'd arrived home two hours ago and called Hilary soon after. That's when she'd learned he'd been searching high and low for her. She'd tried to prepare herself for his visit, knowing he would come. Yet seeing him standing there, his hair looking as if he'd thrust angry fingers through it more than once, his eyes dark and demanding, she wished they could have put off this confrontation until morning.

She tried to keep her voice cool, somewhat distant. "I spoke with Hilary earlier. I wasn't aware I should inform you of my comings and goings."

He felt the anger rising, but banked it, knowing she'd close the door on him if he ranted and raved as he felt like doing. "Do you want to discuss this in the hallway or may I come in?"

She considered sending him away until morning, until he cooled down. But that would only be postponing the inevitable. Better to get things over with now. "You may come in, provided you can behave. I'm reading Shelly a story before bedtime."

Bristling inwardly but with a smile planted on his face, Colby walked past Dionne. "Hello, Shelly." Studying the little girl, he decided she'd lost that sad look that had been such a part of her before.

Hugging her raggedy dog, she smiled back. "Hi, Colby. We can't go fishing anymore. It's too cold."

"I think you're right. Maybe we can go to the Old Mill and pick apples and eat doughnuts and drink cider." He sat down in the chair angled toward the couch. He didn't want to do small talk with this child right now, but there seemed no way out.

"And maybe get a pumpkin," Shelly suggested. "Halloween's coming soon."

Dionne resumed her seat beside Shelly. "Do you like to carve pumpkins?"

"I usually just watched Daddy do it. And we'd bake the seeds in the oven. Do you like pumpkin seeds?"

Dionne's smile was just for Shelly. "Yes, I do. We'll get a pumpkin soon." She picked up the book.

"I can help you carve it," Colby offered.

Dionne looked at him then, wondering how she could keep him from interjecting himself into their lives. After Shelly was in bed, she decided, she'd tell him once and for all. "I hope you don't mind if we finish our chapter," she said, finding her place.

Colby angled his head to read the title. "Oh, *Black Beauty*. One of my favorites. Go ahead." He settled back, stretching his legs, praying for patience.

It was a very long chapter, or so it seemed to Colby. Cuddled into Dionne's side, Shelly followed along in the book, listening intently to the story about the famous black horse. Dionne, he noticed, seemed scarcely aware of his presence as she read on. Except for the occasional twitching of one foot. The fact that she, too, was a little nervous made him feel better.

Questions whirled around in his head. Where had she been on this so-called important trip? Business? An out-of-town patient she'd had to rush to visit? Why did she stop to pick up Shelly before coming home, especially since the child had school in the morning? And would she ever finish reading so they could talk?

Finally, Dionne stuck the marker in place and closed the book. "We'll pick up where we left off tomorrow night," she said, rising. "Let's go, sweetheart. Off to bed."

"Do I get a hug?" Colby asked, standing up.

Still a little shy, Shelly came over, then gave in and hugged him warmly. "Will you be here for breakfast?"

Over her head, he tried to connect with Dionne, but she'd turned away. "I don't know, Shelly," he answered. "We'll see."

He watched her skip after Dionne down the hallway. Even her step was lighter, he noted. Probably because Dionne had brought her over to spend the night. The child certainly adored Dionne. It was evident in every gesture, every look. Well, so did he, for all the good it had done him so far. Restlessly, he paced.

In the hallway, Dionne pulled the door closed and paused outside Shelly's room, giving herself a moment before facing Colby. Since talking with Hilary, she'd been thinking of the questions he would likely ask and of the answers she would give him. She had, after all, left him very abruptly and owed him an explanation. She'd also had over a week to rehearse the scene in her mind, the scene she'd known she'd have to face one day. Colby was nothing if not determined and certainly not one to just let things go.

She'd left him with a hurtful remark, yet he'd come to her. That had cost him, she knew, for he was a prideful man. She knew he cared for her, and she also knew she returned that love a hundredfold. But she must let him go, must turn away. Squaring her shoulders, she swallowed her unease and walked back to the living room.

"Would you like something to drink?" she asked, hiding behind her hostess duties.

"No, thanks."

"Some cake, then. I've got this wonderful chocolate cake that—"

"No." He took a step closer and held out his hand. "Would you please come sit down and talk to me?"

He was being reasonable, so very reasonable. Yet his eyes were stormy even as he attempted to hide his anxiety. Ignoring his hand, she moved to the chair and sat down.

Colby settled on the edge of the couch nearest her, leaning forward and resting his elbows on his knees. "I need to know why you left the way you did, and what you meant when you said there was nothing between us and never had been."

She kept her hands in the pockets of her robe where he couldn't see the way her fingers clenched and unclenched tensely. "I needed time to think, to make some decisions."

"All right. You've had time to think. What decisions have you made?"

It was easier if she didn't look at him, so she stared down at her slippered feet. "I was frantic when I left your house, desperate to find Shelly. Then, when I drove around looking for her in the dark and in the cold and I couldn't find her, I realized something. I love that child deeply."

He nodded. "I knew that just in the short time I've spent with the two of you."

Dionne raised surprised eyes to his. "Perhaps I did, too, but I hadn't faced it. I thought it was just a doctor's concern for a troubled patient. And I was afraid to let it be more because... because of—"

"Because of Denny."

"Yes." He knew her awfully well, she realized, which wouldn't make her explanation any easier. "But that night when I finally found her, when she sobbed out her fears to me, when I realized she'd run away because she was terribly unhappy—and she'd run to me and I hadn't been there for her—I knew I wanted her. Not as a patient or a young friend, but as a daughter."

Colby sat back. This was one he hadn't guessed.

"I called her aunt and uncle immediately, of course. They'd been so worried. Half the town had been searching for her. Joan and Steve Morgan came right over. By then, Shelly had fallen asleep, exhausted. So we talked for a long while." Remembering, Dionne let out a ragged sigh.

"It's a difficult thing to tell two people who've tried very hard for nearly a year to make a child happy that she isn't. They've sacrificed time with their own four to try to answer Shelly's needs, as well as regularly visiting Shelly's father in the hospital for months. Then they had to help her through his death. It was one of the hardest conversations I've ever had."

"I can well imagine." He realized she'd been so preoccupied with Shelly that she hadn't had time to think of him. It wasn't easy to accept, but at least she was being honest.

"We came to some conclusions that night, Steve and Joan Morgan and I. I offered to adopt Shelly." She saw that his expression hadn't changed. "You're not shocked?"

"Not after hearing your story. I knew you cared deeply for her. I always felt you were fooling yourself when you said you didn't want marriage and children."

Dionne swallowed, knowing she was coming to the hard part. "No, I said I didn't want marriage." She held up her hand before he could interrupt. "Let me finish. A child isn't like a husband. She'll be in school and busy going out with her friends. Eventually, there'll be college, perhaps a career, a man in her life. The usual things. But a husband requires much more time, time I need to devote to my patients. I haven't enough energy to deal with my work, a child and still have a portion left over for a man."

Too agitated to sit any longer and unable to make herself look at him, Dionne rose to walk about the room restlessly. "I hope you understand. I'd like to remain friends and—"

He swung her about, catching her off guard. Her eyes, unprotected and vulnerable, implored his. He ignored the plea. "That's a lot of bull."

"No, it isn't. Please, listen to me."

"I have been. I think it's great if you want to adopt Shelly. But what's that got to do with you and me?"

He was being obtuse. Or stubborn, perhaps bull-headed. And he was listening but not hearing. There was only one way to make him see. "There is no *you and me.* I tried to tell you that when I left." She saw the quick jolt of pain in his eyes and almost backed down. But she must not. She must release him. "We enjoy each other's company and we had some fun times. But love and marriage—no! I told you right from the start, I want no part of either. Shelly's enough for me."

His mouth was a breath away from hers. "Is she? Is she really? What about the way you feel when I hold you, when I kiss you, when you lie with me?"

Steeling herself, she hardened her voice. "I don't feel anything for you."

A savage impatience roared through him. "Is that a fact?" He pressed his mouth to hers.

She would not struggle, Dionne promised herself as she fought a silent battle to keep from going under. She kept her mouth a hard line, her body stiff, but he was relentless. His lips moved over hers, taking ownership, fiercely determined. As she drew in a breath, he slipped his tongue inside. Devastating, demanding, it mated with hers until she heard a sob escape from her throat.

Her hands on his back were agitated, the nails raking him, but he paid no heed. He was devouring, out of control as he molded her body to his, his hands touching her intimately through the fabric of her robe. Never had he known such raging need to possess, such wild desire to own, such thundering passion to consume.

Finally, he felt the first hint of surrender in her: the shift in body stance, the lips suddenly moving voluntarily under his. But in moments, he realized it wasn't surrender, but an answering act of aggression. Now she was kissing him, her tongue moving into his mouth and dueling with his. Now she was pressing him closer, her body hot and restless against his. Now her hands that had been wanting to wound were caressing his shoulders, his neck and thrusting into his hair. Now she was branding him hers.

Breathing hard, almost panting, Dionne pulled back, her eyes hot and blazing. "Damn you." She released a sob, fighting tears. "Damn you for coming back, for making me want you. Why can't you let me be?"

His arms held her lightly. "Because I love you," he said, none too calm himself. His hand at the back of her head forced her to look at him. "And you love me, too. Say it. Go on, say it."

She wrenched out of his grasp. "No." Trying desperately to think clearly, she went to sit on the couch. She was trembling all over with need and frustration. Dear God, she didn't want to do this, but she saw now that there was no other way.

He came to sit alongside her and she looked up, forcing herself to meet his eyes. "All right. I'm going to tell you why you and I can never be together. I want you to listen carefully, *really* listen. Will you promise me that?"

It was what he'd been waiting to hear. "Yes."

Taking a steadying breath, Dionne made herself remember what he'd said in the park in answer to her question of how he'd feel if he couldn't have kids. Quickly, before she could change her mind, she plunged in. "I can never have children of my own." There, she'd delivered the bombshell.

He was obviously taken aback. "How do you know?"

Her sigh was ragged, tortured, the words still so difficult to say. "When I was seventeen, I became quite ill with a fever and violent abdominal cramps. When I passed out, my mother discovered I was hemorrhaging and rushed me to the hospital. I'd developed endometriosis and nearly died. But I didn't. I had surgery and recovered nicely. Except for one small problem. No babies, not ever."

He was too quiet. She looked up and saw the sympathy in his eyes. "Don't feel sorry for me." Yes, feel the anger, she told herself. It's so much easier to handle than pity. "I'm just fine. I have work I love, a wonderful family and now Shelly. She's the child I never thought I'd have. She needs me as much as I need her."

Why doesn't he say something, anything? She sniffed once, then swiped a tear from her cheek as she studied her hands. "So you can go now. Shelly and I will have a good life together. And you'll find a woman who can give you the family you've always wanted. I—I wish you well."

Colby rose and took her hands, pulling her to her feet. Her eyes were dewy but steady on his and questioning again. Gently, he touched his lips to hers. Slowly, he rubbed his mouth along hers, kissing the corners, then tasting her fully. He touched her nowhere else except her hands and her lips. He felt her sway with him, uncertain how to react.

Still he kept kissing only her mouth. Tenderly as she deserved. Sweetly, softly, lovingly. At last, he drew back and saw her slowly open her eyes, saw the confusion there.

"Didn't you hear what I said?" Dionne asked.

"Every word." He moved his hands up to frame her face. "I'm sorry you won't be experiencing childbirth, Dionne. But you can still enjoy motherhood. With Shelly. And other children."

She shook her head. "No. This...this is a special case. I have a friend who's a judge and he's helping me. But, despite what you may read, it's still not easy for a single woman to adopt children. The agencies believe two parents are best and—"

"Then let's give them two parents. I love you, Dionne. Please marry me."

She touched his hands, drew them away from her face. "No. Don't you see? You can still have your own children. I couldn't do that to you."

"How could you have been foolish enough to think your fertile or infertile state would be the deciding factor between us? It's you I love, you exactly the way you are. It's like saying I prefer you had brown hair. It makes no difference. I fell in love with the essence of you, not a health record."

She turned then, gathering her thoughts, making herself remember. "Someone else said that to me once. But when it came time to plan the wedding, he left. I—I can't go through that again, the way Nathan made me feel. I won't."

Colby could afford to be patient now. Gently, he led her to the couch and sat her beside him. "I'm not Nathan. I want you for all time. I won't leave. I can pull some strings and we can be married in a day, two tops. How would that be?"

She wanted to believe. Oh, God, how she wanted to believe him. "You'll blame me, in time. You love children. You told me you couldn't imagine anything worse than not having children."

"I still feel that way. When I said I wanted children, I didn't say that they had to be *my* children, did I? If you'd have trusted me sooner, I would have told you that I have nothing against adoption. I'm already nuts about Shelly. Loving her even more won't be difficult. Any children we adopt will become *our* children."

She watched her fingers play with the middle button of his shirt, fighting the hope springing to life inside her. "You're just saying that now. Every man wants his *own* child, a son to carry on his name."

"Damn, I don't know where you get your information. Listen, my father was my biological parent. He never cared for me, not until it was too late. And you certainly were familiar with Lainey's parents and how selfishly they treated their biological child." Colby took hold of her chin. "I'm firmly convinced that if you have a loving heart, you can love any child, one that you have yourself or one who is entrusted into your care. And if you don't have that caring nature, nothing can make up for it."

"What makes you so wise, Mr. Winters?" She was letting herself be swayed—just a little.

He allowed himself a smile. "Born that way, I guess. Dionne, do you remember when we watched that movie here with Shelly?"

"*The Land Before Time,* yes."

"Well, I don't know if you remember the message from that movie, but I do."

She could have recited most of the dialogue, having watched it several times with Shelly. But she let him tell her. "And what is it?"

"If you lose your way, let your heart lead you. When you left me, I was damn mad. I'd told you I loved you, asked you to marry me, and still you'd driven off. I decided I wasn't going to you, that if you didn't want me enough, I'd let you go. Then something happened."

She was listening intently now. "What?"

"They found my father dead in his bed."

Her hands gripped his. "Oh, Colby, just when you might have gotten together. I'm so sorry."

He felt the comfort of her touch. "Yeah, so am I. I stood there in the rain at his funeral and realized I wasn't like him, that I'd quit drinking and made something of myself. But like him, I was alone. He'd alienated nearly everyone with his self-indulgence, his low self-esteem. And I'd let pride keep me from going after you and demanding some answers. Like the movie said, I'd lost my way. So I gave in and listened to my heart. It led me right back to you." He kissed her gently. "Do you believe me?"

"I want to." Dionne sighed and leaned back. "Growing up the way I did, I always wanted a big family, a big happy household with lots of children and dogs and cats and all that. When that option was taken from me, I turned inward. I told myself and anyone who would listen that I was a career woman who wanted no part of all that, that I wanted to go it alone. That, too, was pride, I guess. I didn't want people pitying me or someone marrying me because they felt sorry for me.

"You think I feel sorry for you?"

"No." Shifting, she looked up at him. "My work *is* important to me, but *you* are far more important, you and Shelly."

Colby felt his heart soar. "Say it, please."

Slowly she smiled, giving herself over to the feeling. "I love you. I have from the start, I think. That day you strutted across Lainey's lawn, cocky and flirtatious. Instinctively, I knew I needed to stay away from you if I wanted to hold on to my heart."

"And now?"

"Now I know that I never had a choice after seeing you, certainly not after you touched me. No man has ever made me feel so much or want so badly."

"Tell me again."

She tilted her head up to his. "I love you, Colby. Love you, love you." And she reached for his kiss. It was long and delicious and, as always, stirring. She felt her blood heat slowly as she drew away and studied his eyes. "You're sure, are you? Because if you change your mind—"

"Never." He hugged her close. "You're all I want, you and Shelly. And about five more little faces. Redheads like their mother."

"Five? Hold on, now. My work—"

"You can juggle work and kids and me. You're a talented, beautiful, wonderful—"

"What about you? How about your work schedule? And where will we live? I'm not crazy about Detroit, but your business is there. And my apartment's small. We'll have to get a house, but where?"

He nuzzled her ear, then slid down to her neck. "Details, details. We can work all that out. You forget, I'm a builder, so the house isn't a problem. Only one thing is important." He faced her now. "You and I and our love. We have more than enough love to include Shelly and as many more as you want. The details will work themselves out."

He was right. She would have to learn to trust him, not just with her heart—that he already owned—but with helping to chart their lives. "All right, you win."

Colby smiled, feeling glorious, feeling right. "Good." But he had to consider the child, too. "How do you think Shelly feels about me? She doesn't know me very well."

Dionne thought of the drive home from the state capital, where they'd gone to file the adoption papers in person rather than wait for the mails. "We stayed in Lansing for a couple of days, just for a change of scene. Shelly asked if we could call you. When I told her I didn't think so, she waited a while, then kept sliding you into the conversation. Did I know if you liked horses and riding? Did you ever ask about her? How did you feel about little girls?"

He was grinning. "Did she really?"

Dionne's heart felt the warmth spread. "Yes, she really did."

"Think she'll accept me?"

"Yes. We still have to go slowly with her. Her father died only a short time ago, but she hadn't been with him since the accident because of his coma. I think Shelly started letting go of him back then."

"I'll go slowly. But not with you. How quickly can you get yourself ready to marry me?"

"A couple of months and—"

"Wrong! Much too long."

"All right, one month then."

"Two weeks, tops. My final word.

"But in two weeks it's Halloween."

He grinned. "Perfect."

Lainey Sinclair was a little tired but a lot happy. The wedding had been beautiful. Stopping to catch her breath, she sat down on the edge of her bed, smiling as she slipped off her shoes.

It had been a hectic few days, made more so by the arrival en masse of the entire Keller clan. They'd been everywhere, some staying in the Sinclair house, some with Dionne and the overflow at a nearby hotel. Lainey had had such fun seeing everyone again, meeting the new additions. There'd been dinners and shopping, reunions and rehearsals. There'd been laughter and tears and story telling. And there'd been a getting-acquainted time for Shelly, who'd been nearly overwhelmed by the love and affection from all her new relatives. Then there'd been the wedding this morning.

The bride had worn ecru lace over white satin and had carried a bouquet of pale orange tiger lilies. The groom, who couldn't seem to stop smiling, had worn a black tuxedo. The flower girl had looked much more grown up than most seven-year-olds and had been only a little nervous. Lainey's eyes had been misty as she'd stood to the left of the bride and watched her husband, the best man, search for the rings in the vest pocket of his handsome tux. The groom had been too busy staring at the bride to notice the delay. Rings in hand, they'd turned back to face the minister who'd said the magic words that transformed them into a family.

Then the wedding had ended and the celebration had begun. Papa Keller, telling one and all he had only one daughter to give away and he was going to do it right, had brought his homemade brew and rented a hall, and Mama Keller had found German cooks from somewhere. Neighbors, many of Dionne's patients and their parents and good friends from Detroit and St. Clair had all been wined and dined while wishing the newlyweds a long and happy life. There'd been music and dancing and more laughter, sprinkled with hugs and hand-shakes.

Watching Shelly say goodbye to her new set of grand-parents with promises of visits to Frankenmuth soon had moved Lainey and Dionne to tears. In three days, the child had discovered a new world with caring people, as Lainey had done so many years ago when she'd met the Keller family. They had hearts big enough to accept her and Zac, Colby and Shelly, and even more.

It had been dark out when the last car had pulled away, and five of them had wearily trudged back to the Sinclair house. The bride and groom had rushed to change clothes before leaving for the airport and their honeymoon flight.

"Are you sure you're up to watching Shelly for a week?" Dionne asked as she hurried into the bedroom, unfastening the buttons at the wrist of her wedding dress as she walked.

Lainey wiggled her toes and sighed. "You've asked that question three times. We'll be fine. She's looking forward to helping me with Trixie, grooming her and so on. And I'll drive her to school, help her with her homework, read to her, all that stuff." She stood to help her friend out of her bridal gown. "You are *so* beautiful. I can hardly wait to see the pictures."

Dionne slipped the dress over her head, then turned to face Lainey. "You know, today I *felt* beautiful. I re-membered your wedding day and wondered if all brides feel that way."

"I think they do, every time they look into the eyes of the man they just married."

Dionne reached for her suit skirt while Lainey hung up the dress. "You're feeling all right, aren't you?"

Lainey turned from the closet and touched a hand to her thickening waist. "I feel great, if a little lazy. But Zac's a big help." She moved to stand behind her friend as Dionne ran a quick comb through her hair. "Aren't you excited about the new baby?"

Dionne paused to catch her breath. She and Colby had gone to Judge Tobias last week to finalize the papers on Shelly's adoption, and he'd told them about a little boy, not quite two. A ward of the court, going into a foster home. And he had red hair. That had clinched it for Colby. He hadn't given Dionne a moment's peace until she'd agree to see the child.

"Excited? Overwhelmed. First Shelly, then the wedding and now Michael." They'd fallen in love with the little bundle of energy on sight. She swung toward Lainey. "You don't think I'm crazy tackling so much at once?"

"Are you kidding?" Lainey hugged her friend. "We've both got a lot of love to share, wouldn't you say? And with Colby by your side, why would you worry?"

"Is she worrying again?" Colby asked from the doorway.

"Occupational hazard, dear husband." *Husband.* What a beautiful word. She smiled at him, so handsome in a dark brown suit.

Beaming, he stepped into the room and took her in his arms. "From now on, you leave the worries to me."

"No, we *share* the worries, just like we share the good things."

He turned to wink at Lainey. "I married a liberated woman."

"That you did, my friend," Lainey told him.

Colby kissed his wife lightly, then checked his watch. "We're going to miss our plane if you stay in here chatting much longer."

Dionne slipped on her suit jacket. "I'm ready. Where's the luggage?"

"Zac and I are putting the bags in the car right now." He picked up her remaining case and left the room.

Lainey moved close for one final hug. "You'll love the ship. Cruising's such fun. And I know you're going to be wonderfully happy."

"Thanks, Lainey, for all your help putting the wedding together so quickly. And for watching Shelly." Arm in arm, they walked into the nearby deserted living room. By the door, Shelly waited, still in her silk dress.

Dionne hugged her close for a long moment. "Next time we vacation, we'll all go together, okay?" She hated leaving her daughter, even for a week.

"Will Michael come with us?"

"Yes. By then, Michael will be able to be with us. You be a good girl. We'll be back before you know it."

"Lainey's going to teach me to knit. I'll make you a sweater."

"Great." Dionne kissed her daughter's hair, marveling that this child was hers, hers and Colby's. She smiled as Lainey came up to Shelly, then she walked out on the porch.

"Mom?"

Dionne stopped, not certain she'd heard right. Slowly she turned back and looked through the screen at Shelly.

"Have a good time, Mom."

Blinking back the tears, Dionne nodded, then gave her daughter a big smile. Heart filled to overflowing, Dionne moved to the car, accepted a goodbye hug from Zac and got in.

Colby waved to the threesome now on the porch and climbed behind the wheel. Starting the engine, he glanced over and saw Dionne dabbing at her eyes. "Are you all right?"

Sliding closer, she smiled at him. "In my entire life, I've never been better." She kissed him once, then again. "Let's go. Suddenly I'm anxious to get on with the rest of our lives."

"Me, too, Mrs. Winters."

Stepping on the gas, Colby aimed the car toward the long, winding road.

*   *   *   *   *